"THE BOSS DON'T TRUST HER—SHE'S TOO MUCH TROUBLE."

They were in the pantry by then, less than a foot away, it seemed. My heart pounded, and tears began to squeeze through my closed eyes. But their examination was brief. The door closed again.

More distant now: "I swear she came in here, I followed her."

"The back door."

"Locked. Boss locked it when he came. He kept the key."

Their voices dwindled away. My cramped muscles demanded release, and I finally had to move, to chance that they were gone. I eased myself out of the cupboard and couldn't see a thing. I groped along the wall to the door, then froze and listened. Silence. I found the knob, turned it cautiously, and stepped into the kitchen.

My heart nearly stopped as a hand touched my shoulder and another one clamped itself over my mouth.

Bantam Books offers the finest in classic and modern American murder mysteries.
Ask your bookseller for the books you have missed.

Stuart Palmer
Murder on the Blackboard

Rex Stout
Broken Vase
Death of a Dude
Death Times Three
Fer-de-Lance
The Final Deduction
Gambit
The Rubber Band
Too Many Cooks
The Black Mountain

Max Allan Collins
The Dark City

William Kienzle
The Rosary Murders

Joseph Louis
Madelaine
The Trouble With Stephanie

M. J. Adamson
Not Till a Hot February
A February Face
Remember March
April When They Woo

Conrad Haynes
Bishop's Gambit, Declined
Perpetual Check

Barbara Paul
First Gravedigger
But He Was Already Dead When I
  Got There

P. M. Carlson
Murder Unrenovated
Rehearsal for Murder

Ross Macdonald
The Goodbye Look
Sleeping Beauty
The Name Is Archer
The Drowning Pool
The Underground Man
The Zebra-Striped Hearse

Margaret Maron
The Right Jack
Baby Doll Games
Coming Soon: One Coffee With

William Murray
When the Fat Man Sings

Robert Goldsborough
Murder in E Minor
Death on Deadline
The Bloodied Ivy

Sue Grafton
"A" Is for Alibi
"B" Is for Burglar
"C" Is for Corpse
"D" Is for Deadbeat

R. D. Brown
Hazzard
Villa Head

Joseph Telushkin
The Unorthodox Murder of
  Rabbi Wahl
The Final Analysis of Doctor Stark

Richard Hilary
Snake in the Grasses
Pieces of Cream
Pillow of the Community

Carolyn G. Hart
Design for Murder
Death on Demand
Something Wicked

Lia Matera
Where Lawyers Fear to Tread
A Radical Departure
The Smart Money

Robert Crais
The Monkey's Raincoat

Keith Peterson
The Trapdoor
Coming Soon: There Fell a Shadow

Jim Stinson
Double Exposure

Carolyn Wheat
Where Nobody Dies

SALMON IN THE SOUP

MEG O'BRIEN

BANTAM BOOKS

NEW YORK • TORONTO • LONDON • SYDNEY • AUCKLAND

For
Sal Martinelli,
a man for all reasons.

SALMON IN THE SOUP
A Bantam Book / September 1990

ISBN 0-553-28617-X

Published simultaneously in the United States and Canada

Bantam Books are published by Bantam Books, a division of Bantam Doubleday Dell Publishing Group, Inc. Its trademark, consisting of the words "Bantam Books" and the portrayal of a rooster, is Registered in U.S. Patent and Trademark Office and in other countries. Marca Registrada. Bantam Books, 666 Fifth Avenue, New York, New York 10103.

PRINTED IN THE UNITED STATES OF AMERICA

RAD 0 9 8 7 6 5 4 3 2 1

Some circumstantial evidence is very strong,
as when you find a trout in the milk.
                    —Henry David Thoreau
                        Naturalist, Writer

Some circumstantial evidence is a crock,
as when you find a salmon in the soup.
                    —Jessica James
                        Screw-up, Reporter

Chapter One

It has been said that bad stories often begin with the weather: *The wind sighed through the sycamores . . . the sun poked through and kissed the sullen earth with a smile.*

Well, hell, I don't mean to tell a bad story here, but it's *my* story and *I* know how it began, and it began with the goddamn weather.

It always does, in Rochester, New York.

It was storming. Sheets of it against the windows, the wind howling through the trees outside my apartment, a blind flapping at a half-open window. The stench of lightning in the air.

A clap of summer thunder. Christ. I pulled the covers over my head.

Go to work this morning? No way.

I crawled out again and lifted the phone. Put it down. I couldn't even call in "well." It would be a lie.

It was also a lie, I decided, that sobriety grew easier as time went by. I wanted a drink more than love or money, more than peace on earth. More than a dying man wants a ten-dollar whore, I wanted a drink.

I lay shivering and thought about the fact that there are a lot of reasons to start boozing again when you've been sober a year.

One is that you get tired of being afraid you'll do it—so more and more, it seems reasonable to just get it over with.

Another is that it's a bitch dealing with things without a little oil—dealing with them cold.

I told myself later that if I'd known before I picked up that bottle that Marcus Andrelli was being questioned for murder and would need me, I might not have done it.

Right.

I'd have done it if the Pope were being paraded down Genesee Street on the back of an ass with swords stuck through his palms. If Christ himself were nailed to a cross in Highland Park and pelted with stones, I'd have chosen to take that drink rather than offer a wine-soaked rag to his poor parched lips.

(Lest you be led astray, I feel I should clarify the fact that I'm not in the least religious, nor ever have been. I just want to make sure that anyone, even my old ninny-nunny teachers from Mercy High, could understand the depths of my degradation here.)

My usual was a Genny beer with slices of orange, a Genesee Screw. I thought: I could get hooked again if I start on those. So what if I have something different, something that doesn't have sentimental value, that I don't even like —say a scotch, or a vodka on the rocks?

My list of support numbers hung on the wall by my bed and stared at me. I rolled over and looked the other way. Jesus, what was the big deal, anyway, one Genesee beer?

And who would it hurt? There wasn't anybody it would make a difference to, not really. *One drink.* It was eight A.M. By noon, latest, it would be done. Life would go on as before. No one would know. Not Samved, my guru/shrink, or my support group—absolutely no one at all.

I snaked a hand outside my Puff the Magic Dragon sheet and lifted the phone. It didn't feel like an instrument of the devil. It felt silky and light—the palm of an assisting angel. The number for Harding's Liquors slid out of the gray cells as smoothly. It had been lying suspended in all-too-fertile soil the past year, like skunkweed waiting to bloom.

"Mr. Harding? Jesse. Jessica James. Yeah, a long time. Can you send over a bottle of Jack Daniels?"

I hate Jack Daniels. I wouldn't, therefore, I reasoned,

want very much. What the hell, anyway—as Pop used to say, a little dab'll do ya.

"I'll give the kid an extra ten to bring it over now." I cleared my throat. "Right. Company from out of town. You know how newspaper people are."

When the boy came I ran nervous fingers through my shoulder-length brown hair, which hadn't been combed since the day before. I mumbled my story again about "a fellow reporter from a sister paper" and ignored his snide, knowing look. *No problem, lady—everybody orders Jack Daniels at eight* A.M. I paid him and he went away. I stood by the door in my stained FREE ITHACA! tee from college days and twisted the cap.

The rest was easy.

You don't stand with the bottle and stare into it, shaking, while it rises, inch by inch, to your mouth. That only happens in bad films on TV.

What you do is, you close your mind to it. You tilt the bottle and take the pull.

You don't even enjoy it; that would call for too much acknowledgment of the act.

After a few minutes, though, it hits, and the walls come down, and it's *good, baby, it's good.*

You don't feel bad anymore.

The phone shrilled. I pried open the lid of one eye with something I think was a thumb. The room lurched from side to side. But which room? Where was I? Christ, the bathroom. No more than a postage stamp in size. What was I doing here? I opened the other eye. I was on my back between the sink and the toilet, my head against the wall at a forty-five-degree angle to my chest. One foot was wedged inside the bottom drawer of the linen closet, less than a yard away on the opposite wall. The phone jangled. I couldn't move.

Then I remembered. I'd been standing on the front of the half-pulled-out drawer, trying to reach . . . what? To reach . . .

Something, I didn't know. Something on the top shelf. Then I fell and couldn't get up. My foot and calf had jammed inside the drawer, and the harder I tried to pull, the deeper in they went. I was too screwed up to get any leverage. I had passed out that way.

Shit. If Sister Clarice could see me now.

"Being a woman is something to be proud of, Jessica. Women are the Virgin Mary here on earth, just as men are the Christ. You must always hold yourself high. Be above earthly matters. Look to the sky."

I looked. The sky looked a hell of a lot like a bathroom ceiling to me.

The phone had stopped, but now it began again. It went on and on. I grabbed hold of the pink tile sink counter with one hand and the toilet seat with the other, and pulled. The upper half of my body came a few inches off the floor. My leg twisted in the drawer, and I groaned. I heaved again, ignoring the pain. Long moments later I was on my feet. One of which was still in a drawer.

The phone jangled on and on. "Coming . . . I'm coming!" I yelled.

I stumbled into the living room, limping and rubbing my hip, which felt like tiny little men had been playing lawn darts on my Gulliverlike body as it lay on the bathroom floor. Ran to the counter between the kitchen and living room for my phone. No phone. *Where the hell was the phone?*

"Will you shut the fuck up?" I yelled. I rummaged in a pile of *Rochester Heralds* on the couch that I hadn't read for a week, even though I worked for the goddamn rag.

The papers went flying. Becky Anderson's face smiled vapidly from her column in *Lifestyle*. I wanted to hit her. Stomp on her picture and smash her. But that was another matter.

Beneath the sports section, I found the phone. I yanked the receiver to my ear.

"*What?*"

"Jesse?"

"Yeah." The other voice came from far away, under a tunnel somewhere. Who was it? *"Who is it?"*

"Tark. Where the hell have you been, Jess? I've been trying to reach you since last night."

I'd never heard the hulk's voice on the phone before. Tark didn't trust phones. As far as he was concerned, they were all tapped—and as bodyguard to Marcus Andrelli, Rochester's recently reinstated King of Crime, he'd be the one to know. I squinted at the little travel clock on the bookcase by my desk. It blurred, then steadied. 1:37. Afternoon, it seemed, from the post-rain July sun streaming in through all the windows. It was muggy in here, and hard to breathe. "I had it off the hook," I said, remembering last night's mood of dejection that had gotten me into all this. "Tark . . . what's up?"

"Marcus is in trouble."

I cleared my throat and shook my head . . . neither of which made much difference. I still couldn't make my mouth move right.

"He's at police headquarters," Tark went on. "Vince Russo's there, too, arranging bail, I guess."

"I don't understand."

"Somebody was shot on Marcus's boat. They think he did it, and they've had him downtown since it happened."

"Who? Who was shot?"

A brief pause. "The Sloan lady. Barbara Sloan."

"Baby Cakes?" That one cleared my mind. And I was embarrassed at my almost hopeful tone. *Barbara Sloan.* Tall, blond, cool, beautiful. Intelligent. Marcus's new attorney—and, some said, much, much more. "Is she . . . dead?"

"That's what I hear."

I wiped sweat from my eyes. "Why would they think Marcus did it? I thought he and Baby Cakes . . . What would be his motive?"

"I can't talk about it now."

"Tark, where're you—"

"I have to go, Jess."

"Wait—"

He hung up.

I dropped the phone on its hook and sat on the couch, feeling numb. I surveyed the wreckage of my living room. The four-foot orange tree Mom had sent from California—the one with the dusty leaves and hard green fruit—had been knocked over. I'd have to haul out the vacuum to suck all the dirt off the floor. The Jack Daniels bottle lay on its side by the stereo. A dark stain spread from its neck, where the little liquor I hadn't managed to down had trickled onto the pale gray rug. I'd left the front windows open, and the sheer white curtains there were soaked and twisted from the storm. It was a wonder Mrs. Binty, my landlady downstairs, hadn't called to say the rain was leaking through the floor.

Maybe she had. Hell, how would I know?

I groaned and eased myself to an upright position, then limped into the bedroom, rubbing my bruised bones. On my unmade bed was a pile of notebooks, right where I always kept them to write genius thoughts in before I fell asleep. I picked the top one up and looked at chicken tracks I now remembered scrawling after the first few drinks.

I couldn't read a word.

Well, yes, I could, in fact, read a random word.

One was *Marcus*. The other was *Herald*. The two major problem areas in my life.

One had to do with my obsession for a man who lived outside the law. The other had to do with my work.

Neither one seemed to be going all that well these days.

CHAPTER TWO

I managed a quick hand-held shower, with a floor fan at rocket blast to scatter the humidity. Someone has written that there are only two seasons in upstate New York: winter and the fourth of July. Well, here it was. July. Ninety degrees at seven A.M. Hot as a firecracker poised in erection, by noon.

I stepped outside the clawfoot tub with a slightly clearer head. Glanced down at the scene of my earlier humiliation. Saw that I'd collapsed the web that Lola had been so fanatically spinning between the toilet and sink. Poor Lola. Poor fuzzy eight-legged arachnid. She'd have to begin again.

Poor me. I'd have to begin again too.

I sighed, wondering if I was up to it. A month at St. Avery's treatment center a year ago April, and I'd thought I had it licked. No, that's not true. I hoped I had it licked. There was always that niggling little voice underneath saying: *Don't pat yourself on the back yet, Jess. It's a long cold life, a lot of upsets in the future just by the nature of things.*

I was half right. It's a long cold life, indeed. But the upsets had never really come. Things went, if anything, too smoothly. I found a new job after St. Avery's, at the *Rochester Herald*. They were impressed by the real estate fraud piece I'd done for the *Weston Free Press*, the one that almost won the Pulitzer. *Almost* being the operative word here. I had, a couple of times, *almost* won that most elite of awards. Almost had my fingers on the brass ring, only to see it pass on by and go to the fellow on the pink giraffe behind me, touting feathers in its hair.

Never did I blame my loss on luck. There was something missing in me, I knew. Maybe a hot enough urge to really win. The passion to throw my all into the competitive fray. That predilection had followed me, in fact, from the *Weston Free Press* to the *Rochester Herald*—where I turned down the chance to continue as an investigative reporter and chose, instead, to be a g.a.

The thing is, Investigative on the *Herald* is mostly research if you're the new gal on the block. No matter your reputation, there's a lengthy pecking order to be observed. And I don't know about you, but I grow fungus on my fingers from filing—whereas General Assignments at least got me out on the streets.

Not that I kidded myself I was chasing an officially sanctioned story now. I'd been warned several times by R. B. Chastain, the *Herald*'s new publisher, to stay away from Marcus Andrelli. "The *Herald*'s new thrust is toward the family," R. B. had intoned just last week. "We prefer not to focus on stories about organized crime today. Much better to offer our readership community events and services, positive news. . . ."

"You don't want people to know what's really going on in the city?"

His normally paper-white face became pink. "I didn't say that. What we are speaking of here is a matter of focus."

He had rambled on in that vein, a small man with a preacher's pinched nose. As he pontificated he toyed with a gold watch, taking it in and out of the tiny pocket of his pinstriped suit. In and out, out and in. I began to get an image of an exhibitionist, the watch a phallic symbol. Out and in, out and in. I drew my eyes away with effort.

"I've been receiving complaints about you, Ms. James," R.B. had continued.

"Oh?"

"There seems to be a feeling that you lack team spirit,

that your . . . attitude, shall we say . . . has not been the best lately."

Golly. "Anything specific?" I said.

"In the first place, there's this business of calling in *well* when you don't plan to be here, instead of *sick*. Your humor isn't appreciated by the rest of the staff."

"I got that from a book by Larry L. King—"

"And you can hardly call yourself an objective reporter if you insist on consorting with this . . . this Andrelli, this mobster."

"Yes, sir. The last thing I'd want to do is consort."

His chin wobbled. His nostrils began to drip, and he poked at them irritably with a starched white handkerchief that could put out an eye. Thank God he had stopped the thing with the watch. "That's just the sort of thing I mean," he accused. "This is a newspaper, Ms. James, not a comedy club. From now on, you will be expected at your desk bright and sharp at nine o'clock every morning without fail. And you are to be available for whatever assignments come up —not cavorting around town, doing God knows what."

"I have to see my shrink—"

"And that is another thing. The policy here is for management to follow up on these appointments when time away from work is involved. It seems you haven't been seen nor heard from at the Center for Natural Healing in the past three weeks."

Fuck. Old Samved had *squealed*?

R.B.'s liver-spotted fingers pushed firmly against his desk. "Ms. James, I'm very sorry to have to tell you that this situation does not seem to be working out in a productive manner for either one of us. If matters don't improve . . ."

He left it hanging, but I knew. I'd be fired.

Well, hell, I'm always fired. I've been fired from every job I've ever had, since college. I don't fit in. Can't take orders. Can't follow rules. I would not make a good Marine.

Once upon a time, that might have bothered me. Now

I'm just glad not to have to cut my hair in a buzz and wear those godawful boots.

I had gone back to my desk that day and sat there thinking. The big black and white clock that hung on the wall at the end of the office—a large impersonal area with thirty desks—showed me that it was 11:26. *Tick-tock.*

Tick-tock.

Tiiiiick . . . toooockk.

I drummed my fingers on the gray metal desk. Nicky Ludgett was out on assignment, and so was Carol Bruce. There had been nothing for me, so far. My IN basket was empty; the OUT equally so.

Nothing for me. It seemed I'd been getting fewer assignments than anyone lately. A lot of the problem, I figured, was my own fault. I'd incurred a good deal of resentment by not following the rules.

Or maybe it had something to do with the fact that I was seldom around.

Well, I thought, looking at the clock once more. 11:28. A long day ahead. Not much happening here. And as they used to say in old journalese, "You gotta *leg it*, kid"—you gotta get out and around, talk to people, see what's going on, cover the town.

Uh-huh.

As I left, it had occurred to me that if I got fired, I at least wouldn't have to pack up a cardboard box with photos, plants, nail files. I never kept anything like that at work anyway; it would have been too much of a concession—like saying I thought I belonged.

Tick-tock.

My mind had been straying in a post-drunk haze. I drew it away from the *Herald* and back to Marcus Andrelli. How long had it been since Tark called? Would Marcus still be at police headquarters? Had he been released, or arrested and held? I should hurry.

I peered at my thirty-one-year-old green eyes in the bathroom mirror. They looked dull and puffy, with black shadows beneath. A purplish bruise had begun on my cheek where I'd struck it against something. I scrabbled in the back of my junk drawer for an old tube of that erase-type stuff, left over from the original drinking days. Dabbed some on. Added blush to my white face and dark red color to my lips. Stood back for inspection.

There.

I looked like the hapless survivor of a banana republic war.

Marcus would be thrilled to see me this way, I thought. I pulled on the cleanest things I could find, rumpled white jeans and a red sleeveless tee. They were in the dirty clothes basket, and smelled of mildew. I swallowed bile as my stomach rolled over. Weaved back into the living room. Grabbed up my car keys and locked the door behind me, trotting painfully down the gray, woolly hallway stairs.

As I kicked the old red and white Ghia out of the driveway and into Genesee Park Boulevard, I remembered how I used to tell myself that Marcus wasn't the type to care about looks. But men are always saying that, aren't they? That it's personality they're looking for? A sense of humor?

Well, let me tell you, men lie. When push comes to shove (and other positions of merit), they want Patty Penthouse. They want gorgeous, tall, well-built blonds . . . blonds like Baby Cakes Sloan.

Barbara. Sloan. Dead by Marcus's hand or order?

I couldn't conceive of it.

And as old Samved is wont to expound, "One must conceive to believe."

Marcus Andrelli. Where to begin?

For about three years after my pop died, I'd been cautious, prickly. Not letting anyone get close. I spent my days as an investigative reporter and a drunk, giving fair and equal time to each and going downhill, emotionally, faster than a speeding wooden Flyer. Then a year ago last March, Marcus Andrelli came along, and I let some of the barriers down. Some. Not all. I still don't like dogs.

Which makes it hard on Bastard, a dastardly dog if there

ever was one. Bastard was left behind by a boyfriend who hightailed it out of my life in a panic when I was confined to bed for six weeks with broken ribs. Somehow, I've never been able to get rid of the mutt. Right now, he's on a camping trip with the Flynns, next door to the right, and forgive me, God, but I hope he gets eaten by bears.

As for Marcus, the best way I can describe him is that he's the only upscale mob leader I've ever known. Marcus is caught between two worlds: the one his parents raised him to believe in, where the keynote was truth, honesty, kindness to one's fellow man—and the world he's made for himself as head of an elite new branch of the mob in western New York. Marcus doesn't deal in drugs or the rackets, doesn't believe in street thuggery or violence—yet in a good year he manages to pull off more crooked deals than the Pentagon, the CIA, and the Teamster's Union combined.

It's the new way in organized crime, Marcus tells me, a product of the upscale eighties. Hi-tech is in, gats and molls are out.

So how did I get into the picture? Well, last year, I managed to do a good deed for Marcus—after which he made me an honorary member of his Family (hot damn). Thank God for the New Order: at least we didn't have to slit our wrists and mingle blood.

Mingle we did, though, and with Marcus it was better than good; on a different plane. Marcus was like no one, ever, in my experience. Growing up poor and without power can do things to you, to the way you look at the world and the kinds of fears you have. Just knowing Marcus was there eliminated some of those fears.

But I'd like to think that Marcus, too, got something out of the relationship other than the obvious. One thing about Marcus and me, we could always talk. There was, between us, a sense of loyalty and absolute trust.

In about twenty minutes I was at the Public Safety Building on Plymouth Avenue. I rolled into a slot marked RE-SERVED, COMMISSIONER and eased out of my Campbell's tomato soup can, lifting the door an inch on its broken hinges to close it. I pushed through a mob of fellow reporters outside on the steps, ignored all questions that flew my way, and forged on into the downstairs holding area—certainly one of *my* favorite places to spend a hot summer day. The place was teeming with battered humanity, some of them dressed in blue with badges on their chests. There was no air-conditioning in this older part of the building. Instead, large fans in the corners pushed around fetid air, mingling odors of pastrami and onions from the cops and urine and sour wine from what appeared to be a thousand bums. They must have pulled in all of Dwight Square.

I didn't have time to find out why; Marcus was coming out of an elevator, presumably from the fourth floor, where booking and interrogation went on. He stood talking to Vince, his former attorney and now capo, and he didn't see me at first. His black autocratic brows were pulled tight in anger, the jacket of his dark suit open, white shirt collar unbuttoned, tie loose. He wheeled away from Vince and I stood in front of him, looking up from my five-foot-four height to his trim, hard-packed six feet. The small, ancient scar under his left eye that became visible only under stress was livid now. I reached automatically as if to soothe it, but Marcus drew away.

My hand dropped. "What's going on?" I said.

For a minute he didn't speak. When he did, his voice was harsh. "Where have you been the past three months?"

"I . . . I don't know. I've been around . . ."

"Not around me, you haven't."

I didn't answer.

"Dammit, Jess. I've been worried about you."

"I . . . I guess I didn't think. I mean, if anything, I thought it wouldn't make any difference. If you didn't see me for a while."

"Wouldn't make any *difference*?"

I pushed the hair off my forehead, wiping at sweat, then glanced around the room, hoping for a distraction. Vince was looking in every direction but ours, trying to be discreet.

"Explain. Please." Marcus snapped off the words.

I bristled at his tone, and thought of several things to say, no one of which made any more sense than all the personal shit that had been keeping me away from just about everyone the past few months. In the meantime, Marcus's dark eyes surveyed my hopeless appearance, and one lifted brow reduced me suddenly to the status of carnival flea. I'd never seen him this angry, at least not toward me. I tried to swallow, but my mouth was dry. My head hurt. My legs had begun to shake.

"You know . . ." I mumbled, drawing a circle on the dirty floor with a sneakered toe. "You and Barbara . . . you've been busy."

He was silent for a long moment, just staring at me. Vince interrupted then. "We've got to go, Marc. There are things to be taken care of, people to see." Marcus nodded and turned from me.

"Tell me what's going on, first," I insisted, drawing him back with a hand on his sleeve.

The scar beneath his eye seemed to grow by several centimeters. "Tark's gone," he said. His chin went up in the haughty, emperorlike manner that Marcus does so well. I'd learned that he does it only under attack, or when he's hurt.

"What are you talking about?" I said. "Tark's the one who told me you were here."

Marcus Andrelli, emperor of just about anything he chose to survey this side of the Hudson, bestowed upon me a look that told me I had somehow become the enemy. "You've heard from Tark?"

"Just a little while ago, it's why I came down—"

"Where is he?"

"I don't know."

"You don't know." He bit off each word distastefully.

"No! I don't. He just hung up, he didn't tell me—"

He wheeled back abruptly to Vince. "Let's get out of here."

They barreled through the grimy glass doors to the street,

and I hurried after them, bewildered. The doors nearly slammed in my face. Outside, we were trampled by the fourth estate—a legalized mob that should probably, some-day, be thrown en masse into the clink. I knew most of its members as co-workers from the *Herald*, and recognized the others—the cadre of stringers and photographers that always turns up when anything more interesting than a heat wave comes down. I heard groans coming my way and knew it was because they figured I'd scooped them, and Nicky Ludgett, from the crime desk, pulled me aside while the others were converging on Marcus and Vince.

"What's the skinny, Jess? Did he do it? Did they charge him with first? Did you already call it in? What would Andrelli kill his bimbo attorney for, anyway—"

I cut him off. For one thing, I can't stand people who use terms like *skinny* and *bimbo* and think they're cool. I also didn't like Nicky's wet, fat palm on my arm. "I don't know anything yet," I snarled.

He gave me a cynical look. "C'mon."

"Buzz off." I looked for Marcus, tried to catch his eye. He avoided me and motioned to Vince, pointing to the curb. His limo was there, and they headed in that direction. I did too, fending off the locusts with an elbow. But I didn't make it in time. That door, too, slammed in my face, and Marcus was gone . . . the black, opaque windows forming a barrier as impenetrable as any fourteenth-century moat. The limo purred into action, the wheels turned, the rear end presented itself, like a mare in season. There may have been a cloud of dust as it galloped away—but certainly no "Hi-oh, Silver."

Shit, I thought, with my heart somewhere around my knees. So much for loyalty and absolute trust.

CHAPTER THREE

I ignored the snickers and renewed assaults from my fellow scribes, and tried not to think about how I'd look on *WOKR News* that night. I hadn't even seen the minicams before; there went five minutes of the promised fifteen of celebrity status everyone gets per life, and I'd muffed it by forgetting to powder my nose.

I trudged back into the Public Safety Building. It seemed like it might be a good idea to talk to Grady North in Homicide, see what the hell was going on. Halfway through the chaos of bums in the immense old reception area, however, I was waylaid by an iron grip on my arm.

"Jesse? Jesse, it's me, Howard."

I turned and looked into eyes that were flat and pale, watery from years of fermented rye.

"Howard, good to see you," I said as he gripped my hand. His was all cracked leather and long dirty nails, and I stiffened myself to give him a return grip and a smile. I leaned back, though, when he opened his mouth to speak again and a rotten odor drifted my way. It was so thick I feared for a moment it might enter my body, like a dying soul.

"What's up, Howard?"

"Some bum got hisself knocked off over on the square," he rasped, giving a phlegm-filled cough that got me square on the mouth. I lifted a hand to wipe the spittle away, but he grasped that one too. I tried to breathe only through my nose, keeping my lips locked, but it was hard to do that and talk at the same time. I tried to tell myself that nuns and priests had been ministering to the unfortunate for centuries without getting their diseases. How that related to me I didn't know.

"Howard, bums are dying all the time. Why's the P.D. making a fuss over this one?"

Howard flinched as I spoke, and moved back a pace. He waved an offended hand in front of his wrinkled face. "Jeeesh, you stink, Jesse. You been hittin' the sauce again?"

I sighed. What a gift—t'see ourselves as others see us. I was getting all sorts of lessons in humility this day. "Never mind that, Howard. Just tell me, what's all the fuss about here?"

He shook his head, his eyes going from flat to fanatic and back again as his mind wandered among the spheres. "This's a big one, Jesse. Somebody Important, maybe." His fingernails scrabbled at my arm. "Jesse, remember how you helped us last Christmas, gettin' the shelter and soup kitchen opened up again down here?"

"I didn't do anything, Howard. Just wrote a few pieces, got the right people together." I managed to get one hand loose and rubbed at the spit on my mouth with my thumb.

"Maybe you could do somethin' like that again?" he said uncertainly. "There's somethin' weird goin' on down here." His eyes began to drift again, and he pulled them back with obvious effort, squinting. "It's the kids," he said.

"What do you mean, Howard?"

"I mean where do they go?" His voice began to rise angrily, and he started to shake. "That's what I said, isn't it? I said it clear enough. WHERE DO THEY GO?"

He was shouting, and one of the cops got up from a desk where he was questioning a woman in red sequined shorts and little else. He ambled over with a reluctant air.

"Trouble here?"

I shook my head, but Howard was on a roll.

"Nobody cares anymore!" he yelled. "When I was teachin', things were different. WE DIDN'T THROW KIDS AWAY!"

The cop grabbed Howard by the arm and led him over to a chair near his desk. Howard caved in suddenly, folding into the chair, and buried his face in his leathery old hands. "Oh, God," he said. "God, oh God!" I knelt beside him.

"It's okay, Howard." I touched his arm and then his head. His long gray hair was crusty, and probably loaded with lice. I drew my fingers away. "What can I do?"

He didn't respond. The sobbing continued, and my presence didn't seem to help. After a few minutes, I nodded to the cop—who was keeping one eye out, the other hotly focused on the woman in the red sequined shorts—and left Howard there.

I figured Howard to be in his fifties, although he looked seventy. His body was long and probably once slender, but he had a belly now that would look prosperous on a businessman. On him, as on many of the undernourished, the flatulence was more likely to be caused both by hunger and intestinal worms. Howard had been a high school math teacher, but he'd burned out years ago. I didn't know why—he never told me any more than that. Now he spent his days in Dwight Square, drawing up lesson plans on brown grocery bags and scoring quarters from the successful business people who passed that way on their lunch hours.

Howard was a prime example of meeting the same people on the way up as you meet on the way down. How many of those business people would one day end up in Dwight or Union or Washington Squares somewhere in the world, muttering over quarterly reports or stock market quotes on brown paper bags? With luck, the way the economy was going, maybe only ten percent.

I made it to the stairs this time and headed up, stopping at a moldy green rest room on the third floor to wash my face and run a comb through snarly hair—a victim of all the humidity. The comb snagged, and the pain that creaked through my head when my scalp was pulled reminded me of matters best forgot. For the second time that day my face stared gloomily back at me, too wise for thirty-one, too sharp and cynical for any age. Other than that, it wasn't a bad face. Dark green eyes set off by thick shoulder-length brown curls, high cheekbones, a big enough mouth. A little puffiness and bruising from the morning's adventure, but hard otherwise, hard and crafty and uncompromising.

I bearded Grady North at his desk in Homicide, and I could tell he knew what I wanted when he saw me coming. He frowned and swiveled his chair the other way.

"Hi," I said, sliding into the metal straight-back next to his desk.

He didn't turn around. "I don't suppose you're here for a weather report."

"Hot," I said. "Hot as Hades, everywhere I go."

"You didn't need to tell me that." He picked up the phone and punched three digits. "Skelley? North here. You get the autopsy report on that bum from Dwight Square yet?"

I waited patiently, a long five minutes, knowing the game. He was pissed. It was in every muscle of his taut body, every intonation of his voice.

When he finally hung up, I said, "Hey, why don't you come over for dinner tonight?"

He fiddled with some files. "Busy. Your mobster friend has given me a full plate, thanks very much."

"Marcus?" I pretended innocence, to see what he'd say.

"And don't give me that innocent crap." He swiveled back and looked at me then, drawing sandy brows together over deepset hazel eyes. "You look like hell. Rough night?"

I shrugged. "What's happening? What'd Marcus do?"

"As if you didn't know. He and his attorney apparently had a parting of the ways. He offed her on his own boat."

"Barbara Sloan, you mean?"

"The one and only."

"She was shot on Andrelli's yacht—the *SeaStar*?"

"Last night. At the marina. Pretty stupid, but it was only a matter of time. Andrelli's too damned cocky for his own good. Thinks he runs this town and can do anything in it. I'm here to tell him he can't."

"I thought . . . the gossip around town is that he and Baby Ca— that he and Babs had something hot going. What makes you think he killed her?"

Grady sighed. He leaned back and propped a nicely polished brown shoe on his desk. Since he'd made Detective First, he was dressing better all the time. "You can tell Andrelli it's a waste of time, sending you here. Might as well send any one of his hoods as you."

"You know I don't take orders from Andrelli."

"You don't have to. The two of you work in synchronization, like twins."

Sure. Remembering the doors slammed in my face in the last thirty minutes, I felt more like the middle child, forgotten and insecure.

But the thing about loyalty, for me anyway, is that it's hard to shake. "He didn't do it," I said. "He didn't kill Barbara Sloan."

"Yeah? He tell you who did?"

"I haven't talked to him."

Grady gave a hard laugh and stood, going over to the file cabinet and stuffing the folders in angrily. "Jess, when will you wise up to that guy?"

"I know Andrelli's warts—"

"And you think that underneath them someday you'll find a prince. Well, grow up, Jess. Marcus Andrelli is a ruthless thug—"

"He is not a thug." My voice rose in spite of my efforts to control it. "If it wasn't for him, there would be full-out mob warfare in this town. He keeps a balance, not like the old days—"

"A dead woman's a dead woman," Grady snapped. "Whether you kill her with a machine gun in an alley or a nine-millimeter semi on a yacht."

A nine-millimeter semi? Was that a generalization, or a specific? I pondered it, then asked, "Aren't you even considering alternatives?"

"Barbara Sloan was killed on Andrelli's boat. There was no one there but Andrelli and—he says—that bodyguard of his, Tark. Who, it seems, has disappeared. Andrelli kills the lady over a mob dispute—and the only witness, the only one who can testify against him, takes off on a paid

vacation until the heat dies down. It's all pretty clear to me
. . . and to the commissioner."

"*Fournsey?* He can't find his own ass in the City Hall
men's room. He does what he's told from the top—" I broke
off. "Is Fournsey pushing for Andrelli's arrest?"

He banged the file drawer shut. "I've said all I'm going
to, Jess."

"One more thing. Who're the arresting officers?"

"It's on the record. I'm getting out of here, it's been a
long day. You coming?"

It was either that or sit there staring at an empty desk.
I followed him through the door and into the cluttered
hallway—past scarred wooden benches and anxious relatives waiting for sons and husbands to be released.

"Where you going?" I had to run to keep up with his
long strides. "Harrigan's?"

"Probably."

"Mind if I go with?"

He stopped and faced me. "I thought you weren't drinking."

"I can sit in a bar and have soda water," I said testily.

He sighed. "Come along, then, if you want. But don't
expect me to give you any more information on Marcus
Andrelli's soon-to-be arrest. Your boy is going down, and
there's nothing you can do this time."

"Okay, okay. No sweat. A friendly, nonalcoholic drink,
for old time's sake."

He flashed me a look of total disbelief and turned on his
heel. I followed like a good little sycophant—servile,
flattering—"Gosh, I love your new look . . . sort of like the
all-new Springsteen, on his way to the Grammys." Anyone
watching would've placed me as a police groupie, rather
than a reporter—

That, or a whore.

CHAPTER FOUR

Harrigan's was more crowded than it had been in the old days. We squeezed into a booth with Dick Skelley, who arrived around the same time, and a uniformed cop from Vice, Jack Hoffman. I ordered mineral water with an orange slice, and toasted Grady—firm in the conviction that I would never, in this life or hereafter, drink again. My head felt like a melon patch that had been trampled by seventeen farmers in CAT caps in search of a one-eyed, bushy-tailed skook.

I returned Dick Skelley's smile, noting that his red hair had a few more strands of gray than when I'd seen him last. Jack Hoffman was oddly cool, cooler even than the TV cop he resembled—the bland, freckle-faced Marty Milner, from the old *Adam 12* show.

I'd never really known Jack, just seen him around, and wasn't sure what this seeming antipathy was about. A lot of the Rochester cops knew about my friendship with Marcus, and not all of them, I knew, were as accepting of it as Grady—if you could call him that.

I struggled to keep up with the conversation, pulling apart the orange and sucking on the little pyramids. I pretended the water was my old favorite drink, a Genesee Screw, and almost felt high after a while.

Grady began to ease up too. When Skelley and Jack hitched their belts over beginning, thirtyish paunches and left to pick up another couple of drinks at the bar, Grady said, "Have you eaten yet?"

I shook my head and wished I hadn't. The farmers had

obviously found their skook and shot him the hell to death. Right there inside my skull.

"That's not good for you, Jess. How about a sandwich?"

Harrigan's specialized in thick black bread with cream cheese, Genoa salami, and raw red onions. "Sounds good. I'll have the special, if you're buying."

"Why not? I owe you one for the last fettucine at your place—let's see now, when was that? Saint Joseph's Day?"

I ignored the implication. Saint Joseph's Day was in March, if I remembered the liturgical calendar, and yes, it had been a while since I'd had Grady over. Why was everybody on my case today?

I toyed with the white of the orange, where all the good vitamins are, and watched Grady cross to the bar and order. He and I had known each other for years, and there was a time, before Marcus, when I thought we might end up together. Grady Ryan North is, after all, a man any gal in her right mind would want. A good friend, a brave soul— a straight-arrow, do-it-by-the-rulebook cop. I'd always be sure what I was getting with Grady, and the direction my life would take.

I shudder even now at the thought. It's bad enough having a nine-to-five job.

He came back bearing a number—the modern-day equivalent of prehistoric man proudly fetching home a meal of brontosaurus loin. He also bore a basket of salty snacks. Sliding into the seat opposite me, he dropped it between us and said, "So, how is it these days, being on general assignment at the *Herald*?"

I searched for a sesame stick and made a grimace. "It feels like kindergarten, having to be there regular hours, or when I'm not, checking in all the time."

"You had the option to do investigative reporting," he reminded me for the hundredth time. "It's what you trained for, what you've done for years—"

"Uh-huh. You know what *investigative* means at a paper like the *Herald*? You spend half your life in some dusty library, while all the action is going on outside."

"And the money as a g.a. is good?"

"Barely. But enough to keep paying off Pop's bills and send a little to Mom in California. Not that she seems to want it lately. She keeps sending it back."

"How's it going with her?"

"Well, I went out and saw her in the spring, you know. It was kind of uneasy, but I had to do it, my shrink insisted. Confront the old ghosts, lay them to rest."

"Has she stopped blaming you?"

"For Pop's death? We're making strides."

"And you've forgiven yourself."

"I guess. I'm living with it."

"It wasn't your fault, you know."

"Knowing and internalizing are two different things, at least according to Samved—the all-wise, all-knowing—"

"Your new shrink?"

"Guru/shrink," I corrected. "Maybe someday . . ."

He ran a finger lightly over my forehead, pushing back a stray lock of hair. I gave him a smile. Despite all our differences, our arguments over the way I ran my life, it was impossible not to like Grady North.

"You look like hell today," he said.

Even when he's a pain in the ass.

"You've been drinking, haven't you?" he persisted.

I shrugged.

"Why?"

"Couldn't think of a strong enough reason not to."

"Don't be flip, Jess."

"I'm not. It's the truth. I woke up this morning after a night of depression, thinking that the rewards for not drinking weren't all they were cracked up to be."

"Suddenly? Just like that?"

"I guess it's been coming on awhile."

"Is that why you haven't been around? It's going on a couple of months since we've talked."

"So what's to say? I've been sober. But I'm . . . grouchy, lately. Not fit to be around. The original high of getting all the junk out of my system wore off." I grabbed my third sesame stick, popped it into my mouth, and said through chews, "Hell, I don't know. I'm . . ."

"Bored," Grady finished for me. He took my hand, wiped the salt off it, and pierced me with the Grady North "I know your secrets" probing look. "You're a crisis junky, Jess. Always have been—at least in the five or so years I've known you. If you're drinking again, it's because you needed another emergency to deal with."

I felt myself flush and yanked my hand away. "You're worse than Samved! And you wonder why I haven't been around."

"No, I don't. I know it's because I tell you what you don't want to hear."

"Look, just drop it, okay? My head is pounding. My tongue is so fuzzy I could package it and sell it as a Pet Hairball. Where the hell are those sandwiches?" I cast a frown around, looking for Harve, the bartender.

"He's busy. He'll be along."

I drummed my fingers on the table.

"Is that something new you've picked up?"

I stopped the drumming. "It's . . . time. TIME. It goes so slow these days. Everything takes too long. Standing in lines that go on forever. Driving in traffic that doesn't move. Do you know that people actually pay other people to *wait* for them now? To wait at the DMV, the supermarket, the bank . . . shit, Grady, what kind of a world is this getting to be, anyway?"

His answer was a growl. "I could wring Andrelli's neck." He took a long draught of beer and slapped the mug down on the bare oak table.

"Look, don't start—"

"I know, you've heard it all. But it's true. He's done this to you. You never were like this, before him. You were more relaxed, more easygoing—"

"Shit, Grady, I was *drunk* half the time! Anybody can be easygoing when they're sloshed! I've never been relaxed in my life without some chemical or other running through my brain. In school it was pot. After Pop died, it was alcohol.

Now it's food. Goddamn, where *are* those sandwiches, any-way?" I grabbed a pretzel from the basket of snacks.

"You hungry a lot?" He narrowed his eyes and peered at me like an old family physician.

"All the time. I'll be the fattest reformed drunk in town."

He grinned suddenly. "Not you, Jess. Little Mite?"

"Huh. But you're right. I look like hell. It's no wonder—" I hesitated.

"What?"

"Baby Cakes." I bit at the pretzel angrily. "What did he see in her? She was cold—an ice princess—not his type at all." I stopped as Grady's mouth hardened.

"I have tried and tried to warn you about Andrelli, you just won't listen."

"Dammit, Grady! Marcus stood by me while I was so-bering up. His being there is part of the reason I made it."

"I stood by you," he reminded me.

I looked away. "That was . . . different."

"Right. I didn't show up with roses every week. Jess, it was against the rules, coming up to the treatment center while you were there."

"That's—"

"What?"

"Nothing."

He sighed. "Marcus didn't follow the rules. I know."

It was Grady's turn to drum the table.

I didn't blame him. Nothing about the way I was always comparing Grady to Marcus was fair—or even reasonable. After a few moments, I said, "What's happening with the bum in the park? Why all the fuss? And why is Vice in-volved?"

His mouth twisted. "You don't miss a thing, do you?"

"Well, you were talking on the phone to Skelley right in front of me, keeping me waiting, what was I supposed to do?"

"The bum," he said with the air of someone humoring an unruly child, "was twenty-one years old. Among other things, he'd been working the streets, hustling, since he was fourteen. When he died the other day he looked a hundred."

I hadn't thought to bring the usual pad and pencil, so I reached over to Grady, poked a hand inside his summer suit jacket, and pulled a pen from the inner pocket. It was an old, familiar habit, the kind you acquire with friends, and his slight smile in response to the gesture helped to take the edge off things. I grabbed a dry cocktail napkin and began to write. "What was the kid's name?"

"Con. Constanzio James Argento."

"What was he, a runaway?"

"Yeah. He ran to Chicago when he was fourteen, lived with an aunt awhile, but from what she says, he was never happy with what she could afford to give him. He figured life would be different there, that he'd somehow miraculously have the good things without working for them. When it didn't turn out that way, he got involved with the kiddie porn people; played the part in low-budget movies of the older brother, newsboy, whoever—the one that seduced the little girls, the little boys—"

He shoved his beer aside with a gesture of disgust. "He came back here a couple months ago, the same time the kiddie porn people starting moving in again."

"Wait a minute." A few years ago, the Rochester P.D. had rooted the child porn racket out of the area. I'd worked on the story then. "That scum is back? How come I haven't heard about it?"

"They were pretty far underground this time. But we know who they are now, thanks in large part to Con. Too bad the kid had to die for it."

"He was a snitch?"

"For Vice."

"What'd he give them?"

"A missing link. And confirmation of things we already knew, or suspected." He gave me a steady look. "Two guesses, Jess. Let's see how sharp you can be when you set your mind to it."

I felt my chin go up. "No."

"No?"

"Marcus Andrelli would not be involved in kiddie porn."

"Right. He's the Crown Prince of Good Deeds, I forgot."

"Grady, you don't know Marcus. The way he feels about kids, family."

One day last year I was sent out to cover a six-alarm fire in Marcus's old neighborhood. Actually, I was covering the local politicians, who were making the obligatory rounds, "comforting" homeless blacks and welfare moms, telling them how "everything would be done to relocate them." They were trying to stop a riot from beginning, since it looked as if the whole damned neighborhood was burning down and there was some question about a lack of official interest (up to then) in adequate fire plugs and prevention. The mayor was there; the local assemblyman; Fournsey, the police commissioner; even the governor—all of them clucking sympathetically and patting backs, telling people who didn't have anything to begin with how there would be funds to help them get started again. "This is America. No one goes hungry here."

Sure, and it's a great country for farmers and tool and die workers too.

I was just about getting my fill of it when Marcus showed up with Tark—not in the limo, but in a truck loaded down with food, blankets, clothing.

Marcus's expression when he saw the show that was going on was somewhat akin to mine. They worked into the night—Marcus and Tark, along with some neighborhood wiseguys and a handful of street people—hardly talking, the sky red and their skin and clothes black with smoke. Several older people were overcome by the smoke, and the younger ones—from burned-out vets to single moms, many of them in oddly matched thrift shop clothing—struggled to help the elderly, their faces caked with sweat and soot, everyone coughing and spitting ash.

Finally, the polits became embarrassed by all the media attention the local mob and welfare recipients were getting for doing something rather than talking about it, and they actually mobilized the appropriate agencies to get people into homes or shelters until something could be worked out. They did all this off-scene, of course, disappearing back to their air-cooled offices when the media heat became worse than that of any six-alarm fire.

I guess I'm getting off the track, expounding as I'm wont to do on the absurdity of it all, but what I kept remembering afterward was Marcus in soot-blackened jeans, pacing the sidewalk, his face smudged with dirt and his expression tender as he held a baby while its mother rested. The baby cried, the mother stirred, and I heard a murmuring from Marcus's lips that I had to get closer to catch.

Well, shucks. He was singing an Italian lullaby.

I crept silently away before he could see I'd overheard, but I'll always cherish that picture of Marcus, no matter what. And there was nothing anyone could say that would convince me he'd have a part in hurting kids.

"Marcus is death against child porn," I said to Grady now.

"You're right about one thing, my friend. He's death. To Barbara Sloan, Con Argento, to all the little kids who get messed up in that dirty business—"

"Listen, Grady, if anyone is dealing in child porn here, it's more likely to be Paulie Gandolo, not Marcus. Paulie's the kind of sleaze—"

"Andrelli may be from a different crime family"—Grady studied a rivulet of moisture on his mug of beer—"but we know for a fact he's joined forces with Gandolo on this. And Barbara Sloan was their go-between."

My writing hand paused. "You're kidding." Barbara Sloan—not just a lawyer to Marcus (and much, much more), but a mediator between him and Paulie Gandolo? I didn't know if I bought that—but if true, it could add a whole new dimension to my thinking about Barbara Sloan. For a moment I felt a twinge of sympathy. Anyone in that kind of position would hold a certain amount of power—yet, at the same time, be extremely vulnerable.

"I remember . . ." I began. I stopped to push around some grains of salt, gathering in the memory.

"Go on."

"Oh, a few years ago . . . a brief inner glimpse of Barbara Sloan. Before she went to work for Marcus. She was an attorney for the city then, young and hungry, you know how they are when they first come out of school. She had a lot of drive. I was supposed to interview her about some case she was working on at the time . . . I forget what it was. She was in a hurry, and her attitude was clipped, a little cold. I was kind of pushy myself, I guess, and I got off on the wrong foot with her, way back then. . . ."

I wondered, not for the first time, what had made Sloan leave her position as assistant to the city attorney and go to work for Marcus. I had assumed at the time that it was the usual cynicism—implicit with that particular job—that sets in after a couple of years. City politics could eat you alive. Personally, I prefer mobsters to politicians, figuring that mobsters are at least honest about what they do.

But Barbara Sloan hadn't seemed the type to hobnob with hoods at all. She was kind of prissy—and caught in a dispute between Marcus and Paulie, she probably wouldn't have stood a chance. I knew enough about Paulie Gandolo to know that women are disposable items for him. Paulie was old-style, horse's-head-in-the-bed-type mob. Small, skinny, but with a face that had seen and ordered so much horror you got shivers just looking at it in the papers, Paulie was also a certified nut.

Which brought me back to my original thought. Marcus would never do business with him.

I said as much to Grady. "Marcus and Paulie Gandolo are sworn enemies, opposite poles."

"They may be enemies for the most part, Jess, but you know as well as I that the families join ranks when it means more power for all concerned. And there's a lot of bucks— and therefore power—in child porn. More, even, than in drugs." He pushed the beer aside. " 'Course, I don't know

. . . you think your pal Marcus is into power? Nah, he couldn't be. Not the King of Kind Hearts—"

"Please."

He popped some nuts into his mouth and was silent, chewing, his arms resting casually along the back of the booth.

Apart from the way Marcus felt about kids, I was thinking, he prided himself on not having to deal in the lower rackets—on being able to bring in all the capital he needed through business deals alone.

More than once, I'd heard Marcus on the phone at his penthouse: ". . . launder . . . fix . . . defraud." Those were the things he got off on. Child porn, drugs, the street-level stuff? They were too "old hat," in his words. No challenge.

In truth, I'd always thought street crime was intellectually beneath Marcus. He could be something of a snob.

"What if I can prove Andrelli isn't involved in any of this—in the kiddie porn, in Con Argento's death—and that he didn't kill Barbara Sloan? Will you let up on him? Stop trying to put his neck in a noose every time something goes sour in this town?"

Grady laughed shortly, and ran a hand through his hair. It crinkled back up, the way it always did, in stubborn tufts. His look of impatient despair was almost endearing. "You just won't quit, will you? What will it take for you to see—"

"Let me talk to people, the arresting officers, the witnesses, work with the same information you've got."

"You think you can investigate murder better than my staff—" The effrontery transmitted itself to Grady's back, which stiffened against the wooden booth.

"Don't get all hot under the collar. You said it yourself, I'm trained in investigative reporting—that's not like being an amateur. And I'd approach it from a different angle, maybe. Be more objective."

"Objective!" He nearly choked on the nuts he was munching. Coughing and snorting, he wiped his eyes. "Give me strength."

I turned the napkin over and began to write again, before he could think about it too much. "Who was Con Argento's contact in Vice?"

He was still shaking his head, but he groaned and said something like, "Oh, what the hell . . ." (Or maybe it was, "Jeeesh, you smell." Today, anything was possible.) "Dan Greer," I made out of it at last.

"Danny Greer?" *He of the eyes like a morn in spring and smiling? The kind the song was written for?* Well, hot damn. I felt a surge of female interest. And realized immediately that it was little more than a knee-jerk reaction to the rejection from Marcus earlier.

I may be a fool, but I hadn't gone completely over the edge. I still know when I'm acting like one.

"Danny and I went to school together," I said, trying for a little dignity and omitting the fact that I'd had a terrible crush on that *adorable senior* all through my junior year. "We were on the same softball team. Okay if I talk to him about whatever this snitch—Con Argento—told him?"

Grady muttered, "Why would I mind? And what good would it do?"

I wrote. "How was Argento killed?"

"He was shot, last night, back of that movie theater over on Market."

"No witnesses?"

"No—" He broke off. "Look, I've already said more than I should have. How you manage to wheedle these concessions out of me, I'll never know."

"Just one more thing. Did you charge Marcus today with Barbara Sloan's murder? Is he out on bail, or what?"

"No charges yet. There are a couple of pieces still—"

At that moment, Harve brought our mile-high sandwiches over. He thudded the plates down, and I dropped Grady's pen and nearly broke an arm getting to my Harrigan's Special. My hands took up its thickness, my mouth circled and closed, juice leaked out on my chin . . .

The parallel with other means of oral gratification is inescapable.

But my stomach wasn't quite up to this latest obsession. *Your eyes are bigger than your belly*, Mom used to say.

On this occasion, at least, the need for a food fix was stronger than the available gastric fluids. My stomach did a mazurka, then gave a little bow and died. I put the sandwich down.

Harve stood there a minute, legs rocking in his faded jeans, and just stared at me. Or I think he did. He wore thick, round, rimless glasses, so his eyes were nothing but a blur, but his head was pointed in my direction. His hair was orange, and stood up in puffs like a New Hampshire hill in late autumn.

Harve had been in Nam in the early seventies, and when he got home it took him a few years to put all the pieces of his life, and body, back together. He wandered around the country awhile on a Harley, got tired of being unemployed, and came home. Since then, he had been studying engineering at R.I.T, part-time, for the better part of six years. His theory was that the Army ships you out to blow the countries up first, then sends you back in the Corps of Engineers to put them together again. As an engineer in America, you've always got a chance to work.

He said finally, "You don't look like somebody who's been on the wagon a year."

I wasn't offended. Harve and I go back a long way. "It was a short, unpremeditated fall," I explained.

"Oh. Sorry. I didn't know. What I meant was, you look pretty good."

"I do?" I resisted sticking my tongue out at Grady— mostly because I knew from earlier drinking days that it was probably covered with white slime and would appear real gross.

"Well, you don't look like most of those people in the programs, at least," Harve amended.

"Oh."

His mouth twitched in a beginning grin. "You know how they get, like, strange? Their faces turn all hard and bony-looking, their muscles twitch, and their eyes shift—probably from all the coffee they drink at the meetings. You don't look like that."

I picked up my pace and tone to match his. "I don't go to the meetings," I said.

"No? How're you doin' it, Jess?"

"Private. My shrink's into metaphysics. We decided I've got enough self-image problems without getting up in a meeting four times a week and saying 'I am an alcoholic.' I mean, talk about *imprinting*."

Harve nodded. I went on with the patter.

"So we're working on positive affirmations instead. I practice seeing myself as a beautiful, perfect child of God. No disease, no imperfection. When I need support I have numbers to call, people who support me in the belief that I have no disease, no imperfection—"

I carefully avoided remembering the image of myself on the bathroom floor that morning. As usual with Harve, I was on a roll, and beginning to feel good.

But Grady interrupted. He hadn't heard how this actually worked before, and there was an uncertain tug at his lips. "Are you making this up, Jess?"

"Shit, no. I'm chanting, too."

"Chanting?"

"Uh-huh. Every morning. Mrs. Binty, my landlady, says it's like waking up in a monastery."

"I don't . . . What do you chant?"

"Just sounds. Vibrations, to lift my energy. You know . . . ohhhhm . . . ohhhhm . . . you start at middle C and work your way up the scale . . . OHHHHM . . ."

Grady glanced about nervously, to see, I guess, if anyone could hear and was looking. He caught Harve's wide grin at the same time, and gave a snort. "Jess, how much of this is true?"

I took a sip of my drink. "Everything but the chanting. The guru/shrink was Mom's idea. I think it's all that damned sun out in California; they get weird ideas. Anyway, she sent me the name of this guy a few months ago, Samved, over in Pittsford. Out near the old Nazareth Motherhouse, you know?"

"Uh-huh. And this is working?"

"Well, instead of alcoholic dementia, I get religious visions, but other than that, I'm sober." I sighed, the foot-in-the-drawer mock-up slipping out of the gray cells without warning. "Most of the time, anyway."

Harve pushed his Coke-bottle glasses up on his head, still grinning. Then he gave me a more somber look through ash-colored eyes that might have been fallout from his fiery hair. He seemed to want to say more, but cast an uneasy glance at Grady and was silent. Finally, he brought all the angles of his thin face together in what was probably meant to be a smile, dropped the glasses back on his nose, and sauntered away.

Grady chowed down while I chewed ice, and when he was halfway through, Dick Skelley and Jack Hoffman came back. We shifted to give them room.

"Talked to the M.E.," Skelley said, leaning his elbows on the table. One large, raw hand, dusted with fine red hairs, played with the salt shaker. "Autopsy's in on the Sloan lady. Chief cause of death was the first bullet wound. Came from C dock, just above the yacht, judging from angle and distance. D.A.'s got a witness who says Sloan was on the yacht, talking to Andrelli when it happened—"

He broke off when Grady cleared his throat and slid a glance toward me.

Skelley was silent immediately, but I pounced. "I told you Marcus didn't do it! They were together, the bullet came from somewhere else entirely—"

Grady held up a hand, telling me to wait.

"Who was on C dock?" he asked Skelley. But his tone indicated that he'd already guessed, or knew.

Skelley, looking uncomfortable, said, "Just the one guy, according to the witness."

"Who?"

"You know, the only other person there. The bodyguard.

That Tark guy." He glanced at me, and ran a finger under his tight collar.

"I don't believe it," I said. "Tark—"

Grady interrupted. "The witness see him shoot?"

Skelley nodded unhappily. He and I, together with Pat, his wife, had worked on a Food Bank collection the previous Christmas. Pat was a whirlwind, with auburn hair and a fresh, open smile. I'd gotten the thing started, but she and Skelley made it work. The three of us had become friends that month, sorting out endless cans of pumpkin and beans. Now, even though I'd let the friendship fade—the way I too often do—it was clear Skelley didn't like giving me this news.

"The weapon?" Grady said.

"A nine-millimeter semi, just like we thought. Glock, from Austria. Expensive. A favorite"—Skelley's tone and expression were miserable now—"of the mob around here."

I was sitting across from Jack Hoffman now, so it was natural to look at him as I took a sip from my glass to ease my suddenly dry throat. I caught him unaware, I guess. There was a small smile on his lips, an almost satisfied look in his pale blue eyes. I shivered, and he caught me looking. The smile went away. I glanced somewhere else, across the room, thinking that just moments before, I'd have guessed that Jack Hoffman was pretty much a harmless guy.

I turned my attention to Grady.

"Sounds to me," he was saying, "like your pal Tark did the deed for his boss, then disappeared so he couldn't be made to testify. You still think you can investigate this case objectively?"

"What's left to investigate?" I muttered without any grace. "Seems to me like you've got it all wrapped up."

Jack frowned. "We don't need civilians . . ."

But Grady ignored him, focusing on me.

"There's still the matter of motive to be settled. Maybe Jess could help us with that. Was it a mob dispute—or, let's say, just for the sake of argument, a lovers' quarrel? It was a warm night, the bar was set up—Andrelli and the

Sloan woman were alone on the upper deck of the yacht. There were flowers, candles . . . a romantic setting . . . *but* . . . suppose it was a setup, a trap. And just about the time the lady gets comfortable, she's dead. What do you think of that scenario, Jess?"

Grady waited for me to comment, but Jack's frown had deepened. He slid from the booth, tugging at his uniform tie and saying tersely that he had "some business." I watched him leave, then faced Grady, whose steady, confident gaze was on me.

My resolve about Marcus's innocence wobbled.

I remembered that I hadn't really been around him for the past few months. And I kept seeing his tight face as he had stalked away from me earlier. Feeling the lack of connection. Remembering how he had once told me: "Don't confuse my sometimes better instincts with sainthood, Jessica. That would be a serious mistake."

My world, unsettled and iffy as it ofttimes is, was taking on elements of genuine doubt. The cloud that had been hanging over my shoulders since seeing Marcus descended now, to redarken a day that had begun with an ill wind anyway.

Grady said a few words to Skelley and began sucking down his beer, laughing and seemingly at ease. My depression worsened, and my eyes fixed on Grady's beer like it was a hypnotist's amulet. I could imagine that ice-cold yeasty liquid sliding down my throat, the muscles easing up, my mind quieting, and all the worry and confusion slipping away.

Grady caught me staring. "Jess, you okay?"

I nodded. "I am a perfect child of God," I intoned.

I got my bones out of there fast, and rattled on home.

CHAPTER FIVE

I did not drink that night, if it's of any interest at all. Instead, I ate three Hostess Twinkies with strawberry filling, a pint of coffee Häagen-Dazs, and half a box of Ritz crackers with peanut butter, grape jelly, and marshmallow between.

Ritz Shitz are what Mom used to make for me when I was a kid and felt bad.

I was finally nurtured and stuffed enough to go to bed, but it occurred to me as I tossed and turned and burped that I would have to join Overeaters Anonymous now. That led to the inescapable conclusion that once I gave up food, I'd probably turn to gambling as my next obsession, so it'd be on to Gamblers Anon, and pretty soon my whole wall would be papered with support numbers—accusing, demanding, calling to me:

"Jesse . . . Jesse . . . you've nowhere else to go, now. Time to grow up."

The horror was too much to contemplate, so I pulled my Puff the Magic Dragon sheet over my head and went to sleep.

Chapter Six

Now and then on hot summer days I like to fantasize about spring.

To wit:

They call Rochester, New York, The Flower City, and in spring—which hardly ever comes—the place pops out in lilacs, so many you think they'll never end. People get a little crazy here after the miserable winters, and I'm the worst. I feel like King Arthur in the movie *Camelot*.

I mean, there's crazy Arthur—(Richard Harris does it best)—frolicking in the woods, and Lancelot arrives from France to save the day. He comes pounding in on his trusty steed, handsome as hell and hot to trot, and throws himself at Arthur's feet. "Give me an order!" he cries. (Franco Nero, his blue eyes flashing like aquamarines in fiery pools.) "Send me on a mission! Is there some wrong I can right? Some enemy I can battle? Some peril I can undertake?"

And Arthur—the one I most relate to—says, "Well, actually, there's not much going on today." He sends the astonished Lancelot a-Maying with the queen and her court. "It's the first of May," he tells him. "The season for gathering flowers."

"*Knights* gathering *flowers?*" Lancelot is both astounded and dismayed.

"Well, *somebody* has to do it," Arthur fumes.

And in spring, in Rochester, New York, that somebody is me. The ice melts and the boats are out on Lake Ontario. Trees burst into bloom along the Genesee River, which winds through town. The University of Rochester has its graduations, the high schools have their proms. The place not only blooms with flowers, it bursts right open with caps and gowns and fussy white dresses and suits.

And like Guinevere, I sing out, "Where are the simple joys of maidenhood? Shall I have the normal life a maiden should?"

This absurdity lasts less than three weeks—which is all the spring we get up here. Then it's summer, the heat blisters through, and the thunderstorms begin.

Normal people go back to work. I honestly think that I do too.

But my boss, R. B. Chastain, says I'm still out there a-Maying.

I will never be cut out for nine-to-five.

"Which is probably all the excuse one needs to wake up once in a while and drink," I grumbled, as, cold sober, I pulled on the uniform they make you wear at the *Herald*. It was eight o'clock Monday morning, the dead of summer, and I was struggling into stockings, bra, shoes with heels (no sneakers), regular pants (no jeans). For an old seventies hanger-on like me, a kid who grew up running with boys, this manner of dress is the penultimate death.

It is also *Herald* code. R. B. Chastain—graduate of St. John Fisher, class of '48—has ordained it to be so.

Chastain is a doddering, antiquated fool for a man less than seventy—but a fool with money. And money was what the *Herald* needed last year to stay in business. So they allowed this idiot to buy in, gave him the title of publisher, and within weeks he had instituted (I love that word) a dress code. The only people it didn't hit were the photographers, who still get to dress in their subterranean animal-like way. The rest of us, R. B. maintains, represent the *Herald* when we go out on interviews, and as such we must "keep up."

So here I was, grunting into pantyhose when the temperature even at five A.M. had been nearing ninety. And I *still* haven't learned how to put the damned things on so the legs won't twist and cut off my circulation at the crotch.

I finished with this torture and waddled into the kitchen,

holding my thighs apart so my beige trousers wouldn't sweat. With the renewed but unsteady vigor that comes with twelve hours' sobriety, I looked gratefully around my kitchen, which, like the rest of my apartment, is flooded with light. Every summer I take down the heavy drapes, leaving the windows bare of all but their sheer white curtains and hanging plants. In winter, the drapes go back up, and the place becomes a cocoon.

I didn't, this morning, want a drop to drink. It happens this way with me—or at least, it always did in the past. Total self-destruction one day, then the next, back on track with little trouble at all.

As with most things, however, it's the off days that get you in the end.

I had my appetite back again, and was scarfing down a Danish slathered with butter and some freshly ground coffee, when Toni Langella arrived for her morning visit, her thick dark hair loose and flowing. She plopped the morning edition of the *Herald* down on my butcher-block counter. "He left it in the bushes on our side of the fence again," she said.

Toni is twelve, a budding Olympic gymnast, and she had started hanging out with me this summer, like she didn't want to be at home. Home was the house next door.

"How can you eat that stuff?" she said morosely as I stuffed another bite of Danish in my mouth. She screwed her face up in disgust. "Do you know the kinds of poisons you're putting into your body?" She tossed my coffee grounds into the sink so I couldn't make any more. "The butter alone is three hundred calories, and think of the cholesterol," she complained.

"I take lecithin to counteract that."

Her nose crinkled, and she wiped her hands on her shorts, which were a vivid blue, matching her top. "Lecithin is loaded with fat. It just adds calories." She added this in the same monotone—not putting a lot of energy into it, but as if it were automatic to take care of adults, instead of the other way around.

Toni's coach, I assumed, taught her all the diet crap. Dirsa Presky is a dour, anal retentive little lady if I've ever seen one. All skin and bones, she lives on twigs, and probably insects and grubs.

"I'm only a size eight," I countered defensively. I wiped butter from my chin and sliced an apple, scanning the front page of the *Herald*. There was a short piece about Barbara Sloan—REPUTED MAFIA LAWYER SLAIN IN SHOOTING. and, in smaller print, MARCUS ANDRELLI QUESTIONED. NO CHARGES FILED. I flicked through the rest of the paper. Nothing more. Where were the interviews with witnesses? With family of the dead woman? With Marcus, or his spokesman? The police?

The *Herald* was overdoing its hands-off policy where mob news was concerned.

I put the apple in front of Toni, who was reading the sports pages. She picked up a slice and crunched it between perfect white teeth. "The Red Wings creamed the Chiefs yesterday," she said.

"Did you go?"

She shook her head. "I had practice. Where were you yesterday?"

"Around."

"Your car was out front. Your windows were open, and it was raining. I called. You didn't answer."

It drives me crazy, having people monitor me like that. I prefer to think I'm invisible, that nobody knows where I am or what I do.

"I took a sick day," I muttered.

Her look was sharp. "You're never sick."

"I was yesterday."

"Flu?" Her tone said she didn't believe it for a minute. She was silent. But not for long. "I've been thinking," she said. "Maybe when I come over in the mornings, we could exercise together."

"Exercise." I tried to keep the note of horror out of my voice, but the idea of *exercising, every day*, was . . . well, it was appalling.

"A few sit-ups, a little bending and stretching, that's all. I need somebody to work out with."

"I haven't done formal exercise since second grade—nor do I intend to."

"It'd do you good," Toni said. "We could start out easy, build up to it."

"Sure. And next thing I knew, you'd have me out there jogging or something."

"Jogging's pretty much out now. Walking, maybe."

"I already walk. All over the damned town."

"You probably don't do it right. You have to keep up a certain pace, a good hard stride."

"I've got phone calls to make," I said.

I threw her a black look and picked up the phone on the counter. Dialed Marcus's penthouse for the third time since two A.M., my voice rising this time with indignation.

"What do you mean, he can't come to the phone? He couldn't come to the phone at five, he couldn't come to the phone at seven, he couldn't even come to the phone at fuckin' two A.M. I know, I know, he was busy with Japan then." (Sigh.) "Don't do this to me, Alfred."

Alfred was the finicky receptionist Marcus had hired to impress the so-called legal businessmen he had dealings with.

"My instructions, Ms. James—"

"I don't give a donkey's ass about your instructions. I want to talk to Marcus. *Now.*"

The phone clicked discreetly in my ear. I drummed my fingers on the counter.

"Well, how about it?" Toni said. "We can start tomorrow. I'll come over early."

"Huh?"

"Exercise."

"Oh . . . sure." I heard, and yet I didn't. My mind was on other things.

CHAPTER SEVEN

There wasn't any room left in the tiny *Rochester Herald* lot, so I parked the Ghia three blocks away and walked. The *Herald* is in a gray stone, pre–Civil War building that's been lovingly preserved by the city fathers for its historical significance. Rochester was the major northern terminal for the Underground Railroad in the Civil War, and a lot of buildings are famous for having housed some hero or other of that period—although no one, today, seems to quite remember what said hero had done.

The squeaky 1930s cage elevator, as usual, wasn't working. By the time I got up the stairs to my gray metal desk on the fourth floor, I was drenched with sweat, and my feet—in cheap, hard-sole Italian sandals—hurt like hell. I wasn't in the mood when Charlie Nicks, the city editor, called me into his office.

"I don't see what difference it makes if I'm here or out around town today," I said, still arguing five minutes later. Somebody—I can't think who—has written that reporters are known to be petulant, insubordinate, eccentric, and disturbed. I was trying hard to prove all four points.

Charlie bit angrily into the fourth glazed doughnut from a box of six. He shifted his pink, round little body in his swivel chair and rubbed the sweat off his bald head, leaving a trail of sugar. "You don't have anything hot on the fire," he said, his squat nose turning red at my lack of subordination. "We need you to cover phones for Pete Ransom."

Pete had the three-dot *East-Side, West-Side* column. People called in all day with gossip, and he was out with a bad summer cold.

"Anybody can do that. Give one of the secretaries the experience."

It'd never happen, I knew it even as I said it. Secretaries at the *Herald* are like bonsai trees. At the first sign of growth they're cut to the quick, their tender shoots of independence snipped off and cast away, pearls to the swine.

"How about a compromise?" I ventured. "I'll cover the phones until two, but then I have to go out to Pittsford to see my shrink."

I'd hit on the one thing Charlie couldn't deny me. The one good thing R. B. Chastain had done was *institute* an alcoholism program, probably because so many newspaper people are drunks. Charlie had to let me do whatever it took to stay sober.

So he grumbled a bit longer, hating as always to let me have my way, but finally he agreed.

The trouble was, I didn't really have time to go to Pittsford.

I had to try—yet again—to talk to Marcus. And then I wanted to find Danny Greer.

I went home first to change into shorts and a tee. Then I put another call through to Marcus. This time, the phone wasn't even answered. I tried his place out at the lake. Nothing there, either. I tried Tark next, at his apartment across the hall from the penthouse at the Rochester Towers. Marcus had said he was "gone." Gone where? Gone from the city, from the planet—or just gone from his boss's life?

No answer there, as there hadn't been all day.

Danny Greer was easier. He was off duty, but a call to Joe Pynes downtown told me he was at Carter Park, coaching a Little League baseball game. I walked over, thinking along the way about Toni's plan to save me from myself. The kid was pretty sharp for a twelve-year-old, but if she thought she was going to snooker me into exercising every day in an effort to stay sober, she was wrong.

Nevertheless, as I rounded the last corner to Carter Park, I lengthened my stride and picked up the pace. Just to see if I could do it.

Not bad at all, I thought, my energy rising as I swung into a lope. And a wonderful day! Birds singing, the leaves on the trees a dark, restless green, a promise of summer rain in the air—

"Ow, shit, ow!" I stopped dead and grabbed for my hip as a needle of pain swept through it. "Ow. Goddammit!" I rubbed at the growing cramp, and hopped around on one foot, shaking my leg to work the cramp loose. A pickup truck roared by, loaded with construction workers. "Oooooh, chicky baby," one of them yelled. They tongued a "drrrrrrrrrrr." Hooted. "You wanna ride? *C'mon, baby!*"

I glared and hopped deeper into the park, like a rabbit on the run. So much for power walking.

The baseball diamond was ahead, through a thick stand of trees. I could hear the shouts of players and fans before I actually saw it, and for a moment I had the feeling of déjà vu. Was it really fifteen or more years ago that I'd played on this very field? Or was it just yesterday . . . when all my troubles seemed so far away?

I sat on the grass under an elm, next to a couple of moms who had brought a blanket and picnic lunch. From their chatter, I gathered the game was nearly over, bottom of the ninth. Both women had short-cropped hair, one brown, the other blond. They wore thin cotton tops and shorts, and didn't look a day over eighteen themselves. Springsteen came through the pink Sony portable next to their cold drink jug, and now and then they'd break off their private talk to yell "Go, Jimmy!" . . . "Do it, Andrew . . . yea!" . . . "Andrew, run, run, go, go, go, Jesus, Jesus . . . Oh, no! *NO!*" The latter with a loud groan. "He's safe, dammit, *SAFE!*" But it wasn't any use. It was over, and their team had lost. There was much cussing and vilifying, which warmed my heart.

I waited under the tree until most of the kids, moms, and dads (there were a lot of dads for a weekday—more than when I was young) had drifted out of the park. Then I sort of sidled over to home plate and stood watching Danny talk to a couple of the kids at first base. He was facing my way, but didn't see me at first. His darkly tanned face was relaxed and smiling, and the boys laughed as he clapped them on the back.

Danny is lean, maybe five-ten, with black curly hair and offbeat features that are somehow attractive. In high school, he was funny and charming, always into things. He bartered and scammed his way to graduation with a grin, and everyone loved him. Even now, women and kids flocked around—falling for his easy Irish way.

Danny's nose had been broken in fights as a kid, and he'd picked up a couple of scars somewhere since then. It was a good thing. Without the irregularities, he'd have been too good-looking to be effective undercover, even in Vice.

And yes, it's true I was once a little in love with Dan Greer. But that was sixteen years ago, and my crush was conducted at a distance. Like a lot of girls in eleventh grade, I thought Danny Boy Greer was *hot*. (Or whatever we called it at the time. My grandmother would have declared him the "cat's pajamas"; my mom would have said "groovy." Or maybe not.)

I picked up a ball that had been abandoned at the edge of the field, and fingered it to get the feel. That was when Danny looked over, and I saw his face split into a wide grin. I grinned back, and he sauntered over, hands in his pockets, blue and white cap pushed back on his head.

"Well, now, looky who it is," he drawled. He took the cap off and set it on my head, tilting it far down over my eyes. I shoved it back and saw that there were deep wrinkles at the corners of his blue eyes—the kind major leaguers get from squinting against the sun half their lives. "Haven't seen you in, what, six months?" he said. "At that department charity hop you were covering for the *Herald*."

"You up for a little practice? Wanta toss a few balls?" My fingers were itchy on the one in my hand.

"With you, Jess?" His teeth flashed white against his tan. "Anytime."

I grabbed a mitt off the ground and tried it on for size. It was a little loose, but okay. I wiggled my leg, testing. The cramp was a faint memory now. I backed up onto the field toward the pitcher's mound and started tossing the ball gently, catching Danny's return throws as I walked. He took it easy with me, too, even when I got a good distance away. Guys seem to do that when playing with girls—although once I'd been hit in the face by a fast pitch, and carried the bruise from a broken cheekbone for weeks.

When I was at the mound I stood there a long moment, squinting at Danny's wiry figure in jeans and blue and white sleeveless athletic shirt. I judged his stance to be too relaxed still, as if he didn't expect a lot—after all, it had been years since we'd done this, about fourteen, to be exact. He hadn't even bothered to put on a glove.

So I thought: *What the hell.*

I let him have it—a red-hot comet that zinged across the light summer air at maybe seventy miles an hour and sailed right by his astonished face and casually outstretched hand. It struck the wooden green backboard with a sharp *crack*, and bounced about fifteen feet in the direction of first base. One of Danny's kids, watching, hollered approval.

"Hey, yeah, *do* it!"

"Shit!" Danny stood there, looking first at the ball, then at me, hands on his hips. "*Shit,*" he said again.

"No shit, Danny," I yelled, laughing. "That was a ball. You were *supposed* to *catch* it."

He frowned, then laughed and shook his head. "You always were a handful, Jess." He picked up another ball, and this time he jammed his hand into a glove. He didn't hold back. His first pitch was as fast as mine, and it connected with a good solid *thunk*, stinging right through my glove. I was beginning to feel real good.

In about five minutes I had worked up a free-running sweat, and in ten all the joints were oiled and moving like they hadn't moved in months. It'd hurt the next day, I knew, but it was worth it. That was something I had learned at St. Avery's. Any test of skill, coordination of muscle and mind—any physical activity, shared or otherwise—resulted in the all-important confirmation that one was indeed alive.

Funny how the pressures of everyday life could move in and make you forget that after a while.

Finally, the shadows of the trees began to lengthen, and Danny looked at his watch and held up a hand. "Four-thirty. Break?"

"Sure."

We both fell, sweating, into the shade. He pulled a couple of cream sodas out of a team-sized cooler, and handed me one. "Times sure have changed," he said, rubbing sweat from his eyes with the back of his hand. "I remember when you were nothing but a Munchkin, swaggering around after the boys all the time, acting tough."

"I *was* tough," I protested, breathing just a little hard. I stretched out on the grass and propped my feet up on the trunk of the tree. My hair would be full of twigs, and I'd limp at work a few days from sore knees and thighs—but for the moment I was Guinevere rejoicing in my maidenhood.

Danny grinned. "Yeah, well, you've kept in practice, I'll give you that. You're better than you were fourteen years ago."

"I spent a couple months last year at St. Avery's, drying out, and there was somebody there you'd know real well. From the majors. I was sharkbait for him, but he had to have somebody to practice with or he'd have gone nuts. It got my arm in shape."

"That and then some." He laughed, and glanced at his watch again. "Catherine always has dinner ready at six, but we've got a little time. I guess you didn't come by just to toss a few balls. What's up, Jess?"

I snapped open my can of cream soda, sat straight, tailor-fashion, and took a long swallow. "Marcus Andrelli."

"Oh?" His look told me he knew what most of the Rochester P.D. knew, that Marcus and I were an item, as they used to say. It didn't surprise me; we hadn't exactly worked at keeping low profiles.

"I talked to Grady North," I told him. "He claims Marcus is responsible for setting up the new child porn operation here, probably him and Paulie Gandolo working together."

"That's how I hear it."

"He says the information came from a snitch of yours, Con Argento—the one that just died."

His black eyebrows went up. "Died? He didn't exactly keel over from a heart attack, Jess. Con was shot with a nine-millimeter semi, mafia execution style."

"Uh-huh. You agree with Grady, then, that Marcus did it?"

"Did it, ordered it, whatever. Along with that shooting on his boat the other night."

"Barbara Sloan."

"That's the one."

"You seem awfully sure."

"Nah . . . what I really think is it was just a coincidence, Con gettin' shot after squealin' to me about Andrelli's porn operation. And Barbara Sloan gettin' shot on Andrelli's boat . . . hell, the killer could've been almost anybody . . . Charlie Tuna . . . or maybe Lloyd Bridges, you know, that guy from *Sea Hunt*, yeah, he bobs up—"

"All right, Danny, *enough*. You've made your point."

We were both silent awhile. The sun dipped a little lower, the air became a fraction cooler. A gypsy gull wheeled in from the lake. Finally I said, "So I guess you must have other evidence against Marcus, other than what this snitch, Con, told you?"

"You know I can't talk about that, Jess."

"Why not? Grady's told me most of it anyway." A lie, but worth a try.

"Uh-huh. And pigs sing."

Oh well.

"What about this Con Argento—you recruit him? Or did he come to you?"

"I got him. Almost by accident. He fell flat on his face on Main one day, when I was down there looking for a pimp named Esposita. Con was stoned, but sick, too. I found a half ounce of coke on him, and after I brought him to and cleaned him up, we made a deal."

"You took him on specifically to get information about the kiddie porn people?"

"Nah, that was just accidental. This is off the record, you understand?"

"Okay."

"We—Vice—we've been workin' with the DEA task force on gettin' to the major drug trafficking organizations, tryin' to shut them down. I thought, bein' on the street most of the time, Con could get me something on that." He took a swig of the cream soda and wiped his mouth. "Plus, there's a tie-in between the drug organizations and the kiddie porn, what with the way they use the drugs to recruit them—the kids—and then to keep 'em in."

"And all of it, the drugs, the porn, you think is being run by Marcus Andrelli. Even though you—and the whole damn police force—know he's not into that kind of stuff."

"Well, the way we've got it figured, Jess, is that even Andrelli can't turn down the kind of money that's out there for drugs these days. So he makes a deal with Paulie Gandolo. Andrelli is the brains, he sits up there in that fancy penthouse with his computers, his corporate and banking contacts, and handles the business end. Paulie does the street stuff so Andrelli doesn't have to dirty his hands."

"This is what Con Argento told you?"

He shrugged.

I couldn't think of anything to say that didn't sound kind of silly—like a woman defending her man, while everybody in the family knows he doesn't deserve it.

The trouble was, everything Danny said made sense . . . unless you knew Marcus.

But did I? Did I know him anymore? And how well had I known him in the first place? He was a mobster, after all—no two ways about it. But when it came to drugs,

Marcus had always scorned the dealers, claiming they were too unstable. He'd refused to do business with them.

Danny was shaking his can of cream soda lightly, a thumb over the opening to create more fizz. I remembered him doing that years ago, and I smiled. I had a sudden thought. "You work alone all the time now, Danny, or with a partner?"

"I have a partner sometimes. Nobody steady."

"You ever work with Jack Hoffman?"

"Jack? Now and then."

"What's he like?"

He shrugged. "Oh, you know—a good cop. A little dull, sort of straight for a Vice cop. Not too much good at undercover, but solid otherwise."

"You think so?"

He squinted at me. "Why, Jess?"

"I don't know. I saw him yesterday down at Harrigan's, along with Grady and Skelley. I was curious. What was it old Mrs. Lacey in tenth grade history used to say—'still waters run deep'?"

He laughed. "Jack Hoffman? Nah." He pulled his cap off my head, jamming it down over his own. He rumpled my hair, or maybe he was straightening it. Either way, the effort never made much difference. "We're talking about two different people here. Jack's about as deep as a eunuch in Greenwich Village."

"You think so?"

"I do." He looked at his watch. "Look, Munchkin, I hate to break this up, but I've got to get home."

I nodded and stood, stretching my legs, then took a handle of the cooler to help him with it to the parking lot. We piled it, and some equipment we picked up on the way, into his yellow and black S-10 Blazer, which was parked just behind us on the other side of the trees.

He snapped the tailgate shut and turned, hugging me lightly with one arm, the cream soda still in his other hand. "It sure was good to see you again," he said, brushing my lips with a casual kiss. He smelled of summer sun and dust, of glove leather and sweat. "How about having dinner with Catherine and me? The Havens Inn, Wednesday, at seven? We can talk more then."

I didn't know Catherine very well. Danny had married her right out of high school—she was prom queen, homecoming queen, head cheerleader—you name it, Catherine was the best of it. And she had landed the boy the rest of us loved.

It'd be interesting to meet the woman who had taken Danny Greer's heart and managed to keep it all these years.

"Okay," I said. "Seven? I'll see you there."

But maybe that wasn't the smartest thing I could have done. I was still feeling Danny's kiss on my lips—and it was kind of nice, after yesterday's experience with Marcus and the fine old art of shunning.

I wondered if I'd still be a little jealous of Catherine Greer.

CHAPTER EIGHT

There were a few hours of light left, and I didn't much feel like going home. The evening hours, for me, are the worst when I'm trying not to drink. They drag on and on.

I decided to try Marcus and Tark once more, calling from a phone booth at the edge of the park.

No answer at either number yet. Marcus, I decided, was probably at his cabin on Irondequoit Bay. He often was, in the summer. I could try him there. But my curiosity about Tark was stronger than my desire to see Marcus. Where the hell was Tark—and what was going on?

I thought about how steadfast he always was, implacable, once he'd made up his mind. Physically, Tark was huge— six-four easy, with broad shoulders and an immense chest. He had short, straight, dark hair, and a face that had been pushed in and scarred here and there, remodeled over the years. But his Northern Italian gray eyes had a way of looking amused, and I knew from experience how gentle he could be. Tark was something of a philosopher, maybe even a bit of a mystic. Not your stereotype bodyguard. He had been Marcus's friend long before he'd taken on the job of safeguarding his person, twenty-odd years ago. And as far as I knew, Marcus had never before had reason to question his loyalty.

I wanted to check out Tark's apartment, see if I could find any clues. But the Rochester Towers was on the other side of the city. I headed home to pick up my car, wishing I'd brought it in the first place. The late afternoon sun blazed where there weren't any trees, and my skin felt slick, my hair grimy. My shirt was stuck to my back. I hate walking in the summer. The hot sidewalks rise up and grab you by the throat, and the heat feels like a dead weight on your shoulders, pressing you down. I was relieved when I rounded the corner to Genesee Park Boulevard and saw the Ghia ahead. *It hadn't been stolen today.* Score one for our team, *Yea, team.*

The Ghia: Volkswagen's fleeting tip of the hat to the sports car industry, twenty years ago. Mine was a '68, with a tinny red bottom and rusted white top. Dented and pinged beyond repair. It putters and backfires, coughs and spurts out frightening fumes—but it gets me where I need to go. A solid, faithful little kiddie-car. One you could get used to having around forever.

Right. And just about the time you start thinking that way, look out.

Or, to put it otherwise—I should have known better. I should've taken a bus. But it got me *to* the Rochester Towers okay.

I parked on the street rather than face the valet parker's scorn. Bad enough I had to pass the doorman in my troubled shorts and tee. I tried to do it with pizzazz, at least, squaring my shoulders and looking him straight in the eye. Smiling like I was any blue-chip resident, just in from a relaxing day at the lake. With Herculean effort, I managed to keep my fingers from smoothing my snarled hair.

The doorman, one I had seen a couple of times before when visiting Marcus, tipped his hat and grinned, giving me a knowing look through crinkly old eyes. I wasn't fooling anyone at all.

I ambled across the gold and glass lobby, my beat-up Nikes nearly swallowed by the wealth of red carpeting. I scrabbled in the depths of the navy blue tote I'd brought from the backseat of the Ghia, and found a key inside a black leather holder, which Marcus had given me several months before. It slid effortlessly into the lock of the whisper-quiet private elevator that led to the top floor of the Rochester Towers. The brass doors opened silently, and I stepped in, seeing myself in smoky wall-to-wall mirrors and cringing. I faced the doors as they moved into place, and was swept to the thirty-first floor. The elevator opened, and I faced a plush, private lobby, with mahogany doors on either side. One led to Marcus's apartment; the other, to Tark's. I didn't have a key to either one.

Just on the off chance someone was there, I tried Marcus's place first, ringing the bell then pounding a little, but not until my knuckles were blue. If he had been there, someone would probably have been guarding the lobby.

I trudged across the thick red carpet to Tark's apartment. I rang and knocked there, too, hoping foolishly that Tark would open it, say "Hi, Jess, what the hell are you doing here?", rub a weary hand over his short dark hair, and tell me he'd been sleeping since he called me yesterday. I called out, "Tark, it's me, Jess." No response.

Well, hell, for an enterprising hotshot reporter with a less than legal past, there are always alternatives.

Marcus's apartment, I knew, couldn't be broken into. I'd seen, from inside, the powerful security system he'd set up. But it was possible Tark hadn't bothered. It wasn't likely anything incriminatory would be kept at his place, given Marcus's near paranoia on the subject.

The door had a Drackman lock, the kind they put in about thirty years ago when the Rochester Towers was built, before coded passcards or numbered keypads. I set my tote on the floor and opened it up, pulling out a small spray can of this and a tube of that. There followed a few tense moments and some handy tools I hardly ever use for their cosmetic purposes, but carry around for just such moments as this.

I was smugly pleased to find that I hadn't lost my touch. Of course, when I was a kid, it was cars I broke into most. But in the course of my career the past few years, I've loosened up an occasional house lock, too.

I was in. I glanced around quickly for wires, hidden alarms. Nothing I could see—although I wasn't an expert by any means. My education in this area had come recently, from hanging out with the Genesee Three—the most colorful trio of teenage crooks this town has ever seen. As the months and years since I'd met them passed, I found myself accumulating more and more knowledge in the fine art of housebreaking, ball busting, and plain old state-of-the-art crime.

None of which made me any less nervous now. I felt like a thief, palms sweaty, heart racing. I called out again. "Tark? You home?"

Nothing. Not even the tick of a clock. I took another step forward.

I had never really thought much about Tark's personal life, and what a home of his might be like. He always seemed to be attached to Marcus, like a shade. I knew he had loved a woman from childhood, a relationship that was never meant to be. I knew he was something of a philosopher, and that he was fiercely loyal to anyone who managed to become his friend. But that was all. And one doesn't tend to think of mob bodyguards as living like the rest of us. The stereotypes help to set people like that apart—probably so we won't have to see how much we're alike, how easy it might be to slip through that kind of societal crack ourselves.

I took in the large living room. There was a wide wall of windows with a sweep of open-weave drapery, and the sun spilled through it, casting paler stripes across a white-carpeted floor.

The place was as spotless as a monk's cell. Either Tark was an excellent housekeeper, or he hired one. There was no clutter, no papers lying about, no opened books face down on a coffee table.

The furnishings were a blend of antique oak and modern, and I made a quick but thorough search through a rolltop desk with pigeonholes and lots of tiny drawers. The search should have taken time, but didn't, because there wasn't much there—even in the so-called secret compartments that everybody is told about on the showroom floor. There were stamps, blank postcards, and long white envelopes. A map of the greater Rochester area that looked new and barely used, and this month's utility bills, not yet due. There was a brown leather address book with the pages still stiff, indicating that it probably had never been opened. No numbers or addresses had been written inside.

I opened closets and found a chess set, two shelves of classical tapes and records, winter coats. No sports equipment. I knew that Tark worked out in Marcus's apartment, in a gym Marcus had built in a bedroom. There was nothing in this apartment that would indicate a hobby, except for reading. An entire wall in the living room was lined with books. Jung, Shakespeare, Dickens, and a Kierkegaard that I remembered Tark reading one day, a slim leather volume: *Of the Difference Between a Genius and an Apostle*. Another that particularly caught my eye, a biography of Booth Tarkington. I opened it, and inside was an engraved inscription: "This book belongs to Michael Joseph Bartella." And on the inside cover:

To Michael—Happy graduation! You will always be "Tark" to me. Love, Daphne—June, 1969.

So Tark's real name was Michael Joseph. That answered one question I'd always had, anyway. The name *Tark* had for some reason come from Booth Tarkington—and from Daphne Malcross, the woman I knew he had loved.

On the wall next to the bookcase was a large gallery of what appeared to be family pictures. Tark with an older woman who reminded me of Mrs. Rosetti down the street. Dark, plump, and smiling—the kind of older Italian woman who looks as though she spends her days in the kitchen making superb ravioli and sauce, and her evenings mending altar cloths for the parish church. There were younger children who might have been brothers and sisters, and one of Tark as a young man with a priest, outside a building I recognized as the Jesuit seminary in Penfield. The priest looked like him, but shorter and perhaps ten years older, and without Tark's huge shoulders and thickly muscled arms. I slipped it out of the silver frame, and found written on the back, *Anthony's Ordination Day—June, 1966.*

A brother, I guessed.

The picture of Tark I was putting together was only a small surprise. Marcus would never have suffered a typical mob thug for a bodyguard. He'd insist on someone who could hold his own in intelligent conversation, who could talk about books and understand about family and roots.

In the stainless steel kitchen, a bright red mug had been rinsed and drained. A coffeepot was clean and there were no grounds anywhere, no garbage. A clean bag had been put in the trash compactor, next to the sink. The refrigerator had no perishables: milk, cream, meats, vegetables, or fruits. Yet the freezer was well stocked.

It seemed that Tark had left the apartment that day in the kind of shape one does when going away.

I began to feel tired, and a little depressed. *"Tark's gone,"* Marcus had said. And the look on his face was of someone who had been betrayed.

Was it possible Tark had defected . . . or worse, had actually murdered Barbara Sloan, and left Marcus holding the bag? Did Tark know he'd be disappearing before he went to the *SeaStar* the night Sloan was killed? If he had planned to be gone awhile, and wanted to leave no trace of where he'd be, he couldn't have done a better job.

It was time to see if he'd left any clothes.

He had. An entire twelve-foot-long closet of suits and shirts, in as whistle-clean condition as everything else. Even his shoes were polished and lined up neatly, like in a barracks, on the closet floor. Oddly, there were no casual clothes, not even in his dresser drawers. No jeans, no sweatshirts or tees, and very little underwear or socks.

I went through every suit pocket and dresser drawer for notes, a receipt for an airline ticket, anything that might give me a clue to where Tark might have gone. Nothing.

I turned my attention to the bed, which had a plain oak headboard and was of a curiously narrow size for a contemporary single man. There was a simple nightstand on either side, with reading lights, and shelves below with books. I walked over idly, to check them out . . . and that's when I saw it.

A picture in a brushed silver frame on one of the tables, of Tark—with a woman.

Not just any woman, I thought with shock.

I'd seen this one a couple of times in public, a time or two in the papers. She was dark—dark eyes, dark fall of hair, a beautiful angular face and smile.

A good woman for Tark. Except for one thing.

She was Paulie Gandolo's sister, Bernadette. Her brother and Marcus were sworn enemies.

And in the picture, Tark's arm was around her, holding her close. She smiled up at him . . . with something that looked very much like love.

CHAPTER NINE

Tark and Paulie Gandolo's *sister*?

Paulie Gandolo was the squirreliest little scumbag I'd ever had the nonpleasure to talk to before.

During the FBI sweep of major mob figures in New York state a while back, I endeared myself to Paulie by refusing to testify against him. My reason was that it would mean having to reveal my source for the story I broke about the mob at that time—and my source was a working guy with two kids and a wife. There was a small trail of informers like this in the wake of Paulie Gandolo's long career in crime, and every one was now dead. My source would have met the same fate, if Paulie had found out he'd talked. So Paulie got off, a fact that annoyed our own Rochester cops, including my pal Grady North, no end. The only guys the Feds managed to indict were low-level enforcers, bookies, operators of gambling parlors. And did I feel guilty?

Hell, no.

I knew even then that Paulie was loonier than the original tunes—that given another year or so, he'd settle to the bottom of the pond on his own, gasp his last few breaths, and be eaten by the stronger, feistier carp in town. In point of fact, I knew Marcus was after his hide. So I didn't do Paulie any favors. He'd have been better off this last year in a minimum security prison with the rest of the hoods, playing squash.

But Paulie misunderstood my motives. After the hearings, he nearly insisted on mingling our blood right there in the halls of justice. I brushed off his overtures a little too firmly, I guess, because he took offense.

Now that it looked like there was something between Tark and Paulie's sister, I wondered if my next step in finding Tark might not be a talk with Paulie. I wondered if he'd tell me anything about Tark and Bernadette—if he'd remember even a glimmer of that earlier gratitude. Or would I be putting myself on his hit list to approach him again at all?

The other question was—how did Tark and Bernadette fit in with Grady North's claim that Marcus and Paulie had joined forces?

I was thinking all this as I drove home, with hot air blasting through the Ghia as if it were a sieve. The sun was nearly down, the temperature still most likely in the eighties. I was so thirsty I could barely swallow, but I passed up Harrigan's for a convenience store, where I bought a pint bottle of orange juice.

I sat in the car and opened it, swilling it down, then rubbed my mouth with the back of my hand. I put the half-empty bottle between my bare legs to hold it while I drove, and shivered from its welcome cold against my hot skin. I turned the ignition key.

The Ghia gave one loud backfire, and died.

I groaned.

Tried it again—with the same result. I stood the bottle of orange juice upright on the passenger seat, and got out, yanking up the hood and finding that one of the hoses had blown off. I put it back on, but the car blew again when I tried to start it—and again.

"*Goddamn* winter-beater, goddamn, god*damn*!"

I confess that was me, screaming as I pounded the peeling dashboard and stomped a new hole in the rusty floor of my Ghia, which, after all (and aside from the fact that it has a funky romantic aura to it), is just that: a winter-beater— the cozy term given here to a wreck that people drive around during the salt-on-the-road season, while their good cars are garaged until spring.

It's become quite chic to own a winter-beater, November through May.

But when you have to drive a ruin like that all year round, you feel damned silly. Or like you need a good, stiff drink, the way I did now.

I called a tow truck to haul the Ghia over to Clyde's Mobil. I rode along. I asked Clyde (better known as *Jaws Five*) to call me with the prognosis. He hitched his belt over a mountain of flesh and grinned. "No problem." Which, in *Jaws Five* language, is somewhat akin to "Don't worry, be happy . . . as I fully intend to be when I present you with my bill."

I walked the rest of the way home and got there hot and exhausted, hungry and out of sorts. It was a little after nine P.M., and the temp was holding at eighty-three degrees according to the sign on the Marine Midland Bank along the way.

The first thing I did was lose my clothes. I got into the shower, started at warm and leveled off to cold, and stood there a good ten minutes draining the day away. I dried off and slid into a navy blue tank top, cut-off jeans, and thongs. Then I wandered through the apartment, opening the old windows and putting the sticks underneath to prop them up. I had finished off the orange juice at Clyde's, so I took out a can of tomato, snapped the top, and carried it with me as I watered a few wilting plants, playing for time. But I couldn't put off the inevitable all night, so I finally looked in the pencil jar on my desk to see how much—or, more to the point, how little—was left of my emergency cash.

Not much. Sixty bucks, give or take a tuppence or two.

I went through my desk drawers, a little panicked. I live on a tight budget, and something like a car repair can throw everything out of sync. It could mean that the car would get fixed instead of eating the next two weeks, or in place of paying the phone bill. A reporter without a phone might as well sell pencils to blind men, or pogo sticks to frogs.

So I hoped, foolishly, that I might have hidden a couple of twenties in a desk drawer. Foolishly, because I didn't do things like that anymore. I kept my spare cash in one place and one place only. That was how organized I'd become.

My entire life, in fact, had become dismally predictable in the year that I'd been sober.

To hell with the money, I thought, flopping into the deep chair by my side bay window. Where had all the *fun* gone? God, life was so . . . so . . . *unpremeditated* when I was drinking . . . so *undesigned* . . . so full of flash and sizzle.

I was thinking of one uproarious time in particular, when I fell down the gray wool-carpeted stairs that led from my front door to the porch below, and nearly broke my ass— angrily trying to nab the paperboy, who had thrown my *Herald* into the privet hedge. (This was long before I worked for the *Herald*.) I lost my footing, and the kid got away, so I roared from the porch, "Little son'a'bitch, I'll catch you, I'll catch you, I'll *kill* you, son'a'bitch!" until he was out of sight. I glared at an old man innocently passing by, rubbed at my tailbone, then stumbled back up the stairs—where I called Circulation and gave 'em hell. I held the phone in one hand, what little remained of that week's Irish in the other, knocking back a swallow now and then—and the part I can remember is saying, "Cancel the fuckin' paper if the kid can't get it right, fuckin' paper, anyway, nothin' but gossip, fuckin' yellow rag . . ."

The part that worries me is what I *can't* remember— because they did cancel the paper, and when I called to start it up again, they quite firmly refused. Fortunately, with most big-city newspapers there's real bad communication between Circulation and Management, so I got hired on last summer, anyway. They even send me a paper now and then. And nobody in the lofty offices upstairs has ever even indicated they've heard about my tarnished reputation in the dingy corridors of Circulation down below.

Yeah, those were uproarious times, all right.

I dumped the empty tomato juice can in the trash and got out a cold mineral water. I twisted off the cap, put the radio on, and crawled through one of the two front windows to the wide and gently sloping roof that covers Mrs. Binty's porch.

The leafy branches of two large oak trees in the front lawn shelter this roof, filtering the street lights and offering privacy from the sidewalk below. You can sit here, nestled in the shadows with your back to the window frame, and watch the occasional bus and car pass by. Now and then a neighbor will come out to walk his dog. Lights wink on and off in the windows of the well-kept Victorian homes across the way, and sometimes you feel as though you're moving back a century in time. You might be in any small town, anywhere, circa 1900—except for the now and then shattering sound of sirens in the night.

The radio station was doing a Janis Ian retrospective— all my old high school songs, good for a bad memory or two. This one was all about love being for beauty queens—and not the likes of me.

There was a faint breeze, just enough to make a difference. And actually, as much as I grumble about the heat, Rochester isn't as bad as some eastern cities in the summer. Lake Ontario cools things down a bit, and thunderstorms bring in temporary cool gusts from Canada. But we have our heat waves like everywhere else. This one was in its twenty-third day.

I wiggled against the window frame to ease my back. I thought about how you could be going along, everything quiet and sort of dull, and the next moment all hell breaks loose.

I'm not real good at processing things when too much happens at once. I mean, I have the kind of mind when I'm working that sort of goes into a trance and focuses on one particular thing . . . and I don't always see or hear the cries for help that go on around me. I sometimes hurt people because of that, or wound them in some way that I'm entirely unaware of.

Nowadays, they tell you that's typical fare for the child of an alcoholic. *Adult children of alcoholics.* A.C.A. We're *in* now. The experts know things about us that no one ever knew or even wanted to know before.

All I'd been aware of, growing up, was that my pop was a drunk, and when he drank up the rent money, we were evicted and moved. This happened so often, sometimes I'd start home from school and realize after a few blocks that I was walking the wrong way—back to a house I'd lived in months before. My mom was so busy hustling tables and tips to keep us in food, she wasn't much of an influence then. All my friends were boys, and by the time I was twelve, I knew how to hot-wire cars. We "borrowed" cars for the thrill of it, then dumped them where they'd be easily found. (Well, we did heist a British Sterling in eighth grade, but that's another story.)

We shoplifted, jumped off bridges into the Genesee River, hopped trains (Mickey Ryan and Danny Tree and I once went all the way to Syracuse and back that way), and generally raised hell. All that lasted until I was fourteen and they put me in a temporary foster home. That almost killed Mom. Pop sobered up long enough to look good for the social workers, and eventually I went home.

I didn't start to really drink until ten years later, when Pop died. The "experts" tell me it was the guilt; thinking I'd killed him, and all. That, and the fact that by following in his footsteps, I was trying to keep him alive.

I don't know about that. I just know that even though I'd sobered up in the last year, things weren't all that different. It seems to work that way. You think that being sober is going to change you, but all it does is change the fact that you're drunk all the time. Underneath? It's the same old you.

On the radio, Janis was going on about seventeen-year-olds with ravaged faces. She was the patron saint of us lonely ones, back then.

Well, sing it, Janis. Nothing's changed. Beneath the Estée Lauder there are still the ravaged faces.

I wondered what thoughtless thing I'd done to Marcus to make him react the way he had yesterday. Was it only

that I'd been out of touch for so long? I didn't think so.
Marcus had always given me complete emotional freedom;
it wasn't like him to hold it against me when I needed time
to sort things out. It was more likely, I thought, that he'd
picked up on my ambivalence about our relationship long
before I'd stopped coming around—and that was at the core
of his anger.

I had told him yesterday that I'd stayed away because he
seemed "busy." I had tried to make it appear that I'd been
put off by the addition, in his life, of the beautiful Barbara
Sloan.

Better to seem a jealous bitch than look too clearly at the
truth?

For the truth was that when Sloan and Marcus seemed
to be getting thick, I had stepped back with something like
relief. I wasn't sure why.

I watched the cars pass by below, the lights in the houses
across the street wink off for the night. Janis winked off,
too, with a segue into Old Miles's "Kind of Blue."

I stretched and crawled back through the window again.
Stood there a minute, debating. Then I put a call through
to Marcus, at the lake. He was there, and he came to the
phone. His voice was distant. But mine was too.

I said I'd be out in the morning to talk. He said, "Okay."

I hung up. My hand on the phone was shaking. I still
didn't know why.

CHAPTER TEN

The next morning, a few clouds rolled in. But they were only kidding. They skidded into a curve over the edge of the lake and headed for Buffalo, or maybe Cleveland.

Toni came over at six-thirty, all set to martial me into a rigid hour of exercise before work. I stuck my last raspberry Danish in front of her, along with a huge glob of butter, and said firmly, "Can't today. Got an appointment at the lake. But thanks. Really. Maybe we can do it tomorrow." Or the day after Christmas, 2001.

Her dark young eyes searched my face for signs of growing dissipation. Finding none, she nodded, apparently satisfied. We talked about baseball a little, and when I went into the bedroom to dress, she finally went home.

A while later, I knocked on Mrs. Binty's kitchen door, to ask if I could borrow her car.

"Of course, dear, you know I hardly ever use it anymore. Don't forget to check the radiator, it does run dry in this weather, although I can't get over how much cooler the weather is today."

She was baking Italian crescent-shaped almond toasts— a recipe from Toni's mother.

"Biscotti, they're called," she told me. "You have to dunk them in coffee, or even better, red wine—" She broke off, embarrassed. "I didn't mean—"

"It's okay, Mrs. Binty. I love them with coffee." Just to prove it, I made a pig of myself, drowning four of them in the timid little brew that passed for java with her, and gobbling them down while she talked.

Mr. Purdy across the street, she said, was visiting his sister in St. Louis. The Thomases, down on the corner, were "overseas." Had I heard from my dog? By that, she meant, had the Flynns called to let me know the dumb mutt was all right? I told her no, but they were due home from their camping trip in two weeks. The very thought gave me grief. I felt like a mother, just beginning to enjoy the time off when the troublesome kids return.

As for all the neighborhood news, I couldn't work up much interest. Except for Toni, I don't bother with neighbors much, preferring my own company after work to that of others. I'll smile and nod and be polite, but I don't like people coming to my door unexpectedly and wanting to talk or visit, unless I know and like them. And if I got to know and like them—a *lot*—then what? I'd want to be visiting all the time, instead of reading mysteries or watching old movies on TV, the way I do.

I thanked Mrs. Binty for the biscotti and the use of her car, and climbed into her lumbering gray Olds. It was fifteen years old and had 17,000 miles on it. The engine purred. The exhaust was blessedly silent. It was air-conditioned. Someday, I will steal Mrs. Binty's Olds. I will take it to a chop shop and have it painted, restructured a little, so she'll never know. Then I'll drive it home and tell her I bought it in a used car lot. Let her borrow it whenever she wants. But that wonderful car will be *mine*.

It's a fantasy I have now and then.

In about thirty minutes I'd left the city limits behind and was in the woods, along a seven-mile inlet of Irondequoit Bay that was known locally as Dove's Cove. Marcus had assured his privacy here by buying up the surrounding property years ago and leaving it undeveloped. The land was in someone else's name, and very few people even knew any buildings existed. There was a gatekeeper at all times, and a lookout cabin on the beach that monitored water access to the cove.

I took an unmarked drive that twisted through the woods until it came to a rise overlooking the bay. The trees opened up and I could see, below, miles of crystal blue water glittering in the midday sun. There was a long white beach ringed with evergreens, and tucked into the pines several miles from the main cabin, invisible to the uninformed, was the lookout. Whoever was there today wouldn't be too concerned with me; I'd be stopped at the gatehouse up ahead. The hillside lookout surveyed the boats that wandered into the cove, the would-be picnickers who would be politely told they were on private property and would have to leave.

I drove deeper into the woods, circling the cove to its other side. In about five minutes I had pulled up at the gatehouse to Marcus's cabin. I smiled at Lew, an ancient fellow Marcus had brought in from NYC as a favor to one of his relatives. A gentleman of the old school, Lew always removed his cap to talk to me. His hair stuck up, then, in glistening white tufts, and his pale old eyes would brighten. "Jesse," he would say, "top of the mornin'!" or some other Bing Crosby movie phrase.

He was watching an old black and white movie on a small TV when I drove up. Lew's an old-movie freak like me, although I sort of get away from TV in the summer, preferring to read in the longer evening light. He didn't recognize Mrs. Binty's car, and as I pulled parallel with the gatehouse, I saw that one hand was below the window, reaching for the gun he kept there. When he saw it was me, his eyes lit up and he tipped his hat. But he shook his head.

"If you've come out to see the boss," he said, "good luck." His other hand left the gun and rubbed briskly at the front of his khaki uniform shirt, as if to wipe it free of stains. A box of chocolate donuts was next to the TV; a piece of chocolate clung to Lew's upper lip.

"He's not here?" I said. "But he told me it was okay—"

"Oh, he's here, all right, Jesse, but I've never seen him like he is now. Working round the clock . . . hasn't hardly come out of that barn since the trouble the other day."

"Has Tark been around?"

Lew's deeply wrinkled face moved into a sad frown. He shook his head, giving a *tsk*. "Haven't seen hide nor hair, Jesse. That's what's eatin' him, o' course. Those two were closer than brothers, up till a few months ago. Grew up together, took care of each other . . . It's not right, all this bad blood between them. Things can only get worse."

We exchanged a few words about the movie he was watching: *Leave Her to Heaven*. The original, with Gene Tierney.

"Don't make 'em like this anymore," Lew clucked.

I agreed.

I parked and got out of the car, taking a deep breath of fresh, pine-scented air. There was a peaceful silence here, broken only by the heated ticking of the Olds's motor, and a quiet *whiss-whiss* sound, repeated over and over. It came from the barn, and I knew what it was. I followed the pine-needled path around the main cabin, which was large and sprawling. On the right was a kitchen that formed an L to the rest of the house. An outside deck encircled the entire cabin. Inside, there were huge cushiony sofas before a stone fireplace, sofas I had often sunk into gratefully after a hard day's work out here.

Bypassing the cabin, I headed for the barn. The woods became thicker the closer I got, and alive. A rabbit loped across my path into the underbrush, insects hopped around my ankles making their incessant noise, and the air vibrated with the back and forth communication of birds. *Tweet-tweet . . . hoo-hoo . . . warble-warble . . .*

Jeez.

A thing like that could drive a body nuts.

But the barn, just ahead . . . that was a different matter. Some of the happiest hours I'd spent in my life were here in this barn last summer, when I was fresh out of St. Avery's and still sobering up.

The wide double doors were open, and I made a silent approach, not wanting to disturb the image I knew I was bound to see. I wasn't disappointed.

The barn was sixty feet in depth, its ceiling arched like a cathedral, with windows high up letting in streams of

light. Even the birds were hushed here, and in the middle
of this immensity stood the project Marcus had been working on as a labor of love for over seven years: the Tancook
Whaler. An early Nova Scotia fishing vessel made of wood,
not fiberglass, and with Egyptian cotton sails, not the Dac-
ron most are made with now.

It was truly beautiful, its curves and gentle arcs from bow
to stern like something sensuous and alive. Marcus was
building every inch of the thirty-two-foot Whaler himself
—down to the pintle and gudgeon for the rudder, and even
the anchor, which consisted of a truck axle and other mis-
cellaneous hardware. The lapstrake bottom was of Douglas
fir, the ribs of live oak planking that Marcus had steamed
and bent with his own hands. The inside paneling would
be of soft pine.

Marcus had lived here weekends, in this barn, before
building the cabin. He had lived here building the Tancook,
with no water, no electricity at first, sleeping on a narrow
balcony under the eaves.

The *whiss*ing sound stopped, as Marcus put down the
sander that he'd been using on a plank of pine. I watched
him with something suspiciously like a lump in my throat
as his callused hand ran lovingly over the Whaler's bow,
much the way it sometimes runs over my skin. His shoulders were bare and tanned, with the kind of musculature
that comes only from working out. He didn't look like a
mob leader to me, and he didn't look anywhere near forty.
He looked like someone who had lived a century ago, lived
off the land and grown sure and strong, and maybe died a
hero defending what was his.

I shook myself, the way I do whenever it seems I might
be getting even the least soft or romantic, and Marcus
turned and smiled. Pointing to the mast, he spoke as if he'd
known I was there all along. "Remember that day last summer when we found the tree for that lodged into the bank
of the lake, farther upstream? And we rode it back and
dragged it ashore?"

"My muscles hurt like hell the next morning," I said. "I

had only been sober three months, and I was in terrible shape." I smiled. "I remember you helped me to stay straight that day. I was worried—"

"About your mom. And money."

"Yes." It had been tough, sometimes, trying to send her something every month. She had moved to California four years ago after Pop died—mostly so she wouldn't have to be around me, it had seemed then. I don't know if I sent her money at first to help her out because I was feeling guilty over the way Pop died, or because I wanted to make sure she stayed out there—away from me. My motives are at times selfish, and unclear.

"And you still won't take help from me."

"No."

He frowned. "You hate that job at the *Herald*. How long can you keep on doing it and stay sober?"

I didn't tell him that I'd only managed to do so until two days ago. Instead, I accepted his concern as the peace offering it was.

"We do what we have to do," I said.

"But you don't *have* to work for the *Herald*. If you worked for me the money would be good—"

"I can't—"

"You'd be earning your way. You'd still be independent."

I sighed and shook my head. "It'd never fly."

"It could—if you wanted it to."

But maybe that was the point. What do women want, anyway? as the grand old master of psychology said.

Well, hell, there was only one thing *I* could think of: to be their own men.

"I can't let you influence my life like that." I wished almost immediately that I could call back those words. It wasn't the way I'd meant to begin.

But it was too late. Marcus's mood changed, back to the one I'd seen outside the Public Safety Building when he left me high and dry. His jaw clenched, and a nerve in his forearm twitched. "Which brings up another matter," he said. "Where have you been the past three months?"

"Look, you're the one who walked out on me the other day. I've been trying to reach you ever since."

"The hell with ever since. Where did you disappear to the past three months?"

"Since when do you go and get all possessive?"

He flushed angrily. "How would you feel if the person you'd been closest to for twenty years disappeared, and for three months before that you hadn't even seen the woman you—"

He cut the words off in midsentence, and ran an exasperated hand through his hair. "Sometimes—"

"I needed time alone, to get things worked out about the *Herald*, what I want to do."

"Christ!" He made an angry, frustrated gesture. "It could all be so easy—"

"I can't work for you!"

But he wouldn't let it drop. "Eighty percent of investigative reporting is in the investigation. It's what you like to do. Why not do it for me?"

It was an old argument, going round and round but never ending anywhere. I figured it was bad enough my mom named me Jessica while she was still in and out of the ether and Pop was on a drunk. You'd think she'd have known I'd be called Jesse in school, with a last name like James.

But to work for the mob—become an outlaw for real? Somehow, I couldn't see it.

And as Samved is always quoting in his wispy little guru voice, "One must visualize to become."

"All large companies have their own investigators on the payroll," Marcus went on persuasively, "and as far as the families are concerned, it's the new way. We need experience and intelligence in our structure while we're weeding out the old regime and replacing it with the new."

"Look, can we drop it? I can't talk about this anymore." The truth is, I was afraid to. Marcus was right . . . it could all be so easy.

"Tell me about the shooting," I said, sliding up onto the

workbench. "Who pulled the trigger on Barbara Sloan? The general consensus seems to be that it was you."

With a grimace, Marcus reached for a metal rod on a shelf that held several. Next he'd heat it, I knew, and bend it into whatever shape he needed . . . I'd worked with Marcus on the Tancook often enough to know that he used welding as an outlet for anger. When Marcus couldn't control what Fate created, he created things he could control.

He pulled the propane torch from its box beneath the bench, and holding the rod with pliers, he clicked the torch on. Its automatic ignition spit out a blue flame. He held it to the rod a moment or two, studying it with narrowed eyes. Finally, clicking it off, he bent the rod into an arc and said quietly, "Do you believe I killed Barbara Sloan?"

"I'm trying real hard not to."

He smiled without warmth. "Apparently it was Tark. He's gone over to the Gandolos."

"*Tark?* C'mon."

He squinted at the angle of the rod, then laid it down. Facing me, he said, "Tark sold me out."

"What are you talking about? Tark wouldn't do that. He's absolutely loyal to you."

The small white scar below his eye throbbed. "I guess everybody's got his price."

"Not *Tark*. How can you even think that?"

"I was . . . told by someone. Someone who was up on C dock and saw what happened. According to this witness, the shooter was Tark. And he's gone."

"Gone *where*? And who the hell told you this? An informer? One of your paid snitches? Why would you trust anybody's word over Tark's? You can't even have talked to him about it, if he's been gone."

Nobody I know does "cocky" better than Marcus. His chin went up, and one black eyebrow lifted. "It's interesting that you're defending him so passionately, Jess."

I slid off the bench and stomped to the opposite end of the Whaler, kicking sawdust and scraps of wood out of my path. "I don't need this shit! If you don't trust me—"

"I didn't say that." He punched the torch on again, but singed his hand picking up the rod. The flame clicked off and he dropped the whole lot, giving it up as a bad job.

"Then what's that tone about?" I said.

"I just wonder sometimes . . . this bond between you and Tark—"

"You can't be jealous!"

"No. It's . . . forget it."

"I can't forget it. Tark is *loyal* to you. I thought you knew that."

"Defend him if you want. But Tark did the shooting on the *SeaStar*. Maybe it's a takeover. If I'm sent up—"

"Dammit!" I slapped the graceful bow of the Whaler and felt it shudder. "If you're sent up, Tark will be here taking care of things for you until you get back. You should know that, and if you don't—"

"Then where is Tark now? Why hasn't he shown up since that night, or been in touch in any way?"

"I don't know where he is. But he has been in touch—with me. He called and told me you needed help. That should be enough to tell you he hasn't betrayed you."

Marcus yanked at a new piece of pine, thumped it down on the sawhorse, and began to sand again, his knuckles white. For a long time, he didn't answer. There was no sound in the barn except for the *whiss* of the block of sandpaper, a slow, meticulous delaying tactic. The scent of raw pine filled my nostrils, taking me back to a time the previous summer when Marcus and I had worked together here. We had talked then about things neither of us had shared with anyone before. About betrayal, and its by-product, paranoia . . . and how easy it is to lose trust.

Marcus had told me then how vulnerable he was to betrayal, and I had understood that this was one of the most serious issues of his life. I should have remembered, and reassured him these last months of my own loyalty—regardless of what I was thinking about our relationship otherwise. In Marcus's position, dealing from time to time with lowlifes who would kill over a candy bar concession, the possibility of a double-cross is exaggerated a hundredfold.

But I hadn't reassured him—in fact, the idea never occurred to me, caught up as I was in my own shit.

And I realized now that fear of betrayal was the fuel for Marcus's blind anger where Tark was concerned. The pieces fell into place.

"You know about Tark and Bernadette Gandolo," I guessed. "You think he's gone over to Paulie because of her, and that he set you up for Paulie."

The *whiss*ing noise ceased. He wiped the sweat off his face and chest with a heavy green towel, taking his time. Then he leaned back against the sawhorse, arms folded. "I can't help but think it looks that way."

"And what about Barbara Sloan? What was she up to with Paulie?"

He gave me an assessing look, then shrugged. "I've had her leaking things to Paulie for months, wrong info to botch up some of his sleazier operations."

"Like the kiddie porn?"

A pause. Then, "What do you know about that?"

"Only what I've been told in the last few days by the cops. They think you're the brains behind it, that you run the business end and Paulie runs the streets. They also think you and Paulie had a falling out over business, that Barbara Sloan was in the thick of it, and you had her killed."

He made a scornful sound.

"So how do you have it figured?" I said. "You think Paulie found out that you've been sabotaging him with Barbara Sloan, and he had her shot? On your boat, to implicate you as well?"

"It's one scenario."

"Hmmm." I picked up a handful of sawdust and let it drift through my fingers. "It makes sense. Up to the part about Tark. He wouldn't have shot Sloan."

At his expression, I added, "Not even for Bernadette."

Marcus just looked at me.

"How long has he known her?" I asked.

"Six months. Since March. They met at a get-together at Tark's brother's church near Canandaigua. Tark was trying to build bridges with his family. His sister had gone to school with Bernadette, and she just happened to bring her. Bernadette and Tark met, they talked . . ."

"And now it's serious."

He laughed shortly. "You know Tark. What do you think?"

"I think he probably wouldn't drop her if he cared about her, even for you."

His grim smile flattened out.

"Is that what happened? Did you tell him not to see her anymore?"

He bent and picked up more planks and some molding from the floor, lining them up with controlled precision on the sawhorse. "He was compromising the family," he said flatly, and began to work again.

"How?"

"He wanted to marry her. Paulie wouldn't allow it unless I agreed to a merger."

"Among you, Lucetta, and him?" Jimmy Lucetta was an aging don, the nominal head of Marcus's family. Marcus was the one in charge—at least here in the western part of the state—but Lucetta's opinion had to be taken into account, out of respect.

"Not Lucetta. Paulie wanted me to break away from Lucetta and join him. He wanted my business expertise." His tone was derisive.

"Tell me about the shooting. How did it physically happen?"

"Barbara and I were on the upper deck of the boat, having a meeting. Paulie wasn't supposed to know anything about it. He was getting paranoid, and didn't trust her."

"Tark was at this meeting?"

"Yes."

"On the boat with you and Sloan?"

"No. Barbara and I were on the aft deck, it was dark, and we were shielded from view by a canvas windbreaker —you know that walled-in area around the chairs up there. Tark was up on C dock, which is almost on a level with the aft deck, supposedly keeping watch. Barbara got up and went over to the bar, where she would've been in full view of C dock, but nothing else. She was there less than a minute when the shot came. A few seconds later, all hell broke loose. Marina security guards were swarming all over the *SeaStar* before I could even take her pulse, and then the Rochester police arrived. They took me in, and in the confusion . . . Tark disappeared."

"But you'd expect him to disappear under those circumstances, wouldn't you? So he'd be free to help you? And you've never had any reason to distrust Tark. He's been your friend from childhood—your bodyguard for twenty years."

"In twenty years," he said, "Tark has never been this thick with the family of my enemies, never had his loyalties torn this way before."

"What if whoever shot Barbara Sloan overpowered Tark? What if they've got him and are holding him for some reason?"

"If he was being held somewhere, how could he have phoned you? And you're forgetting the witness. Tark was seen pulling the trigger."

Every question I asked seemed to pull Tark in deeper.

"Who was this witness? You say he told you—personally."

"That's right."

"Then he's not your everyday upright citizen, who just goes to the cops. Why do you trust this person?"

He didn't answer, and I knew by the set of his shoulders that he wouldn't, no matter how I pushed.

"What are you doing about Paulie? How are you handling his setting you up—if he did?"

"I have a few things in the works."

"You want to tell me what they are?"

"Not at the moment, Jess."

"I just asked because I'm on my way to see Paulie," I said.

"*No.*" He dropped the plank he was sanding and stared at me.

"No? No what? No, I'm not on my way to see Paulie? But I am."

His hands balled into fists at his sides. "Don't do it, Jess."

"The way I see it, it's the quickest way to find Tark and find out what really happened that night. If Paulie can't tell me, then Bernadette—"

Marcus said harshly, "Paulie isn't just mad, Jess, he's evil. Some of the things he's been doing . . ." He shook his head as if to clear it of some horror he personally had seen. "That prostitute . . . remember? The one they found in pieces a few weeks ago—decapitated, and with her hands cut off? Jess, Paulie did that. He didn't *order* it. Word on the street is that he did it himself, laughing crazily all the while." His hands gripped my upper arms. "The woman worked for him, and God knows what she did, maybe just looked at him the wrong way, that's all it takes these days."

Boards creaked on the Whaler, dust motes drifted in a stream of sunlight coming through the high arched windows. Marcus's face was so hard it formed an unbreachable wall. Sweat streamed down his forehead into his eyes. He didn't bother to brush it away.

Finally he loosened his grip. "Just let it be, Jess," he said.

In his tone was a message: If I didn't follow orders and stay away from Paulie, I would somehow be part of the betrayal, too.

I wished there were something else I could do. But I'd never been much good at the touchy-feely, nurturing kind of thing—standing by, holding hands, murmuring wishy-washy platitudes. The only solution I could come up with that fit my style was to find Tark.

As I reached the door, Marcus said, "I really want you to drop this now."

I didn't respond. I was too busy planning what I'd say to Paulie Gandolo.

CHAPTER ELEVEN

A couple of well-placed calls, one in particular to Jiddy Knowles, a reporter specializing in the crime families down in the Big Apple, located Paulie for me. I also wanted Bernadette; she could lead me to Tark, if Paulie didn't. Bernadette, however, proved a little tougher to find than her brother. Jiddy said she hadn't been seen around the family compound on Long Island for at least a week. There seemed to be some mystery about where she had gone.

Paulie himself was in Atlantic City, where he owned a small casino. It was 4:20 P.M. I went by the bank, dug into the rent money, and caught the 6:05 USAir down to Philly. The flight took only an hour, but there would be a wait for the connection from there to Atlantic City. I picked up a budget rental, then headed out on the Atlantic City Expressway. The drive took another hour.

Somewhere after Pleasantville, I switched on a local radio station and rolled down the windows, letting dinner jazz fill my ears and the briny air hit my face. I could see myself dancing in the Whatever Ballroom, high atop Atlantic City's own Tropi-cana-dero-schmero-Fountain-Bleu Hotel—swirling in a black chiffon dress and sporting a long creamy string of pearls. It was in that frame of mind that I meandered into town in my rumpled white jeans and shirt, letting the casino tour buses whiz on by.

I found Paulie's place on the boardwalk, a good distance away from either Trump's or Harrah's higher-priced locations. It was a modest-sized building, three floors, and with only one restaurant listed on the billboard in front. Business was bustling, though, and I pushed through the noisy racket. There were slots going *chinkety-chink*, ringing bells, and a trio of pop singers cavorting on a lighted stage. I asked a tired change girl where the offices were, and she hefted her twenty-five-pound money apron and pointed across the red-carpeted room to an area where blackjack and other games were played beneath crystal chandeliers. I headed that way and noted that the mood, even among the polyester crowd at the slots, was intense—the Ballys being massaged and talked to like living things. I felt like I was in a house of ill repute, where all the patrons were making love to machines instead of flesh.

There was a guard by a bank of elevators. I reached to push the UP button, and he put his hand out to stop me before I could touch it.

"Sorry, private elevator. Offices only, up there."

"I'm looking for Paulie Gandolo."

"You have an appointment?" His expression said he was certain I didn't.

"Not yet, but I plan to."

"Offices are closed at night. Call in the morning."

"I can't do that, I'm only here a few hours."

The guard's eyes glazed with boredom. He was young, dark, muscular, and talked with a Brooklyn accent. I guessed he was more likely to be one of Paulie's foot soldiers than an ordinary security guard.

"Look," I said, "I just want a few minutes. At least let him know I'm here." I gave him one of the business cards the *Herald* insisted I carry, the one with my name in the lower left corner, and he looked at it with a flicker of interest. I said, "Tell him it's about his sister."

The eyes narrowed momentarily. He said, "Wait here." He went to a red house phone on the wall and punched three numbers, talked a couple of minutes, then came back and said, "Mr. Gandolo's at the Fantasy Nights Club. Out the front door, turn left, it's on the boardwalk about half a block down."

I thanked him and maneuvered through the casino again.

A jackpot rang, and there was excitement, howls of laughter and fun. At least from some. Others looked sourly at the winner, probably hard-cores who had spent half the day sinking quarter after quarter into that same machine—only to leave it and have Daisy Brill, from Youngstown, Ohio, walk up, pull it once, and win.

It felt good to get out of the artificial air and into the night again. Beyond the flickering lights, the ocean gleamed in the dark—rolls of phosphorescent white competing with miles of neon. The air smelled of cotton candy and caramel corn, and I realized I was hungry. I bought a hot dog from a stand, slathered it with mustard and relish, and was still munching when I reached Fantasy Nights.

It was a dinner club—circular tables with red cloths, candles, dim lights—the sort of thing that looks gaudy and dusty during the day when the chairs are up and the floor's being cleaned. A large stage spanned the far end of the dining area. Its curtains glittered through a smoky haze.

The maître d' glared and opened his mouth, about to turn me and my hot dog away. In truth, his protest might have had something to do with the way I looked: stained jeans, tired running shoes, a cotton blouse by now sweaty from the trip, and my brown hair frizzed from the ocean air. So much for black chiffon and pearls.

"Paulie Gandolo," I said, wiping a smudge of mustard off my mouth and onto my jeans. "I'm expected."

With only a small, disdainful cock of a thin brow, he said, "Of course. Right this way."

I followed along behind his duckish waddle. He didn't lead me to a table, as I'd expected. Instead, he swerved to a lobby on the left and up a flight of winding stairs, the kind you used to see in old movie houses. At the top was a steel door, and he punched in a code. A voice crackled over a speaker. The maître d' answered in a low monotone. The door swung open, and there was Paulie—bathed in a weird red light and hunched on a sofa before a large tinted window that looked down onto the Fantasy Nights' stage. I was ushered in with a stiff wave of arm. I crossed over to

the sofa, hands in my pockets, trying for nonchalant and
failing. I was nervous as hell now that I was actually here,
and now that I saw I'd be tête-à-tête-ing with Paulie-the-
pervert in private. I had pictured it like in the old movies,
where the mobster's in a velvet booth surrounded by broads
and champagne.

He finally looked my way, nodded, and turned back to
the entertainment again. I understood I was supposed to
sit, but there wasn't anyplace to do that except on the sofa,
next to Paulie. I perched on the edge at the opposite end,
leaving a good three feet between him and me.

Paulie twisted a knob on a console, and music from the
stage blared over loudspeakers in each corner of the room.
It was too loud for conversation. He didn't seem inclined
to converse, anyway. There were prancing girls down there
now with bouncing naked breasts, their spangles jangling
to the tune of—inevitably, I suppose—"New York, New
York." When they kicked, their legs swept high over the
front tables, and on the backward kick, it was their breasts
that hung in the customers' faces, jiggling and teasing.

I looked around the red room.

When the door to the stairs had closed, the first thing
I'd noted was that this room was soundproofed. You could
hear the stage music from speakers since Paulie had turned
them up, but not through the walls or door. It was like one
of those crying rooms they once put in theaters for mothers
with babies. Maybe the whole place was a movie house
once, and whoever remodeled it into a casino had left certain things stand. I had a strange, cut-off feeling, not helped
at all by the fact that everything around me was red.

The walls, the floor, the sofa, Paulie, me . . . we were
awash in a glow of crimson lights from the ceiling, track
upon track of them, all over the damned place. And now
that I was closer to it, I suspected that the window was one-
way glass. It had a flat, opaque look, telling me that although
we could see out there, Paulie and I, for all practical purposes, were alone. I focused on him.

He was dressed in one of those iridescent suits that mobsters and pharmaceutical salesmen seem to wear. Under the red lights, it looked purple. He had slick black hair, thinning. A sharp nose, sharp teeth. I knew about the teeth from when he'd flashed them at me in the Halls of Justice last year, not because he was smiling and showing them to me now. While men below were grinning at the women on stage, and even their female companions were smiling, Paulie's mouth was a tight line, his eyes cold. His attention seemed fixed on one dancer in particular; they followed her every move. She had rust-red hair, masses of it falling halfway down her back, and a mole or beauty mark the size of a quarter on her left collarbone. As the dance ended, her chest rose and fell rapidly. The dancers trotted off stage to wild applause from the front row and shouts of "More . . . encore!" They didn't come back. The music died away and a ventriloquist with a dummy took over. For the most part, people went back to their dinners and drinks, losing interest.

Paulie twisted the knob on the console again, and the sounds from below were muted. He pressed another button. "Tell Ginny I wanta see her," he said, and clicked the button off with an impatient flip. He drummed the fingers of one hand on his knee, watching the action below. A man in a black suit threaded his way through the booths and tables to a door at the left of the stage, moving swiftly. I was beginning to realize that Paulie was more than a guest here. His imperious manner was that of an owner, or an investor of standing. The man disappeared, and almost as an afterthought, Paulie turned to me.

"Jesse James," he said. "Long time no see. What brings you here?" He slid closer to me, one arm going along the sofa's back.

"I need a little information, Paulie."

I gave him what I hoped was a friendly enough smile. If Paulie didn't like what I had to say, he could just as easily press another button on that console and have me carted off to a New Jersey swamp.

"Yeah?" He inched closer, and there was no mistaking

the glimmer in his narrowed eyes. "Anything for you, pretty lady. I haven't forgotten how you helped me out last year." He fingered my hair where it fell against my shoulder. His suit jacket was open, his shirt unbuttoned. Gold chains glistened red against a bony chest.

On a coffee table before us was a bottle of champagne and two glasses. Paulie filled the glasses with his free hand and passed one to me. I was tempted to relax the nerve endings with those bubbles, but I set the glass back down and shook my head. I inched back against the sofa's arm, which had the added effect of releasing my hair from Paulie's skinny grip. His mouth tightened and he said, his voice hardening, "Okay. You got five minutes, pretty lady. What's this about my sister Bernadette?"

It was at this point that I realized I held the remains of a cold hot dog in my hand. It wasn't bubbles, but it'd do as a pace-setter—a way to gain control of the interview. *Think of it as an interview*, I had told myself. *And don't let him know you're intimidated.* I brought the hot dog to my mouth, took a nibble, and said, "Five whole minutes . . . and here I thought you'd try and rush me, Paulie." There was a plate of unfinished food on the table, and I picked up a napkin to wipe the mustard off my fingers. "But then, you're a busy man, aren't you? Kind of shorthanded, with Barbara Sloan gone?"

A muscle began to throb in his cheek. "Four minutes," Paulie said.

"Right." I finished off the hot dog, taking my time and glancing at the scene below. I wiped my mouth and said, "God, that was good. There's something about fast food and salt air—"

There was a high-pitched, crazy sound next to me. A *giggle*. I remembered what Marcus had said about the prostitute, how Paulie had cut off her hands . . . her head . . . laughing all the while. I felt a chill right through to my spine, and forced myself to look at Paulie. He was grinning—and in his eyes was a lewd, frenetic light.

"You got *balls*, kid! You know that? I saw it that day when you wouldn't testify . . . you coulda gone to jail, kid, but you . . . you got balls." He shook his head, and those brittle, hot eyes wandered all over me. I saw it coming, but before I could react, he ran a bony finger down my blouse and over a nipple. Paulie laughed again, softly. "Nice," he murmured, leaning closer and laying his palm against me, squeezing. "Anybody ever tickle your belly button from the inside?"

Jesus Christ. I jerked away. For a moment, I thought this might be strategy on Paulie's part. A guy like him could set a woman off balance with something like that. But the eyes . . . it wasn't strategy. It was just Paulie, the Paulie I'd heard about, going shit-ditsy right in front of me. His smile became a hard contortion, and he wriggled closer, giggling softly and reaching again.

My back pressed almost painfully against the sofa arm as far as it could go, and I thought: *Marcus was right.* I was out of my depth here. Over the years, as a reporter, I had trafficked successfully with all kinds: white collar crooks, hard-core criminals . . . but this was something else. I couldn't think for a minute what to do or say, but I remember chanting silently (on the verge of tears or hysterical laughter, I wasn't sure which) *Jesus Mary, Jesus Mary*— the way they taught us to do at Mercy, should our virtue ever be at stake. Funny how it sticks with you, no matter how old, tough, or lapsed you think you are.

Maybe, like King Arthur, Jesus and Mary didn't have much going on that day. Maybe they were out a-Maying and heard my plea. At any rate, I was saved. A buzzer sounded on the console. Paulie's eyes closed briefly, and the hand that had gone for my breast was stayed. He turned angrily to answer the intrusion. "It's Ginny," said a timid voice over the speaker. He pressed a button to let her in —the dancer with the long red hair. She approached us silently, biting her lip, her arms folded in front of her in an attitude of frightened defiance. She wore a skimpy halter now, and her hands ran nervously up and down her bare arms. Harsh lines were visible beneath her makeup.

Paulie erupted. "You were late again, Gin-Gin!" He

lurched to his feet and strode to the area behind the sofa.
"And you looked like a fuckin' cow, plodding around down
there. What the hell's goin' on? I give you a break, and you
give me *shit*?" His voice grew higher in pitch until it was
almost a whine.

"I had to go home and see my kid, Paulie, I told you. I
got stuck in the traffic getting back."

He grabbed her behind the neck and yanked her toward
him. "I expected you, Gin-Gin. You were supposed to be
here two hours before the show."

"I'll make it up, honey," she said. Her tone became whee-
dling. "Okay? After the last show, just you and me. . . . I'll
make it nice for you, honey, okay?" Her arm went around
his neck and she stooped a little to kiss him on the mouth.
"We'll have plenty of time, you'll see."

Paulie made a sound like a low growl, and within seconds
he was all over her—his hips pushing her back into a dark
corner, against a wall. She giggled and whispered and didn't
seem to mind, so I looked away and tried to imagine I was
somewhere else. There were nuzzling sounds, and a moan.
Then the stage music came on again over the speakers. The
lead dancers flounced out, and I heard Ginny say anxiously,
"I gotta go, honey, I gotta get back."

A murmur of protest. A soft laugh. "You are the most
impatient man I know," she said coyly.

"I better be the *only* man you know," Paulie told her.
Ginny laughed, but I thought the sound was uneasy. I heard
her leave and braced myself. I didn't know if she had worn
off Paulie's edge of sexual energy, or simply heated him up
for me.

I needn't have worried. Paulie stood at the window, his
eyes fixed on the stage until he saw Ginny slip into line
there again. It was with obvious effort that he turned back
to me.

"Okay," he said, shooting his cuffs. "Let's get this over
with, I got plans. What's this crap about my sister?" He
cracked his knuckles the way schoolboys will to make girls
shiver, but kept one eye on the stage.

I got up and leaned against the window ledge, my back to the window and stage, facing Paulie. I folded my arms. "We've got some things to discuss first," I said. "For one thing, Barbara Sloan. Aren't you curious about who killed Sloan?"

Paulie said, "I know fuckin' well who blew away Sloan. Your pal, Andrelli."

"You're wrong. Andrelli didn't do it."

"The fuck he didn't."

"He doesn't operate that way."

"Yeah? Well, maybe you don't know Andrelli as well as you think you do."

I laughed softly. "Let's look at it this way. Andrelli is a threat to you. When Lucetta dies—probably not all that long from now, after all, he's an old man—Andrelli will be in charge of all upstate New York, not just the western half. And Andrelli's not as easy to deal with as Lucetta. When he's in charge, you won't be able to push the old rackets through the state the way you do now. All those things Marcus doesn't like . . . drugs . . . kiddie porn . . . you won't have Lucetta's outlet for them upstate anymore. That'll hurt your business, Paulie, it'll hurt real bad. And that makes Marcus a threat to you."

Paulie's knobby hands began clenching and unclenching. I was made aware again of my precarious perch up here in this soundproofed room. I could feel bullet holes at the stem of the brain, cement blocks on my shoes, and swamp mosquitoes nibbling my nose.

I went on, more reckless than brave. "So, Paulie, I've been thinking. It's been several days since Barbara Sloan was shot. By Andrelli's hand, as you say you believe. But if that's so, I'm wondering why you haven't struck back. After all, Sloan was working for you too. And here you are, playing grab-the-titty at the goddamned seashore."

The dancers were thumping away on the stage, sequins glinting in the blinding spotlights. I started walking around the couch, still talking, but glancing up now and then to make sure Paulie was still with me. He was. He had settled on the arm of the sofa, and he swiveled around, his hot eyes on me.

"Now, here's the way I see it," I continued, blocking it out with hand gestures as I paced. "You and Barbara Sloan are having problems. You want her taken out. At the same time, you want Andrelli out of your hair once and for all. And here's Tark, Andrelli's right hand, getting tight with your sister. Maybe he'll even be your brother-in-law one day—and he knows Andrelli's business inside out. Something happens to Andrelli, Tark would be in a position to take over—and you figure he'll do pretty much what you want, to get to marry Bernadette."

The only fly in that ointment was that Tark thought like Marcus. I was certain he'd never fall in with Paulie Gandolo's way of doing business. But if Paulie somehow didn't know that . . . if Tark had for some reason been stringing him along . . .

It was a recent thought. In fact, I hadn't been fully conscious of it until now. I shelved it for the moment—that and both Marcus's and Grady's claim that a witness had seen Tark shoot Barbara Sloan. I wouldn't give much for the veracity of that witness until I knew who it was—or until I talked with Tark.

"So here's what you do," I said. "You have somebody from your own camp shoot Sloan on Andrelli's yacht. You see to it there's no other suspects but Andrelli. And *poof!* You've got both Sloan and Andrelli taken care of with one little pump of a nine-millimeter Glock."

And that's when I knew I had it wrong. At mention of the Glock, a flicker of surprise crossed Paulie's face. He smoothed it out fast, but it was unmistakable. *Surprise.*

Christ. I was on virgin territory, suddenly . . . my scenario had some awful flaw. I felt it in every bone. *It was the gun, something about the gun.*

Paulie saw my consternation, and he took the opportunity to slide one in. He said, "Okay, Miss Smartass, you got it all figured out, but if your little plot was such a great idea, where's my so-called future brother-in-law? Where the fuck is Tark?"

"I was hoping you'd tell me."

"You can hope until your ass turns to ice, just like Andrelli," he said.

"Then what about Bernadette? Where is she?"

His face closed down. "Bernadette is on vacation."

"Where?"

He didn't answer.

"Well, I could always call her later," I tried. "When will she be home?"

No response.

"How about if you ask her to call me?"

He looked at his diamond-studded watch, then at the stage, which had emptied as we talked. "Time's up," he said irritably. "On your way. I got business."

I thought of persisting further. But why? The interview was over.

Paulie didn't even give me a fare-thee-well. "Well," I said, "it's been swell."

He didn't seem to notice my exit, either through the steel door. His eyes were fixed on the empty stage. I made my own way down the movie house stairs—past the snooty maître d'.

As I hit the boards and the humid air, I sighed. Unless I missed my guess, there was one more among us missing: Bernadette Gandolo.

And I hadn't done much, I thought, to move things along with my little trip to the shore.

I was wrong about that, of course. Every action has its reaction—I should know this, with old Samved, my guru/shrink, always drumming it in.

I was on the way back to my rental car, shortcutting down a boardwalk ramp between two abandoned buildings, when they got me.

CHAPTER TWELVE

My neck felt like it was broken, my ribs crushed, and I could see—barely—out of only one eye. I was on a cold floor in nearly total darkness and an inch or so of water, with nothing but an ominous dripping noise for company. I wondered what it was, and if the inch would grow. I thought of sewer rats, of mold and slime and furry flying things that go screech in the night. A trickle of something ran down my cheek. I licked my lips and tasted salt. Blood. My right eye held no sensation at all. The lid felt puffy and wet when I tried to either close or open it, as if there was too much flesh where it didn't belong. I couldn't see out of that eye at all.

What I could fathom from the left eye was, I thought, my knees. I saw the white jean blur, but, oddly, just a few inches from my face.

I had no idea where I was or how long I'd been there. I tried to stand, and only then did I realize I was lying on my left side, trussed, my legs in a fetal position close to my chin. I tried to twist onto my back, to get my cheek out of the water. I could turn my head, but not my body. Something hard and heavy bit painfully into my wrists, which were behind my back. There was a sound of . . . chains. I was chained somewhere, so tightly that I couldn't move.

I was cold and sick, and I bit back a sob of panic as I felt something crawl across the bare skin of my ankle. I rubbed my other ankle against it, trying to kill it. Back and forth, back and forth, trying to catch it, squish it, whatever it was. I heard it crackle. Oh, God.

I thought of my recently dull life at home, and yearned for it. And after a while, when it was apparent I wasn't going anywhere, I thought of my mom, of Marcus, even Bastard the vengeful dog. I thought of my job, and Charlie Nicks, my jerk editor, and how much I hated all that. *God*, I pleaded, *get me out of this and I'll never complain again*. I'll go back and work from eight to five, I won't drink, I'll even be nice to my neighbors . . .

I thought of Toni.

And how, at her age—no, two years older, at fourteen —I had come on vacation to Atlantic City with Aunt Ruth—the woman who was my foster mother that year. They were doing a lot of tearing down in the areas around the casinos then, and Aunt Ruth Donovan (not really an aunt, but she had told me to call her that) was an architect, with a great spirit for adventure. We ambled around, poking into places we had no right to be. I remembered her saying once, "Stick close, Jess. You could get lost under one of these piles of rubble and never be seen nor heard from again." It was like pictures of Berlin after World War II, nothing but broken buildings and dirt.

My guess was that I was in the cellar of one of those still-existent piles of rubble now.

There had been two men—one on each side of me—and they took me so fast there was no time to fight back. They slammed me down on the sidewalk, gagged me, then dragged me up and across a vacant lot. It was pitch black there, and the boardwalk lights spiraled as they threw me to the ground again. Then they began hitting.

One of them straddled my chest and struck me with open palms while the other held my arms. They didn't rape me, and there was nothing sexual about the attack. At one point someone muttered, ". . . teach the bitch a lesson." I finally passed out.

I tried again, now, to move. Pain seared along my spine and the backs of my thighs. It felt like knives cutting through flesh to bone. And I had to pee. God, how I had to pee.

At last I heard a door creak somewhere. A voice said,

"Well, the little lady's awake. Time to rise and shine. Boss is here. He wants to talk."

He carried a lantern that cast shadows on his face, which was ugly and fat. But it was his body I recognized. It was a mound of muscle and blubber, easily weighing in at three hundred pounds. He looked like one of those redneck sheriffs you see in movies about the South, with pants belted low under a stomach that must take in four hundred bucks' worth of groceries a week. I remembered the crushing weight on my chest when he'd sat on me in the vacant lot, and realized now why my ribs hurt so badly.

My chains were undone, and I tried to rub my wrists, but he yanked me across the room and up a flight of wooden cellar stairs. Every limb screamed in pain, and it felt like there was something wrong with my spine. Cramps doubled my legs, making me stumble. At the top of the stairs I was dragged down a narrow passage. It seemed that eyes watched from every dark corner along the way.

My captor shoved me through a doorway into a mostly dark room. I fell against something hard. After a moment I was able to make it out as a scarred wooden table. It held a battery-operated lamp, the kind used for camping. The lamp was shielded on the back and sides. Behind it, in the dark, someone sat. I could see his hands and the cuffs of a black sweater or sweatshirt on the table, nothing more.

"Who is it?" I said hoarsely, my voice shaking. "Who's there?"

"A messenger," the person behind the lamp answered quietly.

"Oh?" I peered into the dark and tried to tough it out. "I don't suppose you're the angel Gabriel."

"Your humor is not appreciated here."

The fat man twisted my arm high behind my back, making me bend from the waist. Sweat trickled into my injured eye, stinging. My teeth clamped down hard on my bottom lip. I tasted blood again.

"Neither is your interference appreciated," the man in the dark said, in what struck me now as an odd, stilted accent. "Is that clear?" My arm was yanked higher. I couldn't stand it, and as I too often do, I struck out recklessly to override the fear. "Nothing's clear! Get your fucking hands *off* me!" I wrenched back with my free arm and clawed at the fat man behind me with my nails. They connected, and he let go for a split second. I twisted around and leveled a kick at his groin. There wasn't much power behind it—pain made me clutch. He yelled, and grabbed for me. I lost my balance and fell backward, striking something hard with the small of my back. Fatso yanked me up, and I struggled, but he held me in a viselike grip around the chest and arms. I gulped for air and felt my legs go weak, like a puppet whose strings had just been cut. I'd have fallen, if I weren't being held.

"We were told to try to reason with you," the voice behind the light said. "Failing that . . ." The hand that I could see made the kind of gesture that goes with a shrug, and the fat man began to drag me toward the door.

"No, wait! Wait, goddammit! At least tell me what this is about. You work for Gandolo? Did Paulie tell you to do this? Tell me what he wants, we'll work it out."

The hand went up in a staying gesture, and Fatso halted.

"You have been asking too many questions," the accented voice said. "Leave the matter of the Sloan woman's death alone."

"Okay . . . just give me a reason."

The hand-shrug again. The arms that held me tightened, one of them going around my neck and clamping, hard. "*Okay.* It was only a story. I agree."

There was a soft laugh. "You agree much too quickly, I think. Perhaps you do not fully understand. If you fail to do as you are told—" He motioned, a flick of the wrist. "Take her back downstairs."

At that moment, the whole house rocked. The floor seemed to buckle beneath my feet. Windows rattled and blew inward. Glass flew. My cheek stung. A red flash lit the room, and I caught a glimpse of the man behind the lamp before a tunnel of hot air wrenched me from Fatso's grip and threw me against a wall. Fatso screamed as huge chunks of plaster fell from the ceiling. He grabbed for his head and came stumbling back, then fell on me. I nearly blacked out from the weight. Then I heard footsteps running.

"What the *fuck*!"

"Check it out! Goddammit, that idiot was supposed to keep watch!"

The fat man was motionless on top of me. Blood from his head dripped onto my face. I pushed upward and shoved. Got free up to my waist. Dragged out a leg. But it seemed like a year before I freed the other. I staggered to my feet, feeling pain all over.

"Get back in there!" came a shout from another room. "Make sure she doesn't get away!"

I was dizzy but standing. I lurched into the hall. At its far end I saw a man, eerily backlit by the neon glow of flames, coming toward me. I spun in the opposite direction and ran. There was nothing that way but the cellar stairs and three doors. I took the one on the left.

I was in a room with an archway to another. The fire outside reflected in on crumbling walls, graffiti, dirt. There were footsteps close behind, and I ran for the adjoining room—directly into the arms of Fatso. A bone protruded from the ridge of his nose. Blood on his face was scarlet from the fire's glare. My throat clamped shut as his hands went around my neck. I made two fists and punched his gut as hard as I could. His hands dropped, probably from surprise rather than pain, and I broke away, bursting through a swinging door. Fatso wasn't more than three feet behind. I swung the door back in the opposite direction, hard, throwing all my weight behind it. I heard him scream as it apparently connected with his already battered nose, and turned to find myself in a kitchen with a back exit. I ran for it, and then screamed myself, in frustration. The handle went only so far. It was locked, no key. Outside,

the fire roared; like an angry ex-lover, it wasn't giving up.
You could almost feel it beating at the air.

One more door remained. I crashed through it and was
in a pantry, the old kind with huge bottom cupboards and
a hutch with shelves. The area was less than ten-by-ten,
and there was no other way out. I was trapped. My pursuer
came through the swinging door.

Somehow, he didn't see me. He was clutching his nose
and shaking his head back and forth. As he lumbered to
the exit door, I yanked open a bottom cupboard and
squeezed myself down into it, thanking fate for once that I
was short and fairly small. It helped—although once in the
cramped position, I thought I might black out from the
effort. I held my breath until my lungs burned, and
squinched my eyes closed as if that would somehow keep
them from finding me. I heard voices in the kitchen. "Save
said to scare her, not hurt her." *Save*. The name meant
nothing to me, and I wondered if I'd heard it right. I
strained my ears, hoping they'd say it again.

"The shit with that. The boss don't trust her—she's too
much trouble."

"Christ, my ass will be fried if she gets away."

They were in the pantry by then, less than a foot away,
it seemed. My heart pounded, and tears began to squeeze
through my closed eyes. But their examination was brief.
The door closed again.

More distant now: "I swear she came in here, I followed
her."

"The back door."

"Locked. Boss locked it when he came. He kept the key."

"The window? Try it."

There was a muffled sound, then, "Shit, it's open. We'd
better check outside."

Their voices dwindled away. My cramped muscles demanded release, and I finally had to move, to chance that
they were gone. I eased myself out of the cupboard and
couldn't see a thing. No window here, no flames to light

the dark. I groped along the wall to the pantry door, then froze and listened. Silence. I found the knob, turned it cautiously, and stepped into the kitchen.

My heart nearly stopped as a hand touched my shoulder and another one clamped itself over my mouth.

CHAPTER THIRTEEN

"Don't yell," a voice rasped. "Are you okay?"

I nodded, and was released. I turned, stunned to see, in the fire's light, Ginny, the red-haired dancer.

"What the hell?" My mouth had fallen open. I closed it and stared.

"I blew up their car," she said grimly. "That oughta keep the fuckers busy awhile." She grabbed my hand and yanked me toward the back door which now stood open.

"Wait a minute! What the hell's going on?"

"Carlo and Manny spread out, they're looking for you all over the neighborhood. Everybody else is gone." She tugged at my hand, pulling me along.

"How do you know? Where the hell did you come from?"

"I had orders to follow you. And I saw what they did to you, back there by the boardwalk. I couldn't help you then, kid. I'm real sorry."

"You saw them—"

"*C'mon.* We've got to *move*, before they come back. I've got my car."

We ran onto a rickety porch, flew down several stairs, and rounded the corner of the house. I saw by the fire's glow that we were indeed in one of the torn-down areas around the boardwalk casinos. The lot around us was empty but for weeds, garbage, and massive hunks of concrete. The surrounding neighborhood was dark. At the side of the house sat the hulk of a car. Flames ate its remains, then spit them into the sky. The house seemed untouched, but wouldn't be for long. I heard the distant wail of sirens.

We sprinted down the street, ahead of shouts: "It's her! Get her, goddammit, there she is!" We stumbled over broken paving, the fire at our backs. Ginny led the way, a foot or so ahead. She ran like mad, and I was breathless keeping up. I could see out of only one eye. My ribs burned.

Ginny stopped short and I bumped into her. "It's open!" She flew around to the driver's side of a small car, and I yanked open the passenger door. We fell into our seats with heavy footsteps pounding down the street behind us. Several loud retorts, and a metallic smack hit Ginny's car.

"Shit!" she cried. "My insurance company's gonna love this." She slammed the car into gear and we tore off, burning rubber and passing two racing fire engines along the way.

Ginny threaded the car through increasingly heavy traffic as we crossed town. After a few minutes I took a more or less normal breath and said, "Why did you do this, Ginny?"

"A long story." She muttered. She glanced my way. "God, you look awful! We've got to get you fixed up."

"I'm okay." I reached into my jeans pocket and found the money I had put there before going up on the boardwalk to see Paulie, so I wouldn't have to carry a purse. It was wet from the water in the cellar, but I counted it. All there. "Just drop me off at the airport, okay? I can get a plane there to Philly, then home."

Her head turned my way a second. "You always take things this cool?"

"I guess I'm in shock."

"Well, that's okay—you left Manny and Carlo in shock, too."

"Airport?" I said.

"Uh-uh. Not yet. We got other plans right now." Her tongue made a clucking sound. "Besides, they wouldn't let you on a plane like that."

I flipped the visor down, and in the passing light from the street, peered at my face in the mirror. God. My right eyelid was swollen to three times its size. Dried blood had caked on my face, in smears like an out-of-control hand had applied dark brown blush. There were beginning bruises on both cheeks, below the eyes. Ginny was right. They wouldn't let me on a plane like this. The other passengers would think I was a terrorist.

"I can give you pancake for the bruises, and dark glasses for the eye," she said. "We'll fix you up."

No airport. Other plans right now, she had said. Was I walking from the fire into the frying pan? "Did Paulie send you after me?"

She didn't answer. Instead, she zigzagged through the traffic, making sure we weren't followed—or at least, that was what she said, giving me cause to wonder how she had become such an expert at that. Some minutes later we were at a high-rise apartment building that Ginny described only as a "safe place, belonging to a friend." She parked in the underground garage, and for the first time I saw that the car was a white Nissan Pulsar, late model. The trunk was ventilated with bullet holes. We took an express elevator to the twenty-third floor. There, we followed thick green carpeting to an apartment several doors down the hall. Ginny let us in with a key.

The door opened to a living room that was simply furnished in black and white hi-tech. It was dimly lit. I took a step inside and then froze. Someone sat in a chair, in near darkness. A woman, with stockinged legs. Her face in shadow. She didn't speak, and I heard Ginny close the door and lock it behind us. I turned back to her. "Who—?"

A door opened from another room. A man stood in the doorway, light from the room outlining a massive figure. For one crazy moment I thought it was Fatso, that he'd somehow gotten here before us. Had my rescuer merely led me into a trap? I prepared to whirl on Ginny, knock her down, and run.

"Hello, Jess," the man said. His voice was soft. I realized, then, that although his figure was massive, it was firmly built. He came forward into the light, and I saw his face and gave a little cry. I stumbled toward him.

"Thank God!" I cried, hugging him in my relief. Then, standing back angrily, "Where the hell have you been!"

"I seem to have heard that question before." His tone was slightly amused. "But first, have you two met?"

He made a gesture toward the woman in the chair, and she stood and came toward me, holding out a hand and smiling. Her long dark hair was shiny, her dark silky dress flowing around a graceful figure. I took her hand and scowled. "I've been wondering where you were, too," I said.

It was Tark and Bernadette.

I sat at a table in a small, efficient kitchen. Ginny checked out my injuries—swiftly and expertly, as if she did it all the time. Tark fussed so much, I finally sent him away. "Go hold Bernadette's hand. I'll be fine."

"Let me know when you feel up to it. We'll talk."

The ribs, Ginny told me, were bruised but not broken. They would be all right. Every time I breathed, however, the pain made me gasp. She gave me a pain pill from an unlabeled bottle—"Got 'em from a doctor I know," she explained vaguely. "They'll work best if you lay down awhile and give 'em a chance."

She tended the rest of my wounds, ignoring a cut on her own forehead. Her skin-tight jeans were smudged with something black, like grease, and her white cotton shirt was ripped in several places. It looked like she'd smeared dirt on it for camouflage. Finally, she clucked like a mother hen until I agreed to rest on the sofa while Tark and I had our talk. She had to be getting back to Paulie.

"He's gonna be fit to be tied," she said. "The prick. First I'm late for his little fuck this afternoon, and now tonight. God knows what he did when I wasn't there for the last show. I got a vision of him up there in that rotten red room, jerking off."

"What will you tell him?" I was worried for her.

"The usual. 'My kid was sick and I had to rush home.'

Home," she said with an arch look, "is supposed to be Hammonton, up on the expressway."

"Do you really have a child?"

She laughed bitterly. "Are you kidding?" She looked around. The kitchen was efficient enough, but bare. It didn't look used at all. "You should see my place—it's colder than this. In my business, there's no time for settling down."

"What is your business?"

She began heating water for coffee in a chrome pot. "Monkey business, kid." She laughed that hearty, husky laugh again, no sign now of the cowed woman who had stood shivering before Paulie several hours before. "Hanging out with apes."

"I'm serious, Ginny. I'm afraid for you, going back there to Paulie when he's angry. He's crazy, you know that, don't you? You know the kinds of things he's done?"

A shadow crossed her beautifully molded face. "Oh, yeah," she said softly, "I know." She laughed again, but grimly. "Don't worry, I know how to handle Paulie Gandolo. The guy's ruled by his dick. All you have to do is take hold and pull. Paulie follows right along."

"But what if he knows you helped me tonight? Manny and Carlo must have seen you, or if not you, your car. What if they tell him?"

"Far as I know, Manny and Carlo haven't made me yet. And besides, Paulie hasn't got anything to do with this shit tonight. Manny and Carlo, they're somebody else's muscle."

"Whose?"

"I don't know yet, but they're not working for Paulie Gandolo. They hire themselves out to the highest bidder, and usually that's somebody from Miami, from the drug world."

She finished with the coffee, then Tark was back again, sniffing around it, and me. "You sure you're all right?" he fretted.

"I'll let you know *after* I've heard your story."

Ginny headed for the door. "Gotta go."

I said, "Ginny . . . thank you for tonight. Your timing was perfect."

She laughed. "I'm a master at perfect timing, kid." She gave me a thumbs-up gesture and grinned. "Say hi to Marcus for me."

Bernadette joined us in the kitchen and sat opposite me. I played with my coffee cup and looked at Tark. He was leaning against a counter, relaxed. His cool gray eyes were amused; his short black hair showed perhaps a few more flecks of steel.

"Ginny works for Marcus?" I said. "Undercover?"

He shrugged.

Of course she did. I should have realized that Marcus would never have let me come here to see Paulie without having an ace up his sleeve. He had planted Ginny in Paulie's camp some time ago, no doubt, and for some other reason. But it was only because she was there that he'd let me come at all. Marcus might allow me emotional freedom—but he ruled the physical world he lived in, and his power extended out to encompass, at a moment's notice, his friends.

"How *is* the boss?" Tark said.

"Okay. Hurt by your seeming defection."

"That's not the way it is."

"Tell me how it is."

He motioned with his head, to the living room. "Let's get you in there on the sofa first."

Bernadette stood. "You go ahead. I'll make sandwiches and bring the coffee."

She was about five-seven, I guessed, but still dwarfed beside Tark. Her eyes were dark, her hair shoulder-length and with a healthy sheen. She wore a sophisticated black silkish dress, and had that kind of good posture that nuns used to teach and only models generally assume now. You could picture her walking down the aisle like an old-fashioned bride, not clomping and waving to the congregation the way a lot of them do these days, but one foot straight in front of the other, shoulders back, hips tucked in. . . .

I could picture her reaching the altar and smiling at Tark, who would be waiting there with a hokey grin on his good-looking, but scarred, mug's face.

And I saw all that in the way he looked at her now, both of them showing the signs of weariness and frustration that come from having been on the run, but together in every important way.

"How long have you been here?" I asked when Tark had settled me back in the deep cushions of the sofa. He had covered me with a blanket that was much too hot—like a nervous mother swaddling a newborn and giving it prickly heat.

I was beginning to enjoy his fussing. Hell, it was good just to be with Tark again. He was a lot like me—except that he broke the rules in *fact* that I only broke in my mind. I'd always wondered if it had to do with size; you tend to think you can have it all when you're six-foot-four and have shoulders that stretch from one county into the next.

"We've been here since the shooting on Marcus's yacht," he said, answering my question. "More or less."

"Why?"

Bernadette came in with the coffee and sandwiches on a tray. He took the tray from her and set it down on the glass coffee table. He waited until she was seated in the black armchair opposite me, then pulled up a stiff-looking designer affair made of chrome and leather, and straddled it.

"The word along the grapevine," I said, addressing Bernadette, "is that you haven't been seen on Long Island for a while. I get the impression you left home kind of fast."

"Faster than you can imagine," Tark said shortly.

"I . . . I was kidnapped," Bernadette added in a soft, husky voice. "Tark found me, and got me away. We've been hiding ever since."

"You were kidnapped? When? Who did it?"

Her eyes went quickly to Tark. He cleared his throat.

"We can't tell you that, Jess."

"Why not?"

"I know how you are," he said. "You'd have to get into it . . . and I need to do this on my own."

I fiddled with one of the sandwiches, pulling out bits of chicken, then looked from him to Bernadette. Tark's expression was resolute. I tried another tack. "The night Barbara Sloan was shot— You disappeared right afterward."

He didn't comment.

"It seemed, on the surface, that you left Marcus holding the bag."

"Is that what you think I did?"

"No. But Marcus doesn't understand what's going on. If it's just that Bernadette was in trouble, why didn't you tell him? Or get his help? Why leave the way you did?"

His voice hardened. "I don't want his help. I can take care of Bernadette myself."

"A matter of pride?" I let my bewilderment show. "That doesn't seem smart, with all the resources at his disposal."

Tark swung to his feet angrily and stalked across the living room. "Christ, Jess, my whole life has been tied up with Marcus, since we were kids. He was always the leader. You know how that feels? And the older I get, the more ridiculous it becomes. I'm a forty-two-year-old man, and all I know how to do is follow somebody around all day to make sure he doesn't get shot or beat up. How long—" He pounded a fist on the frame of the kitchen door, once. Pictures on the wall shuddered. Tark made a frustrated sound and crossed to a narrow window, yanking open the steel-colored vertical blind. He stood there looking out at the lights of Atlantic City, twenty-three floors below.

"Being Marcus's bodyguard is one of the most difficult jobs in the world," I argued. "And you are excellent at it."

"My reflexes are slower now than they were five years ago," he countered. "What will they be like five years from now—" He groaned, and yanked the blinds closed. "Christ, I could be risking Bernadette's life just by looking out this window, signaling that we're here."

After a moment I said, "Have you told Marcus how you feel?"

He shook his head.

"Why not? He knows you have a good mind. He could put you into the business end of things. Give you an office, make you a barterer, a diplomat."

"I don't need Andrelli's help with my future," he said coldly.

I realized then that the split was worse than I'd thought.

"What has Marcus done?"

"From his point of view? Nothing." His tone was a mixture of scorn and frustration. "He took me on as his bodyguard when we were in our twenties and I was out of a job. He was just a wiseguy then, but becoming known, and a lot of the older guys didn't like the way he saw things. They thought he was too inventive, too soft. That he'd change things too much."

"Which he has."

His smile was not pleasant. "Marcus always does what he sets out to do."

I nibbled at a soft piece of crust. "I've always believed you and he had a good relationship."

He shrugged impatiently. "We did. Until recently. Hell, Jess, I don't know, maybe it's just me."

"Marcus said . . ." I glanced at Bernadette. She sat quietly, but her eyes had followed our conversation with sharp intelligence. I was glad for that; I didn't think Tark would last long with the older kind of Italian/Catholic woman who learned to stay out of things. The mobster's wife who really *believed* he got her the new mink coat by just betting on the ponies. "Marcus said there was a problem between the two of you about your feelings for Bernadette."

Tark laughed shortly. "Marcus has always felt he had to look out for me. But you know something, Jess? I'm learning that Plato was right when he said, 'This is the root from which a tyrant springs—when he first appears he is a protector.'"

I was used to Tark quoting philosophers. So was Bernadette, apparently. She didn't raise a brow. But it still seemed strange, coming from this man who had been jousting with criminals all his life.

Tark ran a hand irritably over his bristly dark hair. A few gray strands glimmered in the apartment's dim light.

I answered him, "Plato also said, 'Let there be one man who has a city obedient to his will . . . and he might bring into existence the ideal policy about which the world is so incredulous.'"

Okay, so I stammered a little when I said it. I knew a lot of quotes, but only because I'd had insomnia when I was first sobering up, and spent my nights reading Bartlett's *Familiar Quotations*. I stammered because it always made me feel awkward saying them out loud, like I was showing off.

Tark didn't notice. "You really believe that?" he said. "That Marcus is some kind of savior, some kind of Robin Hood, doing good?"

I countered: "You really think he's a tyrant?"

"Not yet, maybe. But he could get that way—without even working at it. I'm tired of being an apostle, Jess."

An apostle. That had a familiar ring.

Then I remembered. The book Tark had carried with him so often in the last year: *Of the Difference Between a Genius and an Apostle*. The well-worn volume had been in the bookcase at his apartment.

And dammit, he was always testing me like this. "We're on Kierkegaard now?" I said.

But this wasn't a test. It was Tark's life, and Marcus's. Their friendship. Both were at stake.

"Marcus has always been the Genius," Tark answered. "And as long as I'm connected with him, I'm the Apostle. Marcus was born with certain talents and skills, and they give him kind of an authority—almost a Divine Right. While I am what I am, and do what I do, at his authority. As Kierkegaard says—I only carry the word."

"A genius is born, an apostle appointed? I know the theory," I said. "I think it's crap."

Kierkegaard's hypothesis was that an apostle is "called" by God to be such. As a result of this calling, one doesn't become more intelligent, receive more imagination or a greater acuteness of mind. He remains himself, and because of what he is, he serves the genius—who is a man marked out by natural gifts, a man born before his time.

"Think about it," Tark said. "Working for Marcus, I'm constantly given missions to carry out. I'm not supposed to discuss or comment on them, to think them through for myself. 'To criticize when God speaks.' "

"Bullshit."

I dropped the word into this too-elegant conversation on purpose. "Marcus is brilliant, but he's far from being God. And the only reason you're an apostle now is that's the role you've chosen to play. If you choose another role, you could as easily be the one in authority. Someone else would then be following you, carrying your word."

Tark stood with his arms folded. "I have to admit, that thought has been occurring to me more and more."

Ouch. I wasn't exactly inspiring my friend to patch things up with his boss.

"Are you leaving Marcus, then?"

"I don't know, Jess. I'm not even sure where I'd go. What does a mobster do when he gets too old to be one? Marcus dealt with it; he became a financial wizard. While the Feds are busy cleaning up the thugs, he's taking over corporations. His dealings may not be legal, but then, what is these days? Not the government, or most of corporate America."

"You sound like him," I noted. "You and Marcus are more than friends, you're philosophical brothers."

"Sometimes even brothers don't get along."

"You've always admired him." I had to keep trying.

"Because his ideas are good. Even this new way of running things—he was one of the first to do it, and now a lot of the crime families are following. Hell, it's the New Way all over the world. A hundred years from now people will think of this century as the Dark Ages, when people killed each other to get what they wanted, whether it was money, goods, or countries. They'll be moving everything around by computer. Maybe not even that—just exchanging little plastic discs. Imagine how people will laugh then at the old enforcers with their tommy guns and brass knuckles, their bribes and threats."

"Maybe they'll be bribing and threatening the computer operators—the Keepers of the Discs."

"Nah, it'll be foolproof by then, Jess. It'll have to be. Could you imagine the chaos?"

I was feeling tired suddenly. All this mental work taxed my brain and wore me out.

"Are you coming home soon?"

"I can't say. I haven't been able to think much beyond what I'm doing right now—protecting Bernadette."

"From whom?"

He shook his head.

"But what are you doing? What can you accomplish hiding out here in Atlantic City?"

"It's a time thing, Jess. In just a couple more days, it'll all be over. I can't explain."

A time thing. "Something's about to come down? Where?"

He didn't answer.

"Back home? Somebody's holding something over your head—threatening Bernadette if you don't go along—"

"Jess."

"And it has something to do with Barbara Sloan's death, because that's when you disappeared—Sloan's death, and something about to happen—"

"*Jess.*"

His expression was patient, his tone firm.

"Okay, okay, I'll drop it. But I think you should at least talk to Marcus. Tell him what's going on and insist that you want to handle it yourself. He'd understand."

"No, he wouldn't. He can't help himself. You know how he is, he takes over."

Tark was right. Look what Marcus had done here in Atlantic City, having Ginny watch over me. But I couldn't honestly say I regretted that. She probably saved my life.

Was I, too, more of an apostle than a genius? Of course I was. That's why I understood Tark so well. Marcus was the genius among us, one of the gods. He led, people followed. It wasn't such bullshit as I'd wanted Tark to believe.

"You have to promise me," he said, sitting beside me on the edge of the sofa. One huge hand rested on my shoulder. "Give me your word you won't tell Marcus what's going on."

"Dammit, Tark, I don't even *know* what's going on!"

"One thing I can tell you. I've got to get Bernadette away from Paulie. He's been hurting her. And this is something my family would understand, something they'd finally respect me for." His expression became grim. "I've never had my family's respect, not in all the years I've worked for Marcus. Maybe I'm just feeling my age, Jess . . . but I need that now."

"What about Ginny?" I said thoughtfully. "She works for Marcus—won't she tell him you're here?"

"Ginny has her own agenda where Marcus is concerned. She hasn't said a word."

Finally I made the promise to Tark. I wouldn't tell Marcus, either. I guess I had my own agenda, too.

CHAPTER FOURTEEN

I was more exhausted than I'd realized after the flight home to Rochester, and I looked like shit. I called in well, leaving a message with Charlie Nicks's secretary. Then I turned the answer machine on and the phone off, so the inevitable call back wouldn't wake me up. I closed the blinds in my room, tumbled into bed, and pulled the sheets up over my head.

I slept, but kept jerking awake from dreams of rushing water, of struggling to keep above it only to be beaten back down, of fire and pain, and Ginny dancing with wild laughter through the flames.

I gave up around ten. It was easier to control the assorted pains awake and with my wits about me. I dragged myself into the shower, then pulled on some clothes. Ginny had given me a tin of pancake makeup, and I applied it to the bruises, dashed on some dark lipstick, and stuck the sunglasses back on. Gazed into the mirror.

Uh-huh. Just as I'd thought. I looked more than ever like the sole survivor of a third world war.

I checked my messages. Grady North wanted to see me. Would I meet him at Harrigan's today? One o'clock. Danny Greer left a reminder to meet him and Catherine that night at the Havens Inn. And Abe Denton had called—Abe, of the Genesee Three. His message was more obtuse: Seven in the side pocket, twelve o'clock high. I figured he wanted me to meet him at the pool hall on Genesee Street at noon.

Since the pool hall and Harrigan's were in the same block, I could probably manage both.

Before I left the house I almost called Clyde about my car. Then I decided, what the hell, might as well just walk on over and see. I wished I had a nice new sporty Nissan Pulsar, though, like Ginny. Apparently, working for Marcus Andrelli paid well. Maybe I was passing up a good bet, turning down his offer of employment.

Mrs. Binty was in the yard snipping dead buds off her rose bushes. She smiled and called out, and I stopped to admire her latest award winner, a giant white bloom with tinges of pink and a scent that was out of this world.

She hardly said anything at all about my appearance, having seen me with bruises often enough before. It kind of gave her a thrill, and she would tell the neighbors later, I knew, "Jesse's been tracking down criminals again. You should see her *this* time." (All in a conspiratorial tone.) "Don't tell a soul. Her work is *confidential*, you know."

It was a little cooler today, and the walk gave me time to think. I tried to sort out what I'd actually learned from my trip to Atlantic City, and came up with these points: (1) Tark had not killed Barbara Sloan. (2) The "witness" who'd claimed to have seen him do the shooting had lied. (3) The drug boys from Miami—Manny, Carlos, and whoever had sat in the dark behind that lamp in the abandoned house, the one with the accent, were connected to it all somehow. They had warned me away from seeking out Barbara Sloan's killer. Finally, (4) Paulie Gandolo had been truly surprised when I'd mentioned the gun Barbara Sloan was shot with. I didn't know if that meant he wasn't involved, or what.

Add to that the latest ingredient: that Tark and Bernadette had disappeared after Sloan's death, and Tark saying something was coming down in a couple of days—and the soup had begun to thicken.

Tark, Bernadette, Sloan, and the drug boys. They made up quite a pot.

Then there was Tark's silence about Bernadette's kidnapper. If Bernadette had been taken for ransom, her brother certainly would have heard about it. But Tark had said Paulie didn't know a thing. What was the kidnapper's motive, then? And why had all this happened in conjunction with Barbara Sloan's murder on Marcus's yacht?

I was at Clyde's before I knew it. It was an old station, the kind you see in 1930s movies, somewhere out in the desert. Two old-fashioned pumps sit out front, with rounded contours. I swear one of them still says ETHYL. It doesn't matter; nobody ever stops for gas here anyway. Clyde keeps it open primarily for fools like me, who trust him to work on their cars.

Clyde was hunched over a fifties-vintage Chevy, his sloppy torso pressing under the hood. The motor was running, and he didn't hear me at first.

"Clyde!"

He pulled his head out. His heavy face was streaked with grease, right up to his beady little predator eyes. "Yeah? Oh. You come for the Karmann Ghia?"

Clyde knew me from all the times my car had broken down in the last couple of years. But Clyde was a shark, and we'd never been friends. I just hadn't found any other station close by that knew how to work on a wreck as old and Mickey-Moused as mine.

"Be right with you," he said.

I cooled my heels an irritating five minutes while he revved the Chevy's engine from under the hood and fiddled with wires and plugs. Finally, I banged on the hood to get his attention. He straightened and gave me a blank look.

"I've got to be somewhere. Can't I just pay you and go?"

He studied the Chevy's innards again, hands on his elephant hips, listening, I supposed, to the timing. It sounded better than my car ever would.

He wiped his greasy hands on an already oil-black towel and left the engine running. I followed him into the filthy office. It was cluttered with old car parts and newspapers, a Coke and candy machine, a battered desk. Clyde took down an invoice from a clipboard on the grimy wall. "Came to five-eighty," he said, handing it to me.

My jaw dropped. *"Five hundred and eighty dollars?*
What are you talking about? You were supposed to call me
if it went over two hundred!"

"Did. Left a message on your machine." `

"There was no message on my machine, Clyde."

"Yeah, well, I left it. I told you to call by noon yesterday
if you didn't want me to go ahead, and you didn't call, so
I went ahead."

Shit. Tired as I was when I got home, had I somehow
erased that message?

Or was Clyde lying through his teeth?

I looked down at the invoice. "The car's a fucking '68
Ghia," I said, "not a Mercedes. What the hell cost five
hundred and eighty dollars?"

But looking at the explanation of work done didn't help.
There were words like *valves, grind, adjust, ignition,
starter, vacuum hose, seal.* I understood what those things
were, but not what had been wrong with them, or what
exactly had been done. That's the thing with sharks like
Clyde. They know you don't know.

It was my own fault. I never should have brought the car
here, not after what he tried to pull last year. "Needs a
new engine," he had told me then. He didn't know I'd had
one put in when I bought the car. It had 20,000 miles on
it that day—not the 250,000 the odometer read. We argued
awhile, and I finally talked him into doing just a tune-up,
standing there and watching while he worked.

I suddenly wished I were back home in bed.

"Look," I said. "I haven't got five hundred and eighty
dollars. How about if I give you two hundred now, another
hundred in two weeks, and the rest two weeks after that?"

"Can't do it," Clyde said serenely, putting the clipboard
back and picking up the wrench he'd carried in. He turned
to go. "Two hundred won't even pay the labor."

I crumpled the invoice in my hand. "So what are you
saying, you want to keep the damn car here for a month,
while I scrape up the cash? Just let it sit here all that time?"

He headed back to the Chevy. "Up to you," he said.

I calculated quickly. I had $400 in my checking account to pay the gas and electric, the telephone and cable, and to put toward the rent. Another $200 or so for groceries, gas, emergencies. I could write the asshole a check and not send out the utility payments for a few days. Just about the time they might bounce, I'd get paid, and I could cover them—but I had a couple of Pop's old bar bills to cover too. So I'd be short on living money again. I'd never make it to the next paycheck.

I was overwhelmed with anger then, more over a lack of personal power than anything. I wanted to tell Clyde to stick the car up his goddamned ass. I'd ride the fucking buses the rest of my life. Shit, I could get anywhere I wanted to, between the RTS and my own fucking legs. I could even fucking thumb.

I stomped out of there without a backward glance, either at Clyde or my car.

CHAPTER FIFTEEN

At the pool hall on Genesee Street—Jimmy's—I ordered three Cokes in a row to keep from ordering beer while I waited for Abe. The pool hall was dark and dank, an urban cave, and that suited me fine. I didn't want to see anybody I knew.

I stalked the length of the bare wooden floors, stalked outside and paced the sidewalk, then back inside again, studying the rack of cues and the green felt of the tables like they held some answer to my problem with Clyde. All four tables were full. There wasn't much talking. Just the sound of the balls being racked, the snick of a cue connecting, the quiet roll of the ball, the smack as it hit its mark. A few congratulatory phrases, or a groan. I tried to stay out of the way of the old-timers, the hangers-on. Actually, I did know a couple of them, but they didn't talk, not to me or anyone. They were here for serious business —the hustling of fools.

I'd learned long ago not to dally with the likes of them. Syracuse Slim (a seven-foot aging basketball star with chalk dust permanently powdering his long, sad, dark face) wiped out a whole paycheck of mine in one long-ago ignoble afternoon. That was when I was young and dumb and thought it clever and cute for a girl to show how swell she could play pool. Like they do in the movies, you know, where the ingenue strolls over nonchalantly, chalks up a cue, and clears the whole table in one fell swoop.

That was a trick Pop had taught me. Only thing is, once the show is over and all the guys cast admiring glances your way, what do you do for an encore? If you're not too smart, you stick around and get creamed by the likes of Syracuse Slim. He knows all about dummies like me.

Dumb.

How could I have let Clyde do that to me?

I hadn't. I'd gotten the estimate, two hundred dollars, on paper when I dropped the Ghia off. He said he'd left the message that it'd be more; that I should call back if I didn't want him to go ahead. How could I dispute something like that? Were there laws about leaving that sort of thing on answer machines? How did those most helpful and irritating of modern inventions figure into the judicial system? *Did* they—at all? Had any precedents been set?

As a last resort, I could take *Jaws Five* to small claims, I supposed. You didn't need a precedent there. Only the ability to put on a good act.

In the meantime, I didn't have a car.

I ordered another Coke and sat on a cracked leather barstool, staring glumly through Jimmy's grimy storefront window and wondering if it really was turning gray outside, or if it just looked that way through all the dirt. My nose prickled at the smell in here. Fifty years of sweat drifted up from the cracked wooden floorboards. Fifty years of old-timers who poked fun at silly girl things like deodorants, and wore their perspiration as a badge of masculinity.

Syracuse Slim never wore a deodorant. I think that was to throw off his opponents, though. Overcome with the smell, they probably couldn't hit a damned thing.

Of course, these days, you could go into any yuppified pool hall in the suburbs and be overcome by the scent of Armani. Stetson. Old Spice. But that's not what Jimmy's is about.

I stirred restlessly. Where the hell was Abe? If he ever got here, I just might ask him to set up a meet with some local terrorist. Somebody who was so crazy that just for the hell of it, he'd trek on over and scare the bejeezus out of Clyde.

They finally arrived. Not just Abe, but all of them: Percy

Green, the African Rambo; Abe Denton, the smooth talking ball-breaker; and Rack-Jack, the small, wiry martial arts expert. Known hereabouts as the Genesee Three.

They arrived with much slapping of palms between them and the other patrons. I watched from my vantage point at the far end of the bar.

They didn't talk much, or exchange greetings. There was just that touching of hands, and the sharp eye contact. To one person it might be meant as a threat, to another, a nod of brotherhood. *Been hearin' bad stuff about you, bro . . . you invade our territory again, you better be prepared.* That would be one unspoken message, one that always bears repeating on the streets. Another might be, *Heard what you did the other night. A brother doesn't forget.*

These three kids from sixteen to eighteen in age, I think, wield more power at this end of the city than the law—which has all it can handle anyway, with them around. They float like atomic particles among the criminal elements—keeping a sort of order, yet sometimes slipping over the edge, getting out of control. A couple of years ago the Three had appointed themselves my personal guardian angels. They saved me from a mugging once, and even joined me in a caper a year ago, helping me with a break-in that gave me the evidence I needed to put someone behind bars.

I've never been able to get them to tell me why.

They came abreast of me, and Abe slapped me on the shoulder—"Hey, Jess—where you been? We been missin' those crafty green eyes, that mean old mouth."

He took a second look at my battered face. His expression went from surprise to anger. "There somebody you want taken care of, Jess?"

I shook my head and smiled. "Not at the moment. Maybe later."

Percy and Rack made similar remarks of concern and support. I saw a new note of respect in the eyes of some of the guys who were hanging around. Others looked uneasy, their glances sliding away. What had I seen in all the time I'd been waiting? Or heard? And would I report it to the Three?

It's a world of flaming paranoia.

"Bring your Coke over here," Abe said. A pool table had cleared miraculously. He snapped a thumb and middle finger, and the bartender wasted no time setting two illegal beers and a glass of milk along the bar. The milk was for Rack. He was sixteen, and had developed an ulcer—worrying about his family, no doubt. His mom, who'd worked sixty hours a week all her life to feed five kids, had been sick a lot lately. She was on disability, and had refused to take money from Rack, who would have given her the world. A wise woman. Some of it might have been marked.

Percy, in jeans and a black sleeveless tee, racked up the balls. Abe powdered his big dark hands and chalked up a cue. Rack sort of slouched off to the side, leaning against a Ping-Pong table. Even in this weather he wore a studded leather jacket—a thin, expensive leather, but still, it had to be hot. He wore it like armor—protection, I guessed, from the emotional insults you can't see and can't defend yourself against, because half the time you don't even know what the hell they are until they hit. He held something in his hand that cracked and popped, over and over, as he squeezed it. It took me a few minutes to realize it was a Ping-Pong ball. He would squeeze in a dent, then squeeze it out. He saw me looking.

"Gotta do something with my hands," he explained.

Abe called a corner pocket and sighted the cue. You could see his ass tense through the well-tailored cotton ducks he wore. His short crinkly black hair gleamed under the green-hooded lights. Broad back muscles rippled beneath a creamy, short-sleeved, silk shirt.

All of which was planned. Abe is a bit of a dandy. A show-off, too.

"You get me down here just to watch you perform?" I said testily. I was still irritated about the car, and I had better things to do than stand around Jimmy's. Like go home and pull the sheets over my head.

Abe connected with the ball and sent it smoothly to the corner pocket.

He straightened to his full six feet. "Hear a friend of yours is mixed up in this new kiddie porn racket, Jess." His dark eyes held little pinpoints of anger.

"A friend of mine? Who?" It never helps to seem too easy.

"Hear lover boy up to his ears."

"Marcus? C'mon, Abe, don't give me that shit unless you know it for a fact. And you can't know it for a fact, because it just isn't true."

Rack snorted and came forward, squeaking leather. He leaned his hands against the pool table. Rack was small in stature, but you couldn't let yourself be fooled by that. "What kind of fact you want?" he said. "Word's out on the streets. Andrelli's in it with Paulie Gandolo. They're recruiting kids down here, and some of us don't like that much. They want to muck around with fancy little upperclass white children out in the suburbs, that's their business. When they come down to our streets and start messin' with sisters—that be ours."

It was a speech, for Rack. A master at t'ai chi and several of the other martial arts, he was more into striking first—then letting Abe do the talking.

"Look," I said. "I get your point. You want me to warn Marcus off."

"Coulda taken care of him without tellin' you, Jess."

"Sure, right, you can take care of any goddamn thing you want. For Christ's sake, why do you even believe this about Marcus? He's been a friend to you—he's helped out the neighborhood more than once—"

Abe interrupted quietly. "Friends are fine. Till they stop bein' friends. It's like that, Jess." His eyes held me, their anger so strong that for a second I couldn't respond.

"What if I can prove he's innocent?" I said finally.

Abe bent over the table and hit the cue ball so it struck the far end of the table and rebounded to gently drop the five ball into the corner pocket.

Use Your Powers of Deduction!

Follow these clues to the "World of Mystery," and enjoy Agatha Christie like you've never enjoyed her before!

Clue #1—The World's Greatest Mysteries!

Intrigue...murder...deception! No one does it like Dame Agatha! Now savour her most cunning tales of mystery and mayhem in *The Agatha Christie Mystery Collection.*

Clue #2—Beautiful Volumes!

These are collector's editions—not available in any bookstore. Bound in sturdy, simulated leather of rich, Sussex blue, set off with distinctive gold embossing in the finest Victorian tradition. Covers are densely padded—elegant on the shelf, and exquisite to the touch!

Clear, easy-on-the-eye type makes reading a pleasure again! These are stories to be enjoyed. And owning them shows your appreciation of fine books.

Clue #3—Fabulous FREE Book.
Fabulous FREE Read!

Get *The New Bedside, Bathtub & Armchair Companion to Agatha Christie* as your FREE GIFT just for previewing *The Agatha Christie Mystery Collection.* Over 360 pages filled with story plots (but *never* the endings!), photos, facts about Agatha's life, and the many movies and plays of her work. This $12.95 value is yours to keep *absolutely free,* no matter what!

You also get *And Then There Were None* free for 15 days to read and enjoy. Here's your chance to sample *The Agatha Christie Mystery Collection* without risk—enjoy this classic "whodunit," then decide for yourself if you wish to keep it.

No Obligation—EVER!

It all adds up! Send for your no-risk preview of *And Then There Were None.* Enjoy it *free* for 15 days! We'll send your Agatha Christie *Companion* free, and start your *Agatha Christie Mystery Collection* right away. Each volume in the Collection arrives with the same *free 15 day preview. No* minimum number of books to buy. No obligation. *You may cancel at any time!* Mail the reply card today!

The Solution Is Easy!

1. Try the *Agatha Christie Mystery Collection* without risk! Complete the picture on the reply card below (Hint: the missing piece is on the front page of this offer!), then return the card to us and you'll receive *And Then There Were None* to read and enjoy for 15 days FREE!

2. You get *The New Bedside, Bathtub & Armchair Companion to Agatha Christie* FREE when you do! It's yours to keep even if you cancel your membership. Now you have all the facts! Mail the Reply Card Today!

Don't resist our splendid offer! Send for your *free preview* of Agatha Christie's classic *And Then There Were None*, PLUS get your 363-page Agatha Christie *Bedside Companion* FREE! See details inside.

Rack said, "The word's out on Andrelli, and it isn't good. You might want to work on somethin' easier—like waxin' the Thruway."

"Don't give me that."

"The odds're better waxin' the Thruway. You lucky, you get hit only twice by a speedin' car. Then, God shinin' his light on you, your body be dragged only a mile or two by a big rig, and—"

"*Enough.*"

It was a murmur from Percy, but that was all it took.

My eyes met his hopefully. Up to then, Percy had been standing by in Ramboesque silence. It wasn't that he didn't have the smarts; he just didn't see much point in talk. What was there to say, anyway? When the ranch was threatened, you got out the old Winchester and let the bad guys know who was boss.

"You disagree with them, Perce? You believe Marcus is innocent?"

"Didn't say that."

"What, then?"

He shrugged. "I just think it's a little strange that the cards are stacked so high against Andrelli. He's never been no angel, but he's never been caught before, either. If he *is* innocent—and I'm not sayin' he is—then how come the whole world thinks he's not?"

"That's exactly what I've been saying all along. He's being set up."

"Maybe. But by who?"

"I don't know. I thought at first it was Paulie Gandolo. Now I'm not so sure."

"Who else would want to do it?"

There was only one person I could think of, but I didn't want to say it. Grady North had been after Marcus a long time. He had a file a foot thick on his nemesis, one he'd been putting together for years. Had he reached the point where he'd decided to get Marcus—even if it meant twisting the evidence around?

"I don't know yet who else would want to do it," I said.

"Give me some time, will you?" What I meant was, *Give Marcus some time*. God knew, if they tried to take him on, no one would end up winning.

Rack and Abe exchanged looks. Percy shrugged.

"We be around," Rack said.

"Better walk soft in the meantime," Abe added. "And carry one mother of a big stick."

"Yassuh, Mistuh Roosevelt, suh. You got any more little words of wisdom you'd like to share today?"

Rack gave a snort. Percy folded his arms and went back to silent. Abe sighed.

I resisted the temptation to chalk up a cue and show them how I could clear the table in one fell swoop.

CHAPTER SIXTEEN

Grady was at Harrigan's when I arrived, having lunch and looking too elegant in a gray blazer, white shirt, and mauve tie—like he was out for the commissioner's job.

But Grady always had looked good, even in jeans and a sweater. Better, most times, than me.

"I've been meaning to ask you," I said, sliding into the opposite side of the booth, "how're the folks these days?"

"Not bad." He was fiddling with a sandwich, loading mustard between slices of corned beef. "Doing Canada right now in their motor home. Dad misses the force, but Mom keeps him pretty busy traveling."

"Would you do that? Early retirement?"

"Maybe. If I had a wife like my mom, urging me into it—and somebody who'd be as much fun."

"They are like a couple of kids together." I had met them once. They had high hopes for their son, you could tell that right away. Grady came from a long line of cops, and his dad wanted to see him climb the ladder to the top. But he didn't apply pressure. The pressure came from Grady himself, in wanting to please Jim North, whose reputation was heavy-duty on the Rochester P.D.

"So what's up, Jess?" He set the Gulden's jar and knife down, and glanced at me directly for the first time. Funny how people do that; not really looking at the people they know. His eyes narrowed. "What the hell happened to your face!"

"I thought I'd done a pretty good job paving it over," I said, touching my cheek and feeling sweat.

"Well, I hate to tell you, but your powder's starting to run. What the hell happened?"

"I ran into a little trouble. It's okay now." The bruise under my eye itched; I scratched it with my thumb. "So what's up? I'm here at your behest."

He stared at my face a little longer, started to say something, then stopped.

He handed me half of his corned beef and rye. I was starving, and took a huge bite, wincing as my jaw crackled and popped. The rye was soft and thick. I took a swig of the mineral water I'd picked up at the bar, wishing devoutly it were a Genny beer. Damned humidity. It made me want things I'd always associated with hot weather. How does one get through the summer without a Genny beer—not to mention without a car? I wasn't at all sure at the moment that I wanted to—or could.

I waited a couple more minutes for Grady to tell me why he'd summoned me here.

"Not important anymore?" I prompted at last.

He shrugged. "How're you doing on the Barbara Sloan thing?"

"Me? You're the cop."

"Yeah, but you were asking a lot of questions the other day."

"I work for the *Herald*, remember."

"Uh-huh. And Marcus Andrelli—you work for him too, now? Officially?"

"If I did, would I tell you?"

"Just thought I'd ask."

The sandwich was piled too high, my jaw too sore. I pulled a few slices out and dumped them on Grady's plate.

"I just talked to the Three," I told him.

"Spare me."

"They've been kind of quiet lately, haven't they? Staying out of trouble?"

"Or they're getting better and better at making it look that way. Either way, I've learned that when the Three are quiet for any extended period of time, there's some kind of explosion just around the corner."

"They do have a lot of energy," I said proudly.

He didn't even bother to comment.

"They seem to think . . ." I hesitated, unsure of how much I wanted to say. But with Grady you had to give, to get. "They seem to think you're right about Marcus. That he's in the kiddie porn racket up to his neck."

"Yeah? I'm grudgingly impressed. At least they see things more clearly than you."

I chomped down on the sandwich without thinking. Pain shot through my jaw. I fingered it. "Ow."

Grady stopped chewing. He swiped at his mouth with a paper napkin. "I assume you *have* talked to Andrelli," he said angrily. "Did he give you those bruises?"

"Grady, for God's sake! Marcus isn't like that."

"Oh, right, I keep forgetting. He's the Angel of Light and Mercy."

"Just stop it, okay? If you don't, I'm leaving."

He glared suspiciously a moment longer, and I pulled the crusts off my bread. I was getting sick of sandwiches. What I needed was a nice thick juicy steak with baked potato and sour cream, a Caesar salad, a bottle of Cabernet . . .

I dropped the crust. "It occurs to me," I said, leaning toward Grady with my chin on my clasped hands and lowering my voice, "that it's a little odd the cards are stacked so high against Marcus. That everyone has heard exactly the same story. And the story's good. It convinced the Three, certainly, and they're no fools. Problem is, it's too pat."

"Meaning?"

"Meaning, I think someone is deliberately trying to make it *look* like Marcus is guilty. I think he's being set up."

Grady said easily, "That would certainly turn out to be convenient for your friend. Who do you have in mind— Paulie Gandolo?"

"No, I have in mind someone whose job it is to uphold the law—not to railroad innocent people."

Grady lifted the bottle of beer to his lips. His eyes, over it, were unreadable.

"You've been wanting Marcus a long time," I went on. "Maybe you've been getting impatient. Are you up for promotion, pal?"

You could almost hear the clunk of the heavy metal door slamming between us. He shut down, just like that—friend to cop in no time flat. It was a risk I'd had to take.

"Facts are facts," he said coldly. "If they stand up in court—"

"You have no facts. I'd stake my life on it. You're gathering circumstantial evidence around Marcus, hoping to build up public sentiment that will go against him in court."

"Careful, Jess."

"Marcus says a *witness* saw Tark kill Sloan. But I know for a fact that Tark didn't kill her. The witness was lying."

"You've seen Tark?"

I didn't answer.

His mouth tightened in anger.

I went on. "Furthermore, I think Marcus was told about this witness at the Public Safety Building the other day. The day he was questioned by you. Now, I wonder who would have told him a thing like that?"

"Any one of a number of people. Clerks. Janitors. Vince Russo, his capo. He was there acting as Andrelli's attorney. They had plenty of opportunity to talk privately."

"Marcus would have told me if it was Vince, or some clerk or janitor at the station. No, this was someone important—someone whose name he felt he had to keep secret, even from me."

"The whole downstairs area was full of bums that day. Could've been one of them. Andrelli had to walk right through them to get to the street."

"I thought of that. But how—and why—would any of them have been at the marina that night? In the first place, most wouldn't have busfare, and even so, they never stray that far from Dwight Square or the shelters. Not at night."

A guy at one of the round tables between us and the bar

was obviously listening. I lowered my voice. "It just doesn't wash, Grady. It was you who told Marcus that Tark was seen pulling the trigger."

He said softly, "And why do you think I would do that, Jess?"

"First of all, to split the ranks. You think if you can convince Marcus that his right hand has betrayed him, he might feel vulnerable enough to make mistakes. He might do something you can *really* get him on, and that's just the feather you need in your cap to land that promotion you're scrambling for."

Grady began to slide from the booth. "This discussion is over," he said.

"Convince me I'm wrong, make me forget some of the schemes you've perpetrated over the years to get Marcus behind bars."

He was on his feet. He leaned over the table, palms jarring it, his face like a bulldog's a foot from mine. "Every one of which was legal and aboveboard."

"Not quite. There was that little matter of a break-in you planned a year and a half ago to lift a certain set of files you believed would incriminate Marcus. No search warrant, of course—"

"A break-in you got in the way of. I should have locked you up then—"

"And I wonder what it would do to your promotion if the commissioner knew."

He straightened. His expression flew from angry to circumspect within seconds, then smoothed out until there was no sign of anything there—not anger, nor caution, nor even a vestige of our old friendship. It startled me. I thought of how I'd always seen Grady as so uncomplicated. A little like Jack Hoffman. A good, honest cop.

Blind ambition, on the other hand—whether for money or medals—makes liars of us all. It was something I should have remembered.

Grady turned on his heel and slammed past the few captain's chairs and tables in the center of the room. The outside door went flying. It slammed back against Harrigan's tinted blue window and made it shudder.

"Have a nice day," I said.

As I left Harrigan's, I gave a nod to Harve. He was on a ladder polishing the frosted glass mirror behind the bar. He made a gesture that seemed to say, *Wait, I want to talk.* I just wasn't in the mood.

So I waved off Harve, called out "Later," and headed out down Genesee Street. As I neared home I remembered that Grady never did tell me why he'd called me to meet him in the first place.

It wasn't until much later that I realized he had.

CHAPTER SEVENTEEN

The heat wave broke. Thunder rolled across the sky from Canada, and rain pounded in over the lake. I stood on Mrs. Binty's porch, waiting for a cab and watching the lightning and sheets of gray sweep along the street. Steam rose from hot paving; a smell of tar filled the air.

In a half hour, I'd be meeting Danny and Catherine Greer at the Havens Inn. Mrs. Binty had run to get her umbrella for me, since I didn't have one, preferring to stride along in storms unfettered, face upturned to the rain, feet splashing in puddles like a three-year-old.

Except, of course, when I was meeting an old high school hero and his absolutely gorgeous wife, and wanted my naturally curly hair to look like something other than a Boston terrier after twelve days on a dinghy at sea.

The Havens Inn is a white two-story colonial with mullioned windows, surrounded by an acre of green lawn. It was owned by a family during the Civil War who donated it as a hospital, and after that it passed hands as a private home, then a restaurant. There is one large dining room downstairs with a fireplace, mellow oak floors, and windows overlooking a lush green garden.

Danny and Catherine were seated at an open window that was sheltered from the rain by a deep awning. Danny stood, with a wave to me. He was dressed to the nines in a navy-blue summer weight suit, and looked young and vulnerable—like a kid dressed for church, who couldn't wait to get home and put his sweats back on. When I saw Catherine in her white sheath, I was glad I'd worn my one good dress—a red crepe, snug at the waist and flaring out in a soft skirt. The Lady in Red, a boyfriend had called me once—not original, but sweet, and we had a halcyon summer before he went where all men go when they say they'll call and don't.

Catherine, one-time prom queen, cheerleader, and class president—always pretty—had grown into a beautiful woman. She had glossy blond hair that hung to her thighs, and she wore it tonight in a French braid that she continually flicked over a shoulder then pushed back, playing with it sensuously as she talked. All night long men were giving her admiring looks, and she knew it. Her cheekbones were high and pronounced, lending her face a sculpted model's look. Her eyes were a strange light gray. They swam over and around people, aloof as fish in a pond.

Policemen's wives, I know, live with a lot of fear. Tensions run high. Some withdraw into alcohol or drugs, and some flirt with other men—gathering proof of their attractiveness to reassure themselves that if they one day open the door to two cops bearing bad news, their lives as women won't necessarily end.

Danny watched the men watching Catherine, and shifted restlessly in his chair, playing with his fork.

All of this, of course, is how it appeared to me—and although I do have a certain amount of skill in the area of reportorial observation, I have to admit I was looking for trouble—half hoping for some chink in the armor of Danny's marriage. That's not something I am proud to relate, but I try at least to be honest about these things.

Catherine, on the other hand, was more than gracious to me. She invited me to their house afterward for coffee, and wouldn't take no for an answer. They lived not far from me, at the other end of Genesee Park Boulevard, where the homes are larger, the lawns more vast. Their place belonged to Catherine's parents, and was over a hundred years old but remodeled, with a sweeping veranda, sunporch off to the side, and spreading elms—Like a Hallmark card house.

While Catherine was making coffee, Danny told me that they were more or less permanently house sitting while the folks lived, retired, in Florida. "Would you believe they bought this place for twelve thousand dollars when they were married? That'd just about keep a family in rent for two years today."

There were antiques, a fireplace with an arrangement of summer greenery in it, a whole wall of white bookcases. Fresh-picked roses on the coffee table. From a stereo came the soft, seductive notes of Chopin. Sheer white drapes fluttered in the rain-fresh breeze. I thought about my own apartment—the rain spots beneath the windows, the whiskey stains on the carpet, and the orange tree askew on the floor. I still hadn't had time (or the incentive) to clean.

Laura—Danny and Catherine's eleven-year-old daughter— had stayed home with a sitter. The sitter had left, saying Laura was listening to music in her room, and everything was fine. She was a bouncy girl with a scrubbed face and her arms piled high with books. "Summer school," she explained cheerfully when I asked.

There were identical chintz-covered sofas opposite each other at right angles to the fireplace. Danny told me to relax, make myself at home. He disappeared upstairs and I flipped through a *Newsweek*. Danny came down a few minutes later with his daughter, guiding her gently. She was in pink cotton p.j.'s, and she smiled as if she could see me, and said, "It's nice to meet you, Miss James." She had silky blond hair and blue sightless eyes, and Danny was so full of love and pride it nearly split the room. Laura continued into the kitchen to see Catherine, feeling her way with confidence along the furniture. Danny watched her with a passion I hadn't seen in anyone for a long time.

He turned back to catch me watching him, and said with only a little embarrassment, "Laura is the most important thing in the world to me—to both of us."

I'm rotten at coming up with the right words. I made an awkward stab. "Has there been any improvement?" Laura had been struck by a car while riding her bike three years

ago. A piece of bone, pressing on her brain, had left her
blind. There had been some talk around the police department at the time about a collection for an operation,
but it would have been too risky; the doctors refused to
even try.

Danny shook his head. "There won't be any improvement. The only good thing that's come out of this is the
way she's grown up. I've never known a little girl so independent. And brave."

He sat restlessly on the sofa opposite mine—perched on
the edge, elbows on his knees, fingers lacing and unlacing.
"If you could have seen her—like a new star. That's how
she burst into our lives, all five and a half pounds when she
was born."

Catherine called from the kitchen and Danny excused
himself quickly, as if glad for something physical to do. I
got up and wandered around the room, looking at things
to pass the time. On the mantel were two of Danny's baseball trophies. I read the inscriptions and saw they were for
coaching: Daniel X. Greer, 1986, 1988. Several more were
on bookcase shelves, and I crossed over and noted that
some were from high school, Most Valuable Player awards.
A couple more for coaching over the years.

On another shelf were family pictures in silver frames:
A young Catherine with people who looked like they must
be her mother and father, then photos of Catherine and
Danny in high school. More recent ones of the two of them
with Laura: a Laura with sight, mugging at the camera—
thumbs in her ears, fingers wagging, tongue stuck out . . .
and then an older Laura, probably not too long after the
accident. She had a sort of bewildered, unfocused stare.

I looked at the books on the shelf and was delighted to
find Danny's old senior yearbook. 1976. I pulled it out and
flipped through it, searching for group pictures of juniors,
one of which I'd been that year. There it was. And there *I*
was. *God!* I felt myself flushing with embarrassment. My
brown hair, which hadn't yet begun to frizz, hung straight,
long, and limp—and there was one godawful zit on my

chin. It stuck out in a defiant way. The zit. And my chin. I looked at my clothes and squirmed even more. I'd actually worn beads, and a gauzy shirt with fringe. Without a doubt, no bra.

I nearly laughed out loud.

Not too surprisingly, I was barely visible to boys that year. Especially not to Danny Greer.

And there *he* was, on the next page with the drama class—dressed in his role as the Music Man, warning folks about all the trouble on its way to River City—most of it because of him. I could still hear Danny up there on stage, pulling the townfolk in, blue eyes flashing, white teeth grinning. I had kind of a weird, shaky feeling, remembering how I'd sat in the audience night after night, trying to get up the courage to just say hi to Danny Greer.

I felt him behind me then, and turned. He had been looking over my shoulder, so close my hip rubbed against him as I moved. I flushed again, I know. Like a kid. A sixteen-year-old kid. *Get hold of yourself, Jess. Try not to drop the book.*

I stammered something like, "I never could afford one of these." I held it out to Danny.

"Keep it, if you like."

"Really?" I laughed and then shook my head. "That's all I need, my junior-year picture haunting me the rest of my life. I can see it, people coming over, pulling it off the shelf, me trying to explain why I looked the way I did . . ."

I was blabbering. Danny took the book and grinned.

"I'll go help Catherine in the kitchen," I said, turning resolutely away.

But she was coming back in, carrying a silver tray laden with a coffee pot, cups, and tiny chocolate cakes. Danny's wife wasn't just beautiful, she was a great hostess. An elegant homemaker. She had a blind child.

Christ.

I took the cup she offered, and the awkward moment passed. Laura had brought pink napkins, feeling her way along the wall, a chair, an end table, until she reached us.

She and Catherine snuggled into one end of the sofa across from me.

Danny took off his jacket and tie, then opened his collar. You could almost hear his *whoosh* of relief. "Jess, I seem to remember you in high school with your nose in a book all the time. Laura likes to read, too. Mysteries, mostly—the bloodier the better."

"Wait, I'll show you the one I'm reading now—"

Laura jumped up and followed an invisible but sure path to the bookcase. Her fingers counted over from the left-hand side. A quarter of the way along, she took down a large book. She brought it over and flopped down next to me.

"Murder at the Vicarage." She opened the book, and put my hand over a page. The tiny little beads of Braille beneath my fingertips were like black holes leading into a frightening universe, to me. They must have seemed like pearls to Laura.

"They have tapes of most books," she said, "but I love the feel of the paper. Have you read this?"

I nodded without thinking. "Yes."

"I wouldn't want to spoil the ending, if you hadn't. But isn't it great the way she surprises you all the time? I'd like to write that way someday."

"Do you write now?" I couldn't see how, but it was the only thing I could think to say.

She nodded. "On a typewriter. Just stories. Mom taught me to type, and I still make a lot of mistakes, but Daddy corrects them for me. Then he reads the whole story out loud."

If he was any prouder, Danny would have burst. Catherine, listening quietly, looked much the same way.

"What else do you like to do?" I asked Laura.

"I *love* model airplanes. I like the way they feel, so light, like nothing at all . . . and the smell of the balsam . . . I used to make them, before—"

She broke off and shrugged matter-of-factly.

"I'll bet you could learn to do that again," I said. My voice was kind of thick.

She smiled. "My room is just *full* of them. Daddy makes them for me now. Sometimes, I help."

"Good thing you can't see what I've done," Danny teased. "I don't do so good with those tiny little sticks and stuff."

"I know somebody," I offered, "who lives over on Weldon. He's maybe a couple years older than you, and he makes really fantastic model planes. The paper ran a piece about him a year or so ago. I'll introduce him to you, if you'd like. Maybe you two can get together."

Hey, kid, the frail, underused voice of my conscience wheezed, *you being a good neighbor for once in your life, or just wooing Danny's daughter?*

I blamed it, of course, on the red dress. Wearing it had always turned me into both an idiot and a flirt. There was absolutely nothing any deeper going on than that.

Danny sat on the fireplace hearth and we talked for a while, mostly about old times. Laura had curled up in a corner of the sofa, reading, her fingers flying over the pages. Catherine watched her with a soft smile, now and then injecting a word or two into the conversation. In the background, classical music played.

After a little bit, Laura began to nod off. Catherine rose and sat beside her, taking the book gently. Laura's head dropped to her mother's shoulder, pulling at the soft white folds of her dress.

"I'll take her up and put her to bed," Catherine said.

"I'll do it." Danny was already on his feet.

"No, you stay here. I like putting her to bed. Don't I, little princess?" She murmured the words against her daughter's cheek, pushing back her silky hair and urging her to her feet.

"You're tired," Danny insisted. "Let me do it."

Catherine gave a small, stiff laugh. "I don't mind." She said it with a smile, but there was an edge to her voice. A look passed between them, the kind of silent sparring that couples engage in when company's around. *Sure, act like you're home to do this all the time*, the look seemed to say.

Danny shrugged, his mouth tightening. Catherine led her daughter, stumbling sleepily, up the stairs. " 'Night, Ms. James," I heard Laura mumble at Catherine's whispered urging.

Danny's glance followed them every slow step of the way.

" 'Night, Laura," I answered.

Only after they had reached the top of the stairs did Danny turn back to me. "It's been hard for Catherine since Laura's accident. Harder than it might be, I mean, with me being gone so much. A cop's life . . ."

I realized that I'd walked blithely into a family drama, the pain of which I'd had absolutely no concept until now. "I shouldn't have come tonight," I apologized. "I shouldn't have barged in on your night out together."

He laughed shortly. "You saw how that went. She hardly knew I was there."

"Danny . . ." No. *Stay out of it, kid*, the wheezy voice said. *This isn't your business. What's more, you don't want it to be.*

"Can I ask just a few questions about the Sloan case," I said, "before Catherine comes back? Then I'll clear out of here, give you some time alone."

Danny smiled. "I'd almost forgotten that's what tonight was supposed to be about."

"No problem. I was just wondering—can you tell me anything about Barbara Sloan's killing? I mean, aside from the anti-Andrelli line I've been getting from Grady North?"

"You may have to believe what he tells you before this is over, Jess."

"Maybe. But until then, can you tell me anything that I don't already know?"

He began to shake his head, and I said quickly, "Please, Danny. Grady North has shut down. I don't have any other sources in the department I can trust. I'll never tell anyone it came from you."

"Ah, Jess . . ." He got to his feet and ran a finger under

the starched collar of his white shirt. Rolling up his sleeves, he stood at the fireplace. A cool breeze blew through the room and fluttered the roses on the coffee table. A petal fell. It sounded as if the rain had stopped.

Finally Danny said, "I can tell you one thing you might not have heard about, but it won't help you much. It only points to Andrelli's guilt."

"Fair enough. What is it?"

"Off the record—not for publication, okay?"

"Okay."

He sat across from me, leaning forward intently. "The way I hear it, Barbara Sloan had a list. She's supposed to have stolen it from Paulie Gandolo to give to Andrelli. The way the story goes, she refused to hand it over to Andrelli. Either held him up for more money, or lied—said she didn't have it, so she could sell it somewhere else. Andrelli found out, he offed her. Had his pal Tark do it, actually."

"What kind of list?"

"All of Paulie's drug and porn contacts in major U.S. cities."

"Christ. A list like that, in the wrong hands, could shut him right down."

"Well, you know Paulie was running the child porn racket here before. It was shut down and came right back. It's like a lot of things, you don't pour much into it in the way of budget or effort when you know that'll happen. It's taxpayers' money, after all. They grumble about crime, but they don't want to pay us to really make a dent in it. The commissioner—Fournsey—he likes us to be cautious—until, of course, there's a public outcry."

"Where did you hear about this list? Grady North?"

"You kiddin'? He's been playin' things real close to the vest lately. But it's all over the grapevine. You know how those things get around."

"Who would Sloan sell the list to, if not Andrelli?"

"Any one of Paulie's competitors, I guess. But I'm not saying this is what happened—just that there's been a lot of talk about it, so chances are the list at least exists."

I slouched down, propping my feet on the coffee table and folding my arms. "Do you know what Grady's up to?" I said.

He rested his chin on tented fingers. "I'm not sure just what you mean."

"I've been putting together a little scenario. In this scenario, Grady North is setting Marcus up for a fall."

"How do you mean, setting him up?"

"I think he's building a web of circumstantial evidence around Marcus, trying to pin this murder on him."

Danny shook his head. "I hear a witness saw Andrelli's bodyguard do it."

"Yeah, well, you know what I think? I think Grady told Marcus there was a witness to cause a rift between him and Tark. But Grady lied."

Danny scratched his jaw. A dark stubble of beard was already beginning to show. "*Somebody* killed the woman, Jess. Who else was there? Who did it, if Tark didn't?"

"I don't know. One of Paulie's men? Maybe he found out Barbara stole that list for Marcus. Paulie's pretty quick with revenge. He might have had her shot on Marcus's boat to implicate him; get rid of them both at once."

I picked up Laura's book and fingered it absently. "Whatever happened to this list, anyway?"

"Far as I know, it's never been found, unless Andrelli took it off the body and managed to hide it somehow. Tell you one thing, there's a whole lot of people who'd like to get their hands on it. For a variety of reasons, of course."

I put the book down, wishing I had Miss Marple around to help figure this one out. "Danny, will you help me with this? Let me know anything you hear that could help me clear Marcus, find out what's really going on?"

"Jess . . ." His fingers scrubbed his brow. "I know you really want to believe in Andrelli. But the facts are all against you. And as a reporter, at least, you should be looking at the facts."

I said irritably, "If Grady North has facts, why hasn't he

issued a warrant for Tark? Why hasn't he got Marcus behind bars?"

"I can't tell you that. But there's something you should think about. North's got a lot at stake. I don't know how close you are to him these days, so you may not have noticed, but he's going for the big one this time."

"The big one?"

"Promotion. He's got two solid feet on the rungs of that golden ladder, and he's not about to slip at this point."

"Even so, you think Grady would screw around with evidence to put Marcus behind bars and make himself look good?" I needed to hear someone else say it.

Danny smiled easily. "Did I say that? I'm pretty sure you didn't hear me say that, Munchkin."

I sighed. I looked at the clock on the mantel between Danny's trophies. 11:05. At the same time, he glanced at his watch. I picked up my small evening bag.

"I'd better go."

Danny's glance moved to the stair. "Catherine's probably reading Laura a story. Let me get her—"

"No, don't do that. Don't interrupt them."

"Let me drive you, then." He reached into his pocket for his keys.

"It's stopped raining. I'll enjoy the walk."

"You sure?"

"Uh-huh."

"Well." He shrugged. "Okay."

At the door, he pushed my hair behind my ear with a finger. "Listen, Munchkin. Take care. I'd hate it if anything happened to you. Call me if I can help?"

"Sure. Thanks."

He leaned forward to brush my lips, and electricity crackled. I jumped back, feeling awkward and silly. I said, "Please tell Catherine how much I enjoyed the evening." I sounded like Mary Poppins.

Danny held the door, and as I passed through I looked up. A quirky smile turned up the corners of Danny's mouth.

His eyes were crinkling—they were brighter than any old morn in spring.

"I'll be in touch," my old high school hero said.

"Please tell Catherine how much I enjoyed the evening," I mimicked myself as I walked home. Little Miss Goody Two Shoes.

Better that, I supposed on second thought, than walking around with a scarlet *A* on my chest. What was this renewed fascination for Danny Greer?

I kept thinking about Danny and Catherine's marriage. How . . . entrenched they seemed. Drawn together by Laura's blindness, perhaps, but together.

I'd never wear this goddamned dress again. It turned me into a moron.

I looked away from the mess in my apartment and stripped down to basics, dropping the red dress on the floor. It lay there, the crushed petal of an overblown rose. I crawled into bed, feeling wired. I wanted a drink so bad, suddenly, I thought I might be ill if I didn't give in to the need.

I reached for the phone and punched the programmed button for Samved. His answer machine was on, and his ethereal voice intoned: "Good evening, dear ones. I am walking in the moonlight in my garden, and I exhort you to do the same. There is no problem so great, no grief so strong that one cannot be soothed by the glorious partnership of Mother Earth and Brother Moon."

Holy shit.

I squinted at the list of support numbers on my wall. It took four tries before I found one of my group from St. Avery's, Margo, at home. We talked awhile, and the need for a drink passed but I was still restless. A little depressed. I flicked the clock radio on.

They were playing a song about love, and how one knew whether it was true. Crap like that. I tuned out.

Around two A.M., the D.J. announced a giveaway. I caught the tail end.

". . . and the first person to call and identify Dinah Washington's unforgettable 'I've Got You Under My Skin' wins tonight's prize."

Well, I thought—*that, at least, I might be able to do.*

But what was the prize? He never said. Maybe I wasn't listening. Maybe it was a secret. *A secret prize.*

Just for fun, I punched the station's number in, let it ring once, and hung up. I stretched out and listened through four more songs. John Coltrane, Stan Getz. Billie and Ella.

Then I heard it. The unforgettable, unmistakable beat of the drums. The opening to Dinah's song.

I punched the redial on the third beat.

The phone rang three times.

"Hi! Congratulations! You've got it."

"I *do*? I was *first*? Great!"

He chuckled. "Give me your name first, then your address and phone number."

I did, bouncing on the edge of the bed with something like juvenile glee. I'd never done this before.

The D.J.'s voice was low and black and sexy. "Well, Jesse James . . . hey, I love that name . . . thanks for listening. I hope you're not really in need of this particular prize— but on the other hand, I can highly recommend him."

"Great!" I said again. Then, clicking in, "Him?"

"We'll send someone around with your certificate tomorrow. Will you be home?"

"I'm not sure—I guess you can leave it with my landlady, downstairs, but—"

"Perfect."

"Wait a minute, *him*—?"

"Enjoy," he said huskily. And rang off.

I stared at the phone.

Him?

Him *who*?

Now what the hell had I done?

CHAPTER EIGHTEEN

There was a note from Toni on my outside door when I went downstairs. *Where have you been? I've been coming over every morning to exercise. Why is your door locked?*

"So I won't have to goddamned exercise," I groused under my breath. "Ever think of that, kid?" I slunk along the porch to Mrs. Binty's door, hoping Toni wouldn't spot me.

But as I waited for Mrs. B to answer, I noticed my jeans felt tight. It might not be a bad idea to work out a little. Since my fall from grace the other day, I was kind of puffy. I hated that feeling in the summer.

So, okay. I'd give Toni a call when I got home. Apologize. The kid meant well, after all. It wasn't her fault she was twelve years old and had the energy of three atom bombs, while I was tired and burned out at thirty-one.

I'd decided I couldn't wait around for the mysterious certificate to arrive. When Mrs. Binty appeared—in red plastic curlers that made her look like a tiny little cardinal fluttering on a phone wire—I asked if she'd keep an eye out for a delivery person.

She was thrilled. "I have a friend at church who wins those contests all the time. I can't wait to tell her what your prize is!"

Given the enigmatic "him," I wasn't sure her friend from church should be told.

I set out on foot, the plan being to catch a bus at the corner and check out Barbara Sloan's old apartment on the other side of the city. Grady had given me the address, grudgingly, in a thirty-second phone call that left me with a dial tone in my ear.

"It's closed up," he'd growled. "I don't know what you're looking for, but you won't find anything there."

Click.

I was lucky he took my call.

As a matter of fact, I knew I was grasping for straws. But I'd been thinking about Sloan as I lay awake last night. I felt I needed to know something about her personal life. There was always the chance we'd all been approaching this from the wrong angle. For one thing, Sloan was an attorney for the city before she worked for Marcus. She could have made any number of enemies through her job there. Then, too, statistics have shown that most murder victims are done in by a relative or friend. Maybe Grady North was so intent on landing Marcus, he'd been blind to that angle.

I decided at the corner to walk a little farther. It was a wonderful day—sunny, not too warm. I'd get a head start on those workouts. Toni would be proud.

Passing the gun shop on Genesee Street, I remembered something I wanted to ask Marcus. I stopped at a phone booth to call, wincing as my quarter slid down the chute and went *clunk*. I'd never get my car out of hock feeding Baby Bell this way.

He answered at his penthouse in the city.

"I just want to clarify something," I began without preamble, wiping sweat from beneath my eyes.

"And good morning to you too." His old light tone was back.

"You seem in better spirits."

"I am. Why aren't you?"

"I've got a lot on my mind. I thought you did too."

"Well, I wasn't doing myself any good out there at the cabin brooding. I had to get back in charge before someone else did."

"Yeah? You figure that out all by yourself?"

There was a brief silence. "What's wrong?" he said.

"Nothing." Dammit. I sounded like an eighty-year-old curmudgeon. "Ginny says hi."

Another pause. "I know. She reported in."

"She reported in."

"Yes."

"Sounds pretty official."

He sighed. "Ginny is one of my best undercover operators."

"Uh-huh. And this is the sort of thing you want me to do for the Andrelli Crime Family Inc.?" I knew there wasn't a chance his phone was bugged; it was scanned every day with the latest of hi-tech equipment. Not that I cared at the moment, either way.

"Similar," Marcus answered. "But I'd want you in this area, not down there."

"Christ, Marcus! It's bad enough you sit in that ivory tower and never soil your own hands—now you've got all these women working for you too?"

"Jess." The tone became reasonable. A little less patient. "I'm an executive, not a foot soldier. And if I didn't hire women, you'd accuse me of sexism. Why is it I can't win with you lately?"

He was right. But I couldn't let it go. "I just have a hard time figuring how people like Ginny and Barbara Sloan end up working for organized crime."

"Ginny's a damned good investigator."

"I didn't say she wasn't. I could see her with the FBI, maybe, but she's a nice person, and you've got her hanging out with a sick weirdo like Paulie Gandolo."

"Ginny has her reasons for what she's doing," he said.

"What are they?"

Silence at the other end. At least, it seemed clear that Ginny hadn't told him that Tark was at her friend's apartment, or about my meeting with him and Bernadette. *Ginny's got her own agenda*, Tark had said.

I eased open the door of the phone booth and moved it in and out a few times to try to create air. It was one of those old booths, like a hotbox, and my efforts only made things worse. I could already see dark spots on my green blouse beneath the armpits. I felt like a slug.

"Did Ginny tell you about the guys in Atlantic City who grabbed me?" I asked.

He put a threat into the word, "Yes." I half smiled, perversely glad for the implied payback.

"According to Ginny, they weren't working for Paulie. She says they sell their muscle to the drug trade, out of Miami."

There was a brief silence while Marcus fiddled with papers. I could hear them being riffled, and pictured him sitting behind his desk in the vast living room of the penthouse, with the cool blue carpeting and wraparound windows overlooking . . .

Me. Hell, he was overlooking half of Rochester—so he was probably overlooking *me*. I glanced uneasily around as I stood there dripping salt, scratching my nose, lifting the hair off my neck. . . .

It gave me pause. Especially when I heard his gold Cross pen tapping on the glass desk, the way it does when Marcus is calculating odds.

When he gave me his attention again, he said in that voice of authority he uses with rebel foot soldiers, "Jess, this is becoming . . . complicated. I won't have you involved."

"Afraid I'll find the list Barbara stole from Paulie?" I said.

The tapping pen stopped. "What list?"

"Marcus, don't do this."

"I have no idea what you are talking about."

"Uh-huh. You probably don't know anything about a Glock nine-millimeter semi, either."

"Just what am I *supposed* to know about it?"

"Sloan was killed with one."

The tapping began again. "We carry several weapons in the limo," he said. "A Glock was one of those."

"You carry *several weapons*?"

Silence.

"I wasn't implying any criticism," I said.

"We both know you were."

"Wait a minute. You said a Glock *was* one of the weapons in your car?"

"Yes."

"Where is it now?"

"I have no idea."

"What exactly does that mean?"

"It disappeared," he said. "Along with Tark, the night Barbara Sloan was killed."

Swell.

In all the time since this mess began, I hadn't for a moment considered that Tark might be guilty. But now I understood some of Marcus's anger toward him. There were too many unanswered questions, too many suspicions pointing Tark's way.

"I have to go," I said.

"Jess?"

"What?"

"What are you doing for work these days?"

"For work?" Even to me, my voice seemed flat.

"Aren't you supposed to be at the *Herald* right now?"

I said coolly, "Has that somehow, in some way I can't possibly fathom, become some business of yours?"

"Just wondered. Are you giving any thought to my job proposition?"

"Every minute of every day. It's all I think about. *Why not go to work for Marcus Andrelli*? I say to myself. Think of the future you'll have. Firsthand knowledge of the FBI, the Organized Crime Bureau, the Treasury Department, the inside of state prison—"

Marcus hung up.

The cops, I knew, would have swept Sloan's apartment clean of evidence in their investigation after she died. Still, there might be something—some small thing they'd overlooked. A cop who'd been out partying or moonlighting the night before could miss finding something—get careless in his search. And women sometimes hide things in places that men never dream of.

Sloan had lived in one of those rebuilt factories that are often called The Something or Other Galleria. Used brick, lots of trees, with boutiques and courtyards at the street level. A Louisiana-style wrought-iron stairway led up to the second and third floors, which were all apartments opening onto long common balconies.

I had ended up walking the entire way. Toni would not only be proud, she'd be incredulous—and rightly so. Every bone in my body hurt. My feet were flaming lumps.

I limped into the dimness of an espresso shop in the courtyard and ordered a cup to go. Outside again, I flopped onto a green park bench with curlicue trim, and sat in the shade, recovering. The thick, strong coffee was gone in two gulps. My eyes closed, my head went back. Shoulders slumped. Legs went limp. And in less than three minutes, I'd been dumped on by a bird from one of the damn trees. I swore, used a paper napkin to wipe the shit off my shoulder, and wondered why this sort of thing never seemed to happen to other people I knew.

Take Becky Anderson, for instance: she of the *Lifestyle* column at the *Herald*. Take her—please. Becky had followed me to the *Herald* from the *Weston Free Press*, and like Bastard, the dastardly dog, I couldn't seem to get rid of her.

In Weston, Becky had lurked every day behind her desk and her African violets, hating my guts because I thumbed my nose at the very mention of staff meetings. My own antipathy toward her had to do with the fact that the woman had no balls.

Nothing had changed, here in the city. Becky spent most of her time at the *Herald* grousing because I never got in early enough to make the coffee. Nor did I stay late enough to turn off the Xerox machine.

I spent at least half my time trying to get her transferred to the Yukon.

Nevertheless, I couldn't imagine a bird blotch, or for that

matter, a blotch of any kind, on one of Becky Anderson's tidy rayon shirts.

I found a crumpled Kleenex in my pocket and took it over to a water fountain in a brick alcove. I was so intent on wetting it, then rubbing at the bird blotch, I almost didn't see Jack Hoffman—of Rochester P.D. Vice—coming down the iron steps from the apartments upstairs.

He was headed my way, and I shrank back into the alcove, grateful for its shadows. When Jack passed by I got a better look—no uniform today, as in Harrigan's, just a yellow knit shirt and jeans. He hesitated as he reached the sidewalk on River Street, and glanced to either side, then turned left, and was gone from my view.

I had planned to ask the manager to let me into Sloan's apartment. But after seeing Jack Hoffman, I wondered if other cops would be up there. Something going on.

I dropped the damp Kleenex in a trash receptacle and made my way up the stairs. Number 216, Grady had told me. I found the apartment on the second level, at the far end of the common balcony. It had a private location, nestled up against the trunk of a giant oak.

I was wrong about there being other cops here. Sloan's door was locked up tight. No answer to my knock. I glanced around, and saw no one in sight in any direction. I was hot and tired, and I figured, why not? I reached into my pocket and came up with my one credit card. But as a burgling tool it didn't work—which didn't really surprise me. It was seldom good for anything anyway, being, like me, mostly overworked and underpaid. I hadn't brought my tote, and had no other workable accessories this time.

I finally located the manager downstairs and around the back—a Ms. Marcella Wilkes, according to the small tab by her door. It was so small, you had to wonder if she hoped never to be found.

Marcella Wilkes was a woman with long brown hair streaked with gray and a baggy full-length dress that looked like she'd saved it for a Seventies Party and then said, "Oh, what the hell. Today's as good a day as any." I introduced myself as Barbara Sloan's sister, Rosa, from NYC. "The executor said I could pick up some family pictures," I murmured with just the right touch of sorrow.

It had been only a few days since Sloan died. I was counting on her real family not having cleared the place out yet.

The manager's eyes were a little starey, and from the apartment behind her drifted a faint odor of pot. She had one of those smiles that I used to call a shitty grin when I was into the stuff myself.

"You just missed your brother," she said.

"My brother?" I thought for a minute she was hallucinating.

"I told him the same thing I'm telling you. There's nothing personal, no letters, no pictures or stuff up there."

"Uh . . . what did my brother look like?"

She squinted at me. Then she laughed. "You're kiddin'."

"No . . . yes . . . I mean, I didn't know he was coming today. You're sure it was my brother?"

She eyed me suspiciously. "That's what he told me. Blond hair, yellow shirt—I don't remember what else. Barbara Sloan's brother, he said. I guess that would make him yours too."

"He went up to Barbara's apartment?"

"Listen, I don't want any trouble."

"Don't worry—I just thought, if he found anything, that would save me some time."

"He went out of here empty-handed," she said. "If he'd had anything with him, I'd've seen it when he brought me back the key."

"Have you rented the apartment to anyone else yet?"

"Can't. The rent's paid through October, and it stays like it is till the lawyers tell me what to do."

"Can I just take a look, then?" I said.

She shrugged. Infinite patience or lethargy? It was hard to tell. "C'mon in. I'll get the key."

I stepped in and looked around, while Marcella Wilkes shuffled over to a kitchen drawer in worn brown Birkenstocks. It was a large, modern apartment, the kind that someone else could easily have decorated to be classy. In Marcella Wilkes's hands it had entered a time warp. I wondered how often the owner of the place came around to check on his help.

The windows were hung with some kind of orange material. Not a sliver of light showed through. There was a peace poster on one wall and a black velvet painting of Kennedy on another. Beneath it was a lava lamp, resting on a burlap and felt banner. I waited for the Beatles to burst forth with "Help!" from the old hi-fi console and for black lights to flicker on, casting us both in their eerie glow.

It might have been fun. But the manager was pulling a bunch of keys out of the kitchen drawer. "Follow me," she said, sighing. She led the way to the front of the building, then, heavily, up the stairs. It was obvious she'd gotten the word: The war was lost, half the draft dodgers were still happily in Canada where people didn't butt into things that didn't concern them, and there was no place on the planet for activism—or even activity—at least not here or in this year.

She opened the door to apartment 216. "No point my staying," she said. "Nothin' nobody can take, least not without a truck. You need me, you call. And be sure to bring that key back."

She schlupped away, the Birkenstocks flopping.

I glanced around. Barbara Sloan's apartment was the antithesis of Marcella Wilkes's. A big, open, sunny place with polished oak floors, one thick yellow area rug before a fireplace, a couple of ferns. A yellow sofa and chairs, light oak tables.

But Marcella Wilkes was right. After a brief preliminary search—opening cupboards and drawers, looking in closets and beneath bed and furniture—I was satisfied that the only things worth taking would require a truck.

There was a large color television, a stereo system with gigantic speakers and a CD. Even a small computer. But no personal items at all. No clothes, pictures, magazines, food. No digital clock radio, tapes, or CDs.

The question was, what had Jack Hoffman hoped to find here? And why had he lied to the manager about who he was? He couldn't have been on official business. What was he up to?

Looking for Paulie Gandolo's list, was my first and immediate guess. I didn't know why; I just didn't trust Jack Hoffman, not since the other day in Harrigan's.

I tried to remember. I'd been sitting across from him while Dick Skelley was reporting to Grady North about . . . what? Barbara Sloan's autopsy. Then about Tark being seen by a witness, and the weapon . . .

There had been a kind of cold, satisfied look in Jack Hoffman's eyes. Then, while Grady was talking to me, Jack had become angry and left. He hadn't wanted my interference in the Sloan case, that much was sure.

I went back into the living room and sat at Barbara Sloan's desk, which stood beneath a large picture window facing an apartment across the way. I tried to think where she might have hidden something like that list.

I tried the obvious first, turning on her computer. There wasn't much there. Nothing about Marcus, or her work, nothing incriminating that I could see. A few letters to someone named Christopher. I scanned them. They were all in a similar vein: *I love you. We'll be together soon.* Simple messages, simply written, about her everyday life.

Who *was* Christopher? I wondered. There was something about those letters. Were they *too* simple? I wanted to make copies, take them home and study them for some kind of code. But I had already looked in the desk's drawers, and knew there were no disks for making backups.

On the other hand, paper does sometimes get stuck behind drawers. I hadn't gotten around to the next phase in my search: pulling things out, moving furniture around.

I did this now.

The drawers moved easily on their tracks, then had to

be lifted before they could be removed. I dragged them all out, finding nothing. No scrap of caught paper anywhere.

I knelt on the floor, feeling all along the carpet where the bottom drawer had been. Way in the back, my fingers closed over something slick. It was behind the solid frame of the desk, between the desk and the wall, where it would have fallen if it had been accidentally shoved over the back of an overful drawer.

I pulled it out.

A picture. Wallet size. The kind that comes in a package from photography studios.

There were two subjects: Barbara Sloan, and a little boy, about two or three. She was holding him close, their cheeks together, and both had huge smiles. He had dark hair and intense dark eyes, in contrast to her blond, patrician looks.

I turned the picture over. *Christopher Mark, age 3, December, 1986.*

I stared at the picture for what seemed a long time. Then my mind began running at top speed, and all the while I kept telling myself: *Jess, this is crazy.* Just because I'd read Sidney Sheldon's *Rage of Angels* three times and used up every hanky in the house, that didn't mean—

But it was too late. My imagination had begun to draw a parallel, true or not: the beautiful attorney with the mafia leader's kid. Christopher Mark. Marcus was sometimes called Marc.

This is crazy, Jess, crazy.

I built upon the scenario, laying brick after brick of supposition: Sloan had gone to work for Marcus to support the kid, had never told him he had a son, but hoped they would turn out to be close one day. . . .

I thought of Sloan's letters. *We'll be together soon.*

There had been no mention by the manager of a child living here. Where was he? Had Sloan hidden him away this last year or so while she worked for Marcus?

I stared out the picture window. After a minute or two I realized I was facing another window, less than five feet away, in the brick apartment building next door. The drapes were open over there and a television was on.

I tucked the picture of Sloan and kid into my back pocket, turned off the computer, and went back down and talked to Marcella Wilkes again.

She was stringing love beads. I wasn't at all surprised.

"Did Barbara stay here all the time?" I asked. "I mean, do you think she might have had some other apartment in the city?"

If my question struck her as odd, she didn't show it. "I used to hear her come in almost every night. You know, when I saw her apartment the other day, I was surprised how so much of her stuff was gone."

"What do you think happened to it?"

"I didn't take it," Marcella Wilkes said defensively. "Don't go saying I did."

"No, I didn't mean that, of course you didn't take it. But it's strange there's nothing there."

She dropped several beads, and knelt on the floor to pick them up. Her nose nearly grazed the carpet as she peered into its threads. She said, "Yeah, well, maybe the fuzz walked off with it." She picked at the carpet pile. "They do that, you know, take anything they can lay their hands on when a person gets killed and they think there's nobody around to complain."

She hefted herself to her feet, put the beads she'd picked up into her mouth, like a seamstress with safety pins, and went on with her stringing.

I was still puzzled. Money, maybe. It's a known fact that some dishonest cops take money during an investigation, when it's lying around. But a whole apartment full of clothes, magazines, food?

"How long did Barbara live here?"

She looked at me curiously. "Didn't she ever write you?" It sounded like "Dinshevriteou?" what with the mouthful of beads, but I got it.

"We weren't that close." I wondered who Sloan *was* close to. Other than Marcus.

Marcella Wilkes spit the beads into her palm. "She was here about a year and a half."

"Did she ever bring a child here—a young boy?"

"I never saw anybody like that."

Glancing at my watch, I thought that I should stop in at work soon, or I'd be up to my ass in trouble. Hell, I was already up to my ass in trouble. I thanked the manager and hit the streets, running toward a bus that would take me to the *Herald.*

But then I changed direction. There was one more stop I wanted to make first.

The woman who lived behind the window across from Barbara Sloan's apartment was elderly. Her apartment was closed up, with no air-conditioning. It was suffocating and smelled of urine and age. She probably had lost er sense of smell and didn't know this, because she looked as if she tried to keep herself clean. Her face was powdered to the point of chalky, her lips pink, her white hair pulled into a dry, wispy bun at the back of her head. I had to shout and speak slowly to be heard.

"Oh, she moved out long ago," the woman said in answer to my questions about Sloan.

"Moved out?"

"No, she didn't shout. She was a very quiet lady."

"I mean, when did she go?"

"The man below?"

I leaned closer to her ear. "The woman across the way. Blond hair, attractive, a little on the tall side. Did you see her go?"

"I told you, dear. Last week. I saw her packing . . . up all night, she was, and then, next morning, the movers came. I remember, because I was watching *To Have or Have Not* on *The Morning Show.* They don't make them like that anymore."

"When she left . . . while she was packing . . . was anyone else there?"

"No, she didn't take the chair."

I searched for simpler words. "Besides the movers—was anyone there?"

"No one that I saw. Of course, I didn't know the movers personally—so you see, it would be difficult to say."

"And this was last week?"

She nodded.

I would have to look up that movie in the *TV Guide*, see what morning it was on. But I was a nut for old movies myself, and I had seen it listed; I would swear the old woman was right—it was on before Sloan died.

So Sloan had moved from her apartment before the night she was shot on Marcus's boat. The manager had said that her rent was paid up through October. She had paid it in June, four months in advance. Not an unheard-of thing. When people have enough money, and a lease, they sometimes do that so they won't have to think about it for a while.

Women also tend to keep their apartments, if possible, when moving in with a man. Until they see how it all works out.

Given the photo of Sloan and son, and the story my admittedly overblown imagination had put together, the first thing that came to my mind was: she had moved in with Marcus. She had finally told him about her son—their son?—and he had asked her to move in with him until they could work things out.

Of course there were a million other possibilities. I'm not proud of the suspicious way my mind works. But now and again, I get things right.

I thanked the woman—Adelaide Peak, it had said on the mailbox—and headed back to the other side of town and the *Herald*.

CHAPTER NINETEEN

A half hour later I sat behind my desk at the *Herald* in my jeans and sneakers, feet up, contemplating how much easier it is to think when you're not at war with your clothes. Damn Chastain's dress code, anyway.

I wondered if I should call and ask Marcus about Barbara Sloan's kid.

But if Marcus knew Sloan had a son—and even suspected the kid was his—he wouldn't be just angry, thinking Tark had killed her. There'd be a vendetta in the works the likes of which this town had never seen.

There hadn't been that kind of anger in him, up to now. More a frustrated sadness over Tark's betrayal in disappearing.

The question was, if he didn't know about Christopher Sloan, did I really want to be the bearer of these tidings?

I dialed Grady North's number instead, knowing instinctively he wouldn't take my call. Another cop answered.

"This is the mayor's assistant," I improvised in the real assistant, Mary Newberry's, southern drawl. "May ah speak to Grady Nawth, please?"

He must have had me on the squawk box.

"What the hell do you want, Jess?" Grady snarled.

(And yes, it is possible for a person to snarl, I'd learned. Under certain circumstances you can actually see the baring of teeth, the fleck of foam.)

"Did Barbara Sloan have a kid?"

"Don't you ever give up?"

"Did she have a kid?"

"How the hell would I know?"

"She's a homicide victim. You should know every damn thing about her by now, unless, of course, you aren't really trying."

A heavy silence. The gnash of pointed teeth. "The child is a matter of public record. Goodbye."

"Where is he?" I said quickly. "Where's the kid living?"

"With Sloan's mother."

"*Where?*"

An ungracious mutter. "Brighton."

"Look, I know it's got to be difficult, mouthing words and growling at the same time, but can you give me an address? Please?"

"Tmehelmch," he mumbled.

"What?"

The hollow echo of the squawk box rattled like a tin roof in a storm. "2936 Laurel!"

I wrote it down. "I can't tell you how much I do appreciate your cooperation, officer."

"Go to hell."

Did Grady North really say that? *Go to hell?* I couldn't believe my sweet Georgia ears.

I was on my way to the elevator when Becky Anderson waltzed out of the Xerox room, purposely (I was sure) to snag me.

"Charlie Nicks wants to see you."

She said it in that righteous tone she always uses to let me know I'm in deep shit, and it's my own fault, and damn, is she glad.

"Later. I'm on a story," I said, continuing on. I punched the DOWN button and turned back and faced her, waiting with my arms folded.

Becky fingered the black bow on her prim white blouse and gave me the other look I'd grown accustomed to: You think you can get away with anything, but na-na-na-*nha*-na, you're wrong.

I hated her. It was eighty degrees in here, and her short

smooth blond hair wasn't even limp. She looked crisp. Cool. Efficient. All the things I was not.

And on such intricate matters do friendships rise or fall.

"Becky," I said, sighing, "do you *always* do what you're told?"

The turn of her cold, cold shoulder said she did. I watched her teeter away in her tight black skirt, on her high spectator heels. *Spectators.* The perfect shoes, I thought, for tap dancing at the *Herald.*

I wouldn't have felt so bad if men had to wear them too. But they had important work to do, they couldn't hobble around all day. God, I hated this place.

It was just as well, as things turned out.

The elevator was out of order. I had to tiptoe past Charlie Nicks's office to get to the stairs.

He caught me.

"What're you limping for?" he said. "You weren't limping ten minutes ago."

"It comes and goes," I rasped. "I've really got to go home."

"And what's wrong with your voice?"

"A *horrible* summer cold—"

"More like you've been making personal calls ever since you sashayed in here *late* today."

"I gotta go." I turned away.

"Hold it, James. You haven't spent more than ten hours here all week."

"I've been working on something big—"

"Me too. Your termination slip."

He slid it across his desk with a triumphant flourish. Like the cliché, it was pink—nearly as pink as Charlie's bald head.

"I'm fired?" I husked.

"You're fired," he confirmed. "Toodle-oo."

I was rifling my desk drawers for tampons, thinking I wouldn't be able to afford to buy any now, when Mrs. Binty called.

"It's so exciting!" she trilled.

"You heard I got fired?"

"No! You've been fired? I'm so sorry, Jesse, I didn't know."

Bless her heart, she didn't even ask how I planned to pay the rent.

"It's okay, it's my karma," I explained. "I'm moving toward my Life Purpose—professional poverty. Why did you call?"

"Oh, the certificate! It came!"

"Yeah?" The mysterious *him*.

"You'll never guess," she said.

I grinned. "An escort service."

"No."

"A male stripper?"

Shock. "Oh my, no."

"Tell me."

I listened. The grin tugged at my lips. I could feel it growing.

Not bad.

I took a bus home, showered and changed, and borrowed Mrs. B's car to drive to Brighton. She gave me my certificate first. I read the details.

Then I laughed out loud.

Hot damn.

It wasn't bad at all.

CHAPTER TWENTY

I toodle-ooed out into the burbs, driving the Great Gray Chariot and whistling as I neared Brighton. Feeling free for the first time in over a year.

Maybe, I thought, I should stop at the Center for Natural Healing in Pittsford while I was out this way. Tell Samved it looked like my therapy was working.

Actually, I hadn't seen the old fraud in three weeks.

But *something* was working. I felt so good I wanted to park the car and hop the rest of the way.

I restrained myself and ambled along winding, tree-shaded avenues, watching for street names and crossing deer.

It was an area of country clubs, of gentle slopes and quiet wealth. No developer's ax would ever dare dent these trees, no wrecking ball assault the stone and brick facades of these six-bedroom homes.

A mailbox set into a low, stone pillar bore the number 2936 on Laurel Avenue. The main house was two stories of mellow, rose-tinted stone, with sparkling white trim and shutters. It stood back a hundred feet or so from the street. On one side of the house, a sunporch sprawled. On the other, a row of garages—or possibly, a stable. The drive (one would never call it a drive*way*, implying trash cans and lowly asphalt) was made of smooth brick, lined with a riot of English-garden flowers. The lawn was emerald green and looked like it had been rolled by servants (stopping only now and then for afternoon tea) for the past 200 years. Behind the house was a virtual forest of towering trees.

I parked at the curb, turned the ignition off, listened to the silence, and sighed. Much as I loved my independence (and hated compromise), I really dug this sort of thing. Was I becoming a yuppie after all—a little late, if so—or was there, beneath this thick, mean hide, simply a daughter of the ould sod—a country girl, dying to get out?

Either way, my salary at the *Herald* would never have gotten me this. Working for someone with unlimited funds, however—carrying out missions beyond the law and getting paid well for doing it—just might.

Dangerous thinking. I grabbed my tote with pad and pencil, and trudged up the mellow brick road.

I hadn't called ahead, purposely. Taking people by surprise doesn't give them time to think about what they're going to say, or to check up on your story—find out if you're who you say you are.

I rang the bell, heard its solemn tones somewhere far inside, and waited.

After a few moments I felt a presence behind the spy hole. Some hesitation. Then the door cracked open to reveal a woman in a neat white cotton skirt and blouse. *Suburban classique*. Designer, I guessed. Matching white canvas flats. Her short gray hair was carefully permed and shellacked into place. Becky Anderson with bucks.

"Mrs. Sloan?"

"Yes?" The door widened a fraction.

I stuck out my hand. "Hi, I'm Jessica James. I'm sorry to disturb you. I know this is a terrible time for you—"

She took my hand reluctantly, a case, I guess, of upbringing: manners before everything. "What do you want?"

"I just wondered if I might talk with you about Barbara."

Manners or not, her voice turned cold. "Are you a reporter?"

She had probably been hounded to death in the past week. Sometimes I hated admitting to my profession almost as much as I loathed practicing it.

I evaded giving a direct answer and leaned on my somewhat dubious connections with the Rochester P.D. as a credential. "Grady North, the detective in charge of Barbara's case, suggested I stop by."

She hesitated still. I sweetened the pot with a small lie. "I knew Barbara when she worked for the city attorney's office. We were friends. I'd like to help find her killer."

She looked me up and down. I was glad I'd changed into my best navy slacks, raw silk shirt, and Italian sandals. The sandals had those miserable, unbending wooden soles, a fact I hadn't considered while racing through my most hated chore—shopping for shoes. But if I didn't have to think too much, or make any major decisions, I figured they'd be okay.

Finally, she opened the door. "Come in."

I stepped into a cool foyer, with ceramic tile floors and French country furnishings. A vase overflowing with blue delphiniums and white roses dwarfed a fragile fruitwood table. Everything gleamed—floor, furnishings, pewter chandeliers. The house was pleasantly hushed. I wondered where Christopher was.

"Barbara told me she had a son," I began conversationally. We entered a large living room with blue and white flowered sofas, a white, country-style fireplace, an expanse of French doors leading onto a terrace. "How is he doing? Is he here?"

"Christopher is outside. We can talk out there."

I'd been afraid she wouldn't admit to her grandson, that Barbara had kept him a secret even from her closest friends. This was turning out to be easier than expected.

We floated through the living room, or so it seemed. The decor was light and airy, while ahead of us, beyond the flagstone terrace, lay clear blue sky. Once on the terrace, I could see that the woods began farther back than I'd thought. A half acre of green velvet lawn stretched from the terrace to the first stand of trees. In its center, landscaped with rocks and masses of bright flowers, was an oversized goldfish pond. Flashes of orange shimmered as the water lapped and burbled.

Sitting at the edge of the pond on a white bench, looking

overdressed and like something from *Masterpiece Theatre*, was a young boy. Christopher Sloan, I presumed. A woman sat beside him, reading aloud from a book, and they both laughed at something. As we stepped down from the terrace, the woman set the book aside and rose. She came forward and stood facing us. A servant's stance—on duty —awaiting orders. Mrs. Sloan, it seemed, ran a tight ship.

When we reached her, Mrs. Sloan said, "Why don't you take a break now, Janet? We'll be with Christopher."

The woman, who looked perhaps thirty, nodded. She was in white shorts, a tee, and tennis shoes. Her brown hair was pulled into a knot in back. She didn't smile. "I'll be over there if you need me," she said.

She gestured to a table with umbrella and chairs. A cordless phone was on the table, along with a rack of glasses and a pitcher of something that looked like iced tea. Next to them was a thin black briefcase, several pens or pencils, and a tumble of papers.

"Thank you, Janet. I will." Mrs. Sloan turned to me. "Janet is Christopher's tutor," she explained.

Christopher stood before us waiting to be introduced. He displayed as much courtesy and good training as his tutor.

His grandmother said, "Christopher, this is a friend of your mother's. I'm sorry—Jessica—?"

"James," I supplied. "Hi, Christopher."

He was the first to hold out his hand. I shook it, thinking how dry it was, and cool, despite the warmth of the day.

But then he looked at me directly and smiled, and I was mesmerized.

His dark hair clung damply to his forehead in front. It was neatly clipped in back. His eyes were dark brown, nearly black.

Like Marcus's: not topaz in the sun, the way some become. They were intelligent. Challenging. Almost flirtatious as they examined me boldly.

The kid, I had to remind myself sharply, was barely seven years old.

The kid, another voice nagged, *is a youthful carbon copy of Marcus Andrelli*.

"You know my mother?" he asked, smiling in a friendly way.

I glanced quickly at Mrs. Sloan. He had used the present tense "know."

"I . . . uh . . ." It was something I hadn't prepared for, that he might not know his mother was dead. It left me without a plan.

"Why don't we sit down?" Mrs. Sloan said briskly.

She waited for me to take a seat on the bench. Then she sat beside me. Christopher, the perfect gentleman, perched on a rock across from us, knees drawn up, hands folded in his lap.

"Your tutor seems nice," I said inanely. Janet was sipping now and then from a glass of whatever was in the pitcher. She seemed to be relaxing, her head tilted back to the sun. "What are you studying?"

"Janet's not—"

Mrs. Sloan interrupted. "Christopher, why don't you ask Janet to help you pour each of us a glass of iced tea?"

His alert brown eyes swung to her. "Okay."

He slid from the rock, and his grandmother watched fondly as he walked across the grass, shoulders back, spine rigid. I wondered what he'd been about to say.

"You told me you wanted to help," Mrs. Sloan said, addressing me.

"Yes."

"Then it would probably be best, I think, not to talk to Christopher about his mother."

"He doesn't know what happened . . . that she died?"

"It's so difficult to tell a child that age. Especially when he hasn't seen his mother often enough in the past . . ." She didn't finish the sentence. Her expression said she was determined to protect her grandson at all cost.

"You mean because Christopher has been living here with you," I said.

"Yes. It's been hard for him to understand."

"How long exactly has he been here?"

She looked surprised at my question, but answered it. "A year and a half, more or less."

Since Barbara had gone to work for Marcus. "I can see why you'd want to protect him."

"The psychiatrists say it's better to tell children right away these days. I know I have to do it, I just don't . . ." She sighed.

"He's a beautiful child."

"Like his mother," she agreed, her throat catching.

Like his father, I nearly replied.

Oh, hell. Get on with the job.

"Mrs. Sloan—could you tell me who some of Barbara's friends were?"

Her spine stiffened. "You said you knew my daughter—"

"Even friends," I said gently, "don't tell each other the things a daughter tells her mother. Was there anyone who might have had a personal grudge against Barbara? Someone connected with her work, perhaps?"

She made a sour expression, a twist of the mouth. "Barbara didn't talk much . . . and especially not after she went to work for that—that evil man."

I said carefully, "You mean, Marcus Andrelli?"

The expression became ravaged—the look of someone who'd been raped, who'd had her entire life taken away. "I don't want to talk about him," she said harshly. "It's because of him my daughter . . ." She let the sentence die.

"How do you know Andrelli is responsible for what happened? Couldn't it have been anyone, someone from her old job—"

"I don't want to talk about this," she repeated.

"I'm sorry, Mrs. Sloan, truly, I am." I looked at Christopher, who was chatting with Janet and pouring iced tea from the pitcher into four glasses. Mrs. Sloan's eyes followed mine.

"Barbara was afraid," she said softly. "She was afraid something would happen to Christopher because of her connection with that filthy business. She wanted him clear of it—"

The words were choked off as she turned her back to me. Her shoulders trembled.

Christopher called out, "Gramma, it's almost ready."

I saw that a glass had spilled, and Janet was helping now as he tilted the heavy pitcher.

"We'll have tea," Mrs. Sloan said politely. Her eyes, when they met mine again, were dry. Both she and her manners were in control. "Before you go," she added pointedly.

I followed her across the grass.

Four lawn chairs, thickly padded with blue cushions, surrounded the table. Christopher stood politely behind his grandmother's, holding it out for her. Unaccustomed to the graces, or *Masterpiece Theatre*, I was already sitting when he reached me. He made a small, courteous gesture of sliding in further, although the grass didn't allow my chair to really move. I smiled, glanced back up at him, and said, "Thanks."

The kid, for God's sake, winked at me.

We sipped our tea . . . all four of us . . . without speaking, the way the upper classes tend to do—making every libation a ceremony. From the woods came a chatter of birds, and now and then the fish pond went *plop*. The fringe of the umbrella swayed like a hula dancer in the small breeze that drifted across the lawn. Somewhere in the neighborhood, a lawn mower buzzed, its sound muted. I suppose a dog barked somewhere too.

Our silence wasn't relaxed. Barbara's mother was still clearly tense. Her powder had caked into creases that before were invisible, and her thin fingers toyed restlessly with her glass. Janet, on the other hand, seemed watchful to the point of paranoia. Her eyes darted continuously across the grass to the woods, then to the house, then back to us again. Her hair, still pinned in a knot, fell in damp tendrils over her forehead. She didn't bother to push them back.

"Do you like ice skating?" Christopher asked me suddenly.

"Yes. I love ice hockey."

"What about figure skating?"

"It's my favorite."

"Mine too. My mother's going to take me to the Ice Capades when they come."

My tea went down the wrong way. Mrs. Sloan's eyes closed briefly.

"On Labor Day weekend," Christopher said blithely.

"That's . . . wonderful."

"Christopher . . ." his grandmother began.

My stomach clenched. *God, don't let her do it while I'm here*, I pleaded silently. *I know it's not fair to let him go on thinking, planning, and sure, the kid has to be told, but not while I'm here.*

I was still living with the look in my mom's eyes when she found out Pop had died. I would carry it to the grave.

"I can get tickets through my paper," I said quickly. "Maybe I could take you . . . I mean, go with you and your mother . . . if you'd like . . ."

I blundered on in that vein for uncountable moments in time.

Finally, I sensed that Mrs. Sloan was staring at me. I turned to see that her blue eyes were icy. Accusing. She set her tea down abruptly. "I know who you are now. You're that reporter."

I opened my mouth, then realized there was nothing I could say.

Her voice shook. "I recognized your name, and I thought it was because you were a friend of Barbara's. But you're not. You're the one people talk about, the reporter at the *Herald*." Her face became engorged with rage. "Barbara told me about you. You're a friend of that mobster!"

I set my glass down, my own face flaming. I dried my hands of its frost on my pant legs.

"I really do want to help—"

I glanced at Christopher, who was watching with that keen gaze again. His attention swung from his grandmother to me, like that of an avid journalist hoping to get the straight scoop for a change.

"I didn't mean to upset anyone," I said lamely.

"You and that man are friends!" she repeated. She pushed herself away from the table and jumped to her feet. Her chair tumbled backward. Christopher seemed awed by his grandmother's anger.

"Get out of my house!"

"Mrs. Sloan, please. What happened—it may not be what you think—"

"Get out of here!" she screamed, reaching protectively for Christopher. "Janet—!"

But Janet, Christopher's "tutor," was way ahead of her. Before the words were even out of Mrs. Sloan's mouth, I saw movement in that direction. My head jerked her way.

She had stepped a few paces back from the table, no longer part of the scene but outside it. The black briefcase was open. The woman held a gun. It was pointed down, but both hands firmly gripped it. It wouldn't take much to bring it to firing level—a split second, no more.

"I'll have to ask you to leave," she said. Her tone was polite but flat. It brooked no interference. "Leave. Now."

"You're—"

"I'm Christopher's bodyguard. And I am fully prepared to remove you from the premises. It would help if you'd leave of your own accord."

She had been guarding Christopher, I realized now, ever since I'd arrived. I said as much.

"You would never have been allowed near him otherwise," she replied. "No one is. Remember that, in the future."

"I didn't come here to hurt Christopher—"

I looked at him. He had paled a little, but he stood facing

both of us bravely, his shoulders back, chin high. He seemed to have placed himself between us and his grandmother, and I thought as he took on this role of protector that he looked more like Marcus than ever.

"I would never hurt Christopher," I said.

Chapter Twenty-One

Janet escorted me to Mrs. Binty's car. After the initial shock, I wasn't that surprised by her place in the Sloan home. Women are more and more in demand as executive bodyguards. They "fit in," blend into upperclass backgrounds in a way that men like Tark, with his size and worked-over face, can't. They pass as companions, secretaries—and, apparently, as tutors.

So the questions running through my mind as I drove back into the city took other forms. Was Janet just one more of Marcus's employees, like Ginny? Did he know about his son, after all? Had he managed to keep the secret of Christopher all the time I'd known him, and had I been so stupid I'd never even picked up a clue?

For that matter, why did Christopher Sloan *need* a bodyguard? Was Mrs. Sloan simply being cautious since Barbara's death? Or had Marcus placed Janet there for reasons of his own?

Christopher's grandmother obviously hated Marcus Andrelli. This might be because she knew he was Christopher's father and hadn't assumed responsibility for his child in all these years. But if that were the case, would she allow him to invade her home with Janet that way? Or had her hatred begun recently, because she believed him responsible for her daughter's death?

My mind was a muddle. I needed a drink for one of those flashes of brilliance it sometimes brought. Not that I consciously planned for one as I pulled into a parking space along the curb a half block down from Harrigan's. I honestly thought I'd dismissed the idea.

Mrs. Binty's Olds was air-conditioned, but the short walk from it to the bar was suffocating. I welcomed the coolness of Harrigan's with its blue-tinted windows that were like those of the grottolike bars at the shore. At the bar, I slid onto a stool and grabbed a cocktail napkin to wipe the sweat from my face and neck.

There were only a couple of people in Harrigan's: television cable installers in uniform, having an after-work beer. Harve was at the far end of the bar, juicing oranges into a frosted pitcher. When I was drinking (before St. Avery's), I'd taught him how to make Genesee Screws with fresh oranges and Genny beer. The idea had caught on with some of the regulars, especially in the summer. It rose up to haunt me now as my tongue flicked out and licked dry lips. My throat felt like it had been throttled, and yes, I do know how that feels. It happened to me, not all that long ago—when Daphne Malcross was missing.

That, too, had involved Marcus Andrelli.

Why did violent things keep happening to the women in Marcus's life?

And why did Barbara Sloan go to work for him in the first place? It didn't look, judging from her family home, as if she'd have needed the money.

Ambition?

Or was it, as I'd been thinking, a way to get Marcus and Christopher together?

So easy to arrange: Sunday picnics on the yacht. Mother, son, and father. They would grow close. In time, she would tell Marcus that Christopher was his.

No. Marcus would have seen himself in Christopher right away.

So, then. Was that what had happened?

And if so—did Christopher know? And how would he feel—when he was old enough to understand—about having a mobster for a father?

I'd had a drunk for a father, and that had been pretty bad. But would I rather not have known Pop? In many ways, he was good. When he died nearly five years ago, it was my fault—or I'd thought it was. And I still missed the old sot. I missed him a hell of a lot. He used to take me to circuses, six-pack in hand, and to watch the Red Wings play.

I thought about Christopher, whose mother had promised to take him to the Ice Capades. Who would take him now? Marcus? Sure—him and a whole cavalcade of bodyguards. If he wasn't in jail by then for killing his son's mother.

Poor little kid.

I came out of my reverie to hear Harve saying, "You look like you lost your best friend."

I leaned my chin on my palm. "It happens, sometimes," I said.

"Anything I can do?"

"I guess not. Thanks anyway."

"Something to drink?"

The biting scent of fresh-squeezed oranges tickled my nose. I stole a thirsty glance at the pitcher of juice and imagined it mixed with the malty taste of a Genny beer. Harve's thick eyeglasses followed in that direction. Then they came back. He slid the glasses up on his fiery orange head, and fixed me with bland, ash-colored eyes.

"Some juice?" he said helpfully. "A nice tall chimney glass filled with crushed ice and orange juice? Pick you right up."

Bartenders know you too damn well. They know who drinks too much, and who's trying to quit. They know when you fall off the wagon. They know, even, who's never going to make it—no matter how hard they try.

My tongue flicked out again. I couldn't help it. I looked at Harve. He'd never say what he was thinking. But you have to be completely without shame to drink in front of a bartender who knows you've been to a treatment program.

"Sure, juice. Okay." I could hold out, I supposed—if only another day.

Harve filled a chimney glass as promised and set it down, ice clinking, pulp freezing, before me. I took a deep swallow and felt the acid frost hit my stomach and slide on back to my spine.

"There's something I've been wanting to talk to you about," Harve said. He wiped his hands on a towel and stood with them spread on the bar, leaning a little close. His tone was confidential.

"What's up?

Two cops came through the front door, talking companionably and pulling at their shirt collars. Undoing top buttons. Off duty. Harrigan's was the one place around where they could hang out comfortably. The owner, Jake Wiley, had been a beat cop for twenty years. He was hardly ever here, but Grady had told me Jake gave orders to each new bartender: Make sure my boys are taken care of.

Harve, however, seemed nervous at the cops' presence as they headed for a booth. "Not here," he said. "Let me take care of these guys, then meet me, kind of casual like, in the back room, okay?"

"Okay . . ."

Everybody seemed to have secrets these days.

Which brought me around full circle again to Christopher Sloan. And I'm not sure why I decided what I did. Maybe I felt guilty for Marcus, in some strange way. He should be taking the kid places, like my pop did with me. Or maybe it was just that I wanted to do something like my pop did for me.

Then again, maybe both those explanations were too complicated—or too simple—and maybe I didn't need to make any goddamned explanations at all.

I carried my glass to the phone, stuck a quarter in, and called the War Memorial. I asked for the ticket office. "The Ice Capades," I said, feeling stupid and sentimental. "I'd like two tickets. One adult, one child, for Labor Day weekend. Best seats you've got." I held the cool glass against my still flushed cheek.

"Those tickets aren't on sale yet," the woman told me.

Swell. "When do they go on sale?"

"August first—but be sure and call early, they'll sell out fast."

August first? Three weeks from now? I'd never remember to do it; I was terrible that way. Becky Anderson was always trying to get me to use an appointment book, the way the upwardly mobile do. I personally think that it's lugging those heavy things everywhere that gives them early heart attacks.

I said to the woman at the ticket office, "Look, can't you just take the order now? That's several weeks away."

"No, ma'am. The booking's just been confirmed this week. The tickets aren't even made up yet."

I sighed. So much for my one good deed of the day. And just as well. Thinking of Becky Anderson reminded me I didn't have a job. How could I afford tickets to the Ice Capades?

I hung up just in time to see Harve slip into the back room. The two cops were in a booth, engaged in heated discussion, with full mugs of beer. The cable installers seemed happy enough watching Phil Donahue on TV. No one was at the bar. I sauntered as casually as possible after Harve.

The back room, though large, was not much more than a storeroom. The two kinds of sandwiches Harrigan's served were made up at the bar. Back here, there were cartons of bread and booze, a white oversized refrigerator, a desk piled high with manila file folders and scattered invoices. In the center of the storeroom was a round table that looked convenient for the weekly poker game or two.

Harve motioned me away from the door and stood with one hand on the knob, visibly agitated. He pushed at his glasses, leaving smudge marks, and began without preamble. "Look, Jesse, I'm no hero. The last few years I've been minding my own business, goin' to school, workin' here, staying out of trouble. What goes on, I don't see. The gambling, all that, it's run of the mill for a local bar like this—"

"Harve, I assumed all that. What the hell's wrong?"

He was opening the door as he talked, looking out, then closing it.

"The point is," he said, "there's no way I can go to the cops about this. For one thing, I don't even like cops. Cops live by rules, I hate rules. Cops ask too many questions, like where were you on the night of, and I hate questions."

"Okay."

"The other thing is, I can't trust any of the cops I might talk to about this. Not anymore."

"Meaning?"

"Meaning, cops are in on it."

"On *what*? For crying out loud, Harve—"

"The drugs, the porn, the kids—I wouldn't even say anything about the drugs, maybe, but when it's kids—I saw too damn much of kids being used like that in Nam, there's no way I'm gonna let it happen here and not try to do something about it. I thought maybe—maybe if something leaks, like, not to the cops, but to the papers—"

"Hold it." I pulled a chair out from the table and straddled it. "Start at the beginning. I won't tell any cops."

"Not even North," he insisted.

I felt a little jolt at the implication that I couldn't trust Grady, even though I'd been thinking the same thing myself recently. "No," I agreed. "Not even North." I drank my juice.

He pushed his glasses back, studied me a long moment, then nodded. "Okay. Listen. This is the way it goes down."

He told me the whole story, every now and then doing the nervous-making thing with the door.

It seemed there had been meetings going on here the last couple of months, regular meetings between Fournsey, the police commissioner, and Jake Wiley, the owner of

Harrigan's. There was also a third guy Harve didn't recognize, but who figured from the conversation to be a cop, and a fourth—someone who spoke with an accent.

The meetings were after hours, when the place was locked up. They would come in through the back door, arriving separately, leaving their cars somewhere else. At least, Harve had never seen one of them park at the curb, nor in the alley behind the bar.

Harve had never been asked to leave, either, during these meetings. He'd worked for Jake Wiley a long time and seen a lot of things, none of which he'd ever talked about until now.

His voice rattled faster, becoming more and more strained.

"After Nam, Jess, all this two-bit shit seemed pretty small potatoes. No way you're gonna be shocked by numbers running, payoffs, crap like that, once you've seen kids and old people with their faces blown to bits. Christ, you ever see little kids' eyeballs scattered around you on the ground? They pop, you know, there's not much holding them in—"

"Harve, please." I was holding the pulpy dregs of the orange juice, looking into them. My stomach did a flip-flop.

Harve seldom got like this anymore. They say when he first got home from the war, he was this way all the time. Guys came back with different problems; Harve was one moment normal, the next borderline nuts. Paranoid. Expecting land mines over every hill. At the same time, he was so smart it was scary—top of his engineering classes every time at R.I.T.

As he continued, he pushed at his glasses, then rubbed his hands on the bar apron he wore over his jeans.

"You've actually been back here when these meetings are going on?" I said.

"Nah, I'm out there cleaning up, but sound carries like crazy in this old place once it's closed up for the night. I've picked up things. Enough to know Fournsey's involved in running drugs through the city, and that they use these drugs to recruit little kids for those dirty movies and things."

Fournsey. He'd been police commissioner for years. Shit. "And Jake Wiley, your boss?"

He shrugged. "It's his place. The meetings are here. I don't think he's in charge of anything, though, at least I don't hear him talk much."

"Fournsey would be the one in charge."

"Him, and that other guy, the one with the accent."

"What does this man with the accent look like? You ever see him?"

"Just once, when I was taking trash out to the alley and he came out the back door. Kind of a small guy. Dark clothes, dark hair. But it was night, so I never really got a good look at his face."

The accent, the size . . . It sounded from the description as if he might be the man who'd sat behind the table talking to me at the abandoned house in Atlantic City. My impression was that he'd been small. And Ginny had said that Manny and Carlo usually worked for the drug people, out of Miami. If this was their boss—and he was coming up here for meetings—something big must be about to come down.

"What do they talk about?"

"In the beginning, it was figures, then more meetings. These people meet more than your average Bausch & Lomb VP. They discussed how the operation works. The drugs come up from Miami, then the mob distributes them around the city—to a main man first, who takes his cut, then moves them along to the porn producers and so on down to the lower levels—the photographers, directors, recruiters, like that. They got it worked out smoother than a baby's ass—" He broke off. "Sorry."

"This main man—you think he's the real boss?"

"Shhhh." He held up a hand as footsteps sounded, then squinted through the open crack of the door. His thin shoulders tightened, then relaxed. The door closed and he leaned against it, his face pale. "It's okay. Just one of the cops, gettin' a beer. Jake lets them do that sometimes."

"The real boss," I prompted.

"Yeah, yeah, well, see, from what I can figure, he's never been to a meeting. But he's local. He's the one who gets the drugs up here and deals them around."

"You've never caught a name?"

"Nothing I can remember."

I was thinking about what Manny—or Carlo, whichever—had said when I was hiding in the pantry at Atlantic City and the car outside was burning. *SAVE said not to hurt her, just scare her.* I'd begun to think of the word in caps—an organization, perhaps.

"How about the word SAVE?"

Harve thought a minute. "You know . . . now that you mention it . . . I remember the one guy, the one with the accent, using that word."

"What did he say?"

His angular face twisted as he tried to remember. A chapped-looking hand ran over his blaze of hair. Actually, I happened to know the hand wasn't chapped, and that it looked like that in any season. Back during those years after Nam when Harve was wandering the states, he'd nose-dived his Harley into a fuel tank in Nebraska. An accident—I think. His hair, which had been blond and straight until then, had grown out this fiery, kinky orange. His hands, which had automatically flown to protect his face as he landed in the resulting fire, had been scarred so badly the skin would never again be the same.

"I can't remember," he said finally.

"Did you get the impression SAVE was a man, or some kind of name for an organization?"

"I think I assumed they were talking about the people in charge of the operation around here. I don't know, Jess, I only picked up bits and pieces. Something about shipments coming to this person, or thing, called SAVE . . . a head honcho, him gettin' the biggest split . . . yeah, that's right. He's supposed to get the biggest share, they said, so it was a him."

A code name, then.

"Like I said," Harve went on, "this's been goin' on a long time, the meetings, I mean—the past couple of months. But now"—he took his glasses off and rubbed at them with his stained apron. It couldn't have done much good, and was probably a nervous tic. "Now, they got a big drug shipment coming in, and soon. This is why I decided to tell you, Jess. It's the biggest this city's ever seen, I hear. They're planning on using the drugs in a major move to recruit kids—not just street kids, you know, the runaways, like they do all the time, but in the movie theaters and malls, the pizza parlors—all the places kids hang out. And Fournsey's guaranteed the cops won't do anything to stop it."

I could well imagine. There would be millions in it—for everyone involved.

The question was, just how far did this rotten-apple-in-the-barrel effect trickle down through the Rochester P.D.?

To Grady North?

I didn't want to believe it. Setting up Marcus for a fall was one thing; dealing in drugs and porn another. But then, Grady's M.O. was that he always followed orders. And what about Jack Hoffman? His mysterious visit to Sloan's apartment?

Harve said, "I've got to get out there, Jess. Jake Wiley catches me in here talking to you—" He let it hang. "I just thought—well, they've got another meet set up here tonight . . ."

"Uh-huh. And you thought I might like to listen in. Be a bug on the wall."

"Something like that."

I saw no point in telling Harve I no longer had a job at the paper—nor a license to poke around.

"What time are they meeting tonight?" I asked.

"Midnight."

I unwrapped myself from the chair. "You got any place

private I can listen from? Or do I have to lurk over there behind the Smirnoff?"

He grinned, visibly relaxing for the first time. "You'll do it?"

I shrugged. "I'm not all that busy tonight."

He pointed with his head, off to the left. "The perfect place. The men's bathroom. On the other side of that wall."

"Behind that *Playboy* calendar?"

He actually blushed. "It's over a peephole."

"A peephole? To the *men's* bathroom?"

"Jake is an old pervert," he said.

Jeez. The people you thought you knew.

CHAPTER TWENTY-TWO

"Don't fall in," Abe muttered. It was actually a guttural grunt.

"Very funny," I muttered back.

I'd done a lot of things for a story in my relatively short career, but this was the first time I'd stood on a men's urinal, peeking in reverse direction through a peephole. Harve had cut a small hole in the calendar—large enough to see through, but small enough not to be easily noticed.

Miss July, on the other hand, might object. She was missing a tit.

Harve had also left the television on in the bar, to help cover our noise. We didn't have to worry about how to hear the conversation in the back room. Rack had planted a bug earlier in the evening, under the poker table. Abe and I each wore earphones that plugged into a tape recorder. It sat nestled on paper towels in a sink, revolving smoothly.

In the back room, sitting at the table, were three men: Donald Fournsey, Rochester's police commissioner, was one. The guy who had questioned me in the dark in Atlantic City was another. I'd had no doubt, after hearing him speak, that that was who he was. The third attendee was one of Rochester's finest: Jack Hoffman.

I had asked Harve: "Has that third guy been here before?"

He said, "Hoffman? Hell no, I know Jack like the back of my hand. I'd've told you."

Was Hoffman, then, the one the other two had talked about in meetings—the one who went by the code name,

SAVE? The main guy, who was handling the drug shipments to this area, and distributing the stuff down the line
to the porn people? Somehow, I couldn't see Fournsey
taking orders from Jack Hoffman. Surely there was someone
over them both. Someone closer to the mob.

The dialogue continued. The tape turned.

Atlantic City: "You eliminated the Sloan woman?"

Fournsey: "She had the list. She could have held us
up for it. And she knew about this shipment."

Atlantic City: "The delivery is set for tomorrow
night."

Hoffman: "Ten o'clock all right?"

"Yes. You have found a new meeting place? Where?"

Fournsey gave a description of Dwight Square, the
one down at Midtown where the bums hang out.

A.C.: "This is the largest shipment, ever, to the
Northeast area. A major portion of our organization is
involved. We would not have risked it without your
assurance. What about the reporter?"

Hoffman: "The James woman? The orders were to
frighten her off . . . not kill her."

A.C.: "I don't like it. The man is soft. He should get
rid of her once and for all, the same way he did the
Sloan woman."

He. I looked down at Abe. His eyes had narrowed. He
mouthed the word: *Andrelli.* I shook my head, but my
mouth went dry. They weren't talking about Paulie Gandolo. He'd never be accused of being soft. Especially not
about me.

Who, then? *Not Marcus. Please, not Marcus.* I'd almost
rather it were Grady than Marcus.

A.C.: "If anything goes wrong this time, there will
be no more shipments from my area."

Fournsey, hastily reassuring: "The appropriate people have been apprised."

I was still looking at Abe. He nodded. Cops. Cops would be looking the other way.

I had seen all I needed to see. I stepped down from the urinal, lowering myself wearily to the bathroom floor and leaning my back against the wall. Abe, moving lazily, eased down next to me.

I listened with growing disgust as they continued to talk. Figures, percentages. A corporate meeting, as Harve had said. A fucking market report. The abuse of children being columned in cold, painless digits.

I felt sick. I kept hearing, *Too soft . . . should have killed her, same as the Sloan woman.*

Was it Marcus, then? Tark had quoted Plato in saying that when a tyrant first appears, he is a protector.

Had Marcus slipped over the edge into that area where protection becomes tyranny?

It was easier to see Marcus going that way than Grady. Marcus was in the frame, so to speak, already. For Grady, it would take a giant leap.

The voices continued. The Atlantic City guy was talking, and my ears pricked up at the word *SAVE*.

"If he learns about the double cross," Fournsey said, "before we pull it off . . ."

Jack Hoffman: "Dead meat. We'll all be dead meat."

Atlantic City: "You are certain he knows nothing about our changing the time of delivery?"

Hoffman: "I told him it was at midnight tomorrow. We'll do the exchange at ten, and you can pocket the dough and be out of there before he knows what's up. Christ, I gotta pee."

Atlantic City: "And when he discovers he has been double-crossed?"

Hoffman snickered. "What's he gonna do? Run to the cops?"

Fournsey and Atlantic City went on with their recitation of figures.

"I gotta pee," Jack Hoffman said again. A chair slid back on the wooden floor.

I felt Abe's hand grip my arm, and with a jolt, I remembered. *Shit! There was no bathroom in the back room.* We'd never even given a thought to what might happen if somebody had to pee.

We stumbled to our feet. Abe grabbed the tape recorder from the sink. I tore off my headphones. The back room door opened and closed. I heard Harve's voice above the TV, but couldn't make it out. Hoffman's baritone answered. Heavy footsteps came our way. The doorknob turned.

We looked around wildly. Hide in a cubicle? Christ, how do they know, when they do that in the movies, which one the villain won't choose?

They let their feet show, dummy.

But Harrigan's was closed for the night. There wasn't supposed to be anyone here but Harve.

All this thought took place, on my part at least, in the split second before the door opened.

There was nowhere to hide.

"Wait!" Harve yelled from the outer bar. "No! You can't!"

Oh, God, he was panicking. The motion at the door ceased.

"You can't go in there!" Harve yelled, "I just mopped that floor!"

"Christ, man, fuck off. I gotta pee." The door began to open again. My muscles were so tight, I couldn't have moved if I'd wanted to.

I gave Abe a frantic look. But he was shaking his head. "Be cool," he whispered. *Let Harve work it out.*

He had more faith than me.

Harve was rattling on in a nervous, panicky voice. "The

plumbing's bad. Yeah, that's what happened, the toilet ran over and I had to mop the floor. It's still stopped up, you can't use it."

Jack said, "Man, I don't care if I have to pee in the *sink*. I'm gonna fuckin' pee."

You could practically hear him hopping around out there. The door moved inward again. Harve cried, "You better watch it, there's rats in there, all that water and shit!" I moved behind the door, ready to hit Jack if I had to so we could make a run for it. But Abe was motioning to the ceiling. It had been torn out at some time, and green fiberglass panels had been laid across the beams. One of the panels, over by the wall, was loose. Bare lights showed through a foot-wide crack.

Abe grabbed my arm and yanked me over there, pointing upward. I nodded. I jammed my foot in his cupped hands and he hoisted me onto his shoulders. I pushed against the loose panel. Harve gave a shriek. "Rats!" he cried. "I saw one, Jesus Christ, close that door!"

By that time I was through the panel and prone on a beam, grabbing the tape recorder and earphones Abe was handing me. He gave a jump and caught the beam next to mine, clearing the ceiling just as Jack Hoffman backed through the door muttering curses at Harve. "Crazy motherfucking jerk!"

Jack slammed the door behind him and made a beeline for the sink, muttering all the way. "*Rats.* No goddamned rats. Christ, that guy is screwed." I heard a zipper, and then the sound of peeing in the sink. Abe's face was only an inch or two from mine. He rolled his eyes. *The things I do . . .*

There had been no time to pull the panel back in place. Neither one of us was really hidden. All Jack had to do was look up to see Abe. I was above a panel, but between it and the lights, so my shadow would be clearly visible from below.

In the outer room, the TV began to blare. Harve had

MTV on, or something like it, and I could hear him rapping along—loudly:

"*So you think you wanta do it, babe, you wanta buy the store, well, look at all the things you got, you got a whole lot more . . . so you think you wanta do it babe, you wanta buy the store . . . well, you got a piece of me, babe, you got a whole lot more . . .*"

I wondered if he'd finally gone nuts.

The zip again, then Hoffman ran water in the sink. Abe, looking tense as hell, held a finger up. *One minute.* It'd be over. We could get out of there.

I nodded, and as I did, I guess my arm shifted. One of the earphones I'd propped under it slipped and fell through the crack of the fiberglass panel. It clattered onto the floor of the cubicle below. My heart clattered with it. I squinched my eyes and clutched the beam with both hands, trying stupidly to make myself invisible.

Abe said in a normal tone, "Fuck."

Hoffman turned the water off. For several seconds, I didn't hear him move. I gripped the beam so tight it was a wonder my knuckles didn't crack. My back suddenly cramped. I needed to move my legs to ease it, but couldn't. The pain kept getting worse.

The door of the cubicle below me opened. I dared to open one eye and look down. Hoffman was there, his blond head only a few feet from mine, squinting into the toilet. The earphones had bounced behind it. A wire stuck out from the shadow of the commode. All he had to do was move his head a couple inches, and look on the floor.

The bathroom door banged open. It smacked against the sink. Hoffman whirled around. Harve stood there with a mop.

"Shit, man, you ever gonna be done in here? I gotta go home, and I can't go until this floor's done! The morning crew would have my ass!"

Hoffman stood looking at him a moment, then shook his head.

"Crazy fucking jerk," he muttered.

He shoved past Harve, out the door.

Harve looked around. Then he looked up. He saw us. He grinned.

"Crazy fucking jerks," he said.

CHAPTER TWENTY-THREE

I was up all night, so wired I couldn't do anything but pace the floor. Abe had taken the tape to have copies made. He'd keep one copy in a vault somewhere that only he knew about (probably in some batcave beneath the sewers), and I'd get the other. The master would be mailed to Mrs. Binty, to be opened by the attorney general's office in the event of my death.

Which all sounds overly dramatic. But when you're actually in the middle of one of these things, the possibilities become all too real. So does the paranoia.

Abe dropped off my tape around noon. He looked well rested enough, which didn't fool me at all. Abe never sleeps in the middle of a scam. He swung out of a newly purchased white 'Vette, strutting up the walk in white pleated pants and corresponding shirt, whistling a happy tune. I heard Mrs. Binty call out cheerfully. She liked Abe, a lot. She liked his style. I didn't bother to tell her how he managed to afford all that style.

"Here it is, lady," he drawled, tossing me the package as he waltzed through my door. "You hear any ticking, it's only because this is one big bomb."

"Let's hope it doesn't go off in our faces."

We had talked after Harrigan's last night—Abe, Rack, Percy, and me—and we had our plans all lined up for Dwight Square tonight.

"The one thing that bothers me," I said, "is doing this alone." I poured both of us strong coffee. "Who'll believe us, first of all, even if we do manage to get pictures of the exchange? It's not like any of us are A Number One where the law's concerned. And Fournsey could always come up with some story to cover his ass—he and Hoffman could say they were in some kind of undercover sting to bust the delivery—"

"You think they might be, Jess?"

"*Fournsey?* I've never trusted him. He's a real jerk. And Hoffman, he's just a worker bee, he hasn't got the skill to pull off something like that. He'd have had to have been acting last night, and I just didn't see it."

"I agree." Abe drank the hot coffee in one gulp. "Good *druuugs*," he growled appreciatively.

"Another?"

"Keep it comin'. Gotta stay juiced."

"You didn't sleep at all?"

"Lady, when I finally sleep, you ain't gonna see this mean black hide for a week."

"Swell. We'll be in excellent shape tonight. I can just see us, tap dancing all over Dwight Square like some goddamn frenetic Gene Kelly movie."

"Cool, lady, be cool."

"And the other thing is—what the hell do we do when the meet tonight is over? Hold them at gunpoint? Make a citizen's arrest?"

"You worry too much. We'll play it by ear."

"I don't know. Why do I feel so damn vulnerable with this thing?" But I did know. It was because there was no one I could call for backup. Always before, there had been Grady North. Or Tark. Or Marcus.

I'd be glad when this was over with. It wasn't even a story anymore. Not primarily. It was the answer to a lot of questions in my life.

Abe and I talked awhile longer, but I didn't feel any easier when he left.

I finally decided that since I was an apostle—as I'd recently admitted to Tark—and not a genius, I needed to talk to someone in authority. Maybe not Divine Authority—but authority, nevertheless.

* * *

There were four boys still on the field at Carter Park. I hadn't been much in the mood to watch kids play ball, but I found myself relaxing. I began to feel good, watching Danny with the kids—in a way I'd never felt with either Marcus or Grady. It was an uncomplicated thing, and nice that way; the usual tensions weren't there.

A storm was brewing. A cool breeze swept across the park. I sat, knees drawn up to my chest, just watching. The game was over, and the remaining team players were messing around. The kid batting, a six-foot giant, hit one that would've been a homer in any major ball park in the world. It sailed like a meteor, aiming straight up toward a storm cloud. A spot of rain fell almost immediately. For a brief moment, I actually wondered if the ball had pierced the cloud.

"Isn't he great?" Danny said, joining me. He was grinning. "He'll go on to the majors after school."

"Don't you ever work as a cop anymore?"

He laughed. "The department gives me all kinds of time off in the summer, to run this league. You know, the older I get, the more I'd rather be here than hot in pursuit of the criminal element."

I had suspected this about Danny, after seeing him with Laura. It was obvious he loved kids. That was the main reason I'd decided to take him into my confidence. (Okay, okay, so I wanted to see him again. So what? Shut up.)

"Danny, we have to talk."

"What's up?"

"After they leave—"

Big drops of rain began to fall. As if they were made of sugar, the boys took off in all directions. Running. A real macho bunch.

"Hey, this equipment's gotta be put away!" Danny yelled.

One kid yelled back amiably, something like, "Later. See ya tomorrow."

Danny sighed, but he didn't look all that displeased. "Help me put this stuff in my Blazer, will you? Darn kids. They're all alike. Try and get a little work out of 'em . . ."

We lugged the equipment—gloves, bats, balls, towels, cooler—to the Blazer, and stuck it in the back, getting caught in the cloudburst ourselves.

"Give you a ride home?" Danny yelled over a clap of thunder.

"Sure." I scrambled into the front seat.

He climbed in too, and put his key in the ignition. I touched his arm. "Wait a minute, okay? I really need to talk to you."

He looked at me curiously, then settled back. "Okay, Munchkin."

I still didn't have the right words, even though I'd been thinking on the subject all night. I waffled. Asked him about Catherine, and Laura. He answered patiently. The rain beat down.

"You might as well spit it out," Danny said finally. He gave me one of those looks: *What in the world are you messed up in now?*

"This has to be confidential," I said. "Just between you and me."

"Does it have something to do with what we talked about the other night? Andrelli? Grady North?"

I nodded.

He shook his head. "I don't know, Jess. I can't promise."

"C'mon, Danny, I need your help."

"Why me?"

"You're the only one I trust."

He thought about it awhile. Took out his keys and tapped them on the steering wheel. Finally he said, "Tell me first. I'll keep it confidential if there's any way I can."

I told him what I'd seen and heard the night before, then reached into my tote. "I want to play the tape for you."

He slid it into the cassette and punched a button. The tape began, Fournsey's voice, then Hoffman's. Pulling up totals on all the kids they'd destroy. Danny's eyes were at first wide with surprise, then angry. He drummed the wheel.

When the tape was over, he sat silently. I didn't say anything. The tape played on without sound. Finally, Danny punched the eject button. The radio took over. His fist made a loud smack on the wheel.

"Hoffman," he said with disgust. "I've worked with him. But not lately. He's been different lately."

"He's not alone in it," I said.

"Fournsey? That doesn't surprise me at all."

"Danny . . . forget Fournsey. What about Grady North?"

"You don't really believe North's involved?"

"I don't want to."

"Well, there're other ways it could be. You said before that you thought he was trying to set Andrelli up. Maybe he got orders from Fournsey to set him up. Fournsey and his mob friends might want Andrelli out of action once and for all. Of course, North might not know why the commissioner wants Andrelli, but he'd have to follow orders."

"Blindly?"

"If he wants that promotion."

"I suppose that could be."

"Try this on. Maybe North isn't involved in this drug thing directly. But he's looking the other way. You know how easy it is to take payoffs, Jess. It's just money changing hands, and all the old cops did it. You think North's old man was lily-white? He owned half this town before he retired."

"Grady's *father*?" Jim North was the one person, aside from Grady himself, I'd have trusted with my life. My perceptions in the last few drinking years must really be screwed.

"Hell, Jess, it's always been that way—from the top down. You know how the crack houses manage to stay open, and the kiddie porn comes back every time. There have to be payoffs going on, and up high."

I was silent. Then: "There's a meet tonight, Danny."

"I know, I heard it on the tape."

"How about if we show up for it—you and me?"

"You mean, unofficially? Without telling the department? Hell, Jess—" He shook his head.

"Danny, *think*. Whom can we trust in the department now? If this starts with Fournsey, who knows how far it's trickled down?"

A long silence. I had known it was asking a lot. A cop could lose his career, turning on buddies. You never knew if you'd end up with a medal or a boot out the door.

Danny sighed. He reran the tape, listened, then fast forwarded to the appropriate part. Fournsey's voice came over, talking about Dwight Square. Then Hoffman got up to pee. The tape went dead. Danny pushed the eject again.

"They're probably meeting at the bandstand," he said. "By the children's playground. It's pretty torn down now, rotted away. Kids used to play there in the mornings, but it's full of port bottles and beer cans, piss and old newspapers now. A lot of drugs change hands there."

He drummed the wheel some more.

"I guess . . . I guess I could just go to the park . . . hang around. Unofficially."

I sighed and relaxed, leaning back against the headrest.

Danny reached behind me into the cooler and brought out a cream soda and a beer. He handed me the soda. He popped the beer.

"I'd rather have one of those," I said. I'm still not sure why.

He gave me a look, hesitated, then reached in back again.

The Genny felt good and cold in my hands. I savored it a moment.

"Something on your mind?" I asked as he watched me.

He shrugged. "Not a thing."

Everybody's an expert on alcoholism these days. You can't pick up a paper without reading how it doesn't help to criticize. How when drunks are ready, they quit, and there's not much point in saying anything, meanwhile.

I popped the Genny and took a deep, cool draught. Then I shivered.

Danny reached in back again for a towel, and threw it over my hair—rubbing it dry the way one does with a dog. I laughed, spilling a little beer, then came out from under and shook my hair free.

"Is this a perm?" he said, fingering the tangle of curls I hated.

"It's called Vidal SasStorm."

"I like it. Hair *should* curl when it's wet. It looks more natural that way."

"Hmmm. Daniel X. Greer, I do think you say the sweetest things."

We sat there drinking, the rain coming down in torrents. The radio played: the same station I'd had on all week. They were still doing the Janis Ian retro.

"God, do you remember that?" Danny began to sing along to "When the Party's Over," and I tapped the backs of my nails against the window, keeping time, my elbow propped on the arm rest. Sipping the beer, I began to hum. The tempo picked up, or maybe it didn't, really, but only seemed so because the rain was beating faster on the Blazer's roof.

When the song was over, we looked at each other, laughing. Danny's black hair was wet from the rain; he pushed it off his forehead.

"Imagine," he said reflectively, "that it's 1975. We're both juniors—"

"But I was a year behind you—"

"Never mind that, this is *my* fantasy. Sooo . . . we're both juniors, and we've been to a party—no, wait, to the prom. It's spring. This is a spring rain, the kind that opens the lilacs—" He glanced at me. "You love lilacs."

That gave me a start. "How did you know?"

"I told you, it's my fantasy—"

"No, but I do! I love lilacs—"

"That's what I said." His eyes twinkled. They were as

blue as Laura's—his child's—and I swallowed a lump in my throat.

"So, before the prom, I brought you a big bouquet—which, of course, I stole from old Mr. Lewis's backyard—you remember him?"

"Do I remember him? We used to sneak in his back door and up to his attic, Danny Tree and me, and drive him nuts. He thought he had squirrels, and he was always calling the exterminators—"

"You were one bad woman, Jesse James."

"I wasn't even a woman. I was thirteen years old at the time."

"I'm talking about the night we went to the prom. You were seventeen. I brought you these lilacs, and you broke a little piece off and stuck it in your hair—"

"And we danced and danced—but now the party's over, and we're sitting in your old Mustang—wasn't it a Mustang?"

He grinned and nodded.

"And we're sitting in it outside my house, with the rain coming down in buckets—"

"Your father is waiting up with the lights on—"

"My father—" I heard the tear come up from my throat before it actually appeared. I brushed at it automatically. I was getting used to this reaction when Pop's name was evoked and alcohol was running through my veins. The combination was deadly.

"Hey, what's wrong?" Danny said.

I shook my head.

"Tell me."

"Oh, it's just . . . my pop. He always did wait up. He was a drunk, you know."

"No, I didn't know."

"Really? I thought everybody at school was talking about it all the time."

"I don't think anybody knew."

"I can't believe that."

"Your pop," Danny said gently. "He's watching . . . what? Johnny Carson? Does he know we're out here?" He said it insistently, pulling me back into the fantasy. I was grateful.

"I don't think so. It's dark, and it's raining too hard to see. Or maybe he thinks we're waiting for the rain to let up—"

"So you won't ruin your dress."

"My prom dress, yes."

"It's a beautiful dress."

"You think so?" I smoothed my jeans as if they were a bouffant skirt. "My mom made it. She worked on it nights, after her job at the restaurant—"

He nodded. "There wasn't much money at my house, either."

"But none of that matters tonight. We're here, together in the rain, and we've just been crowned king and queen of the prom—"

"King and queen of the prom? I don't know . . . that's not in my fantasy," Danny said.

"Shut up. It's in mine." I'd never been to a prom.

"Well," Danny noted, laughing softly, "I think you should know your crown's crooked. Here, let me straighten it . . ."

He reached with both hands to my hair, pretending. I don't think he meant it to be more, it just grew. He stroked my hair, then his hands slid down to my face, one on each cheek. His lips followed. A light kiss on the nose that ended at my mouth.

For a long moment, I was seventeen again. The smell of a rough, adolescent boy—baseball sweat, clothes that were thrown on the floor after a game, then worn the next day without benefit of soap . . . hands that grope and cover the breast . . .

I broke away, shaking. "It's . . . it's been a great evening," I said, "a swell prom." But images of Catherine and Laura were clamoring in my brain. I reached with adolescent panic for the door. "I've got to go."

"Don't go," Danny murmured, drawing me back.

I resisted with more strength than I'd thought I had. "I have to. The rain's slowing down. Pop will be out here to see what's going on."

"Silly Munchkin. You don't have to do everything he says."

But I wasn't seventeen anymore, I was thirty-one. Going on a hundred.

"It's that kind of thinking that killed him," I replied.

CHAPTER TWENTY-FOUR

Walking home, the sky was like soup. Fish soup. Gray and oily.

Appropriate enough. It was a fine kettle of fish I'd gotten myself into this time. *A married man, for God's sake. By the time I hit thirty-five, I'll have run through every cliché.*

I did a lot of thinking about Marcus and Grady, too, about the way I'd screwed up over the years by trusting the wrong people. And how—no matter what the shrinks said—that had killed off Pop.

Time after time, I had done the wrong thing. How could I turn that around?

I pondered it all the way home. Finally, nearing Genesee Street, I thought: *With life—as with soup—when the pot starts to boil, it's time to skim the scum off the top.*

I stopped at the first pay phone and made one call, designed to do just that.

CHAPTER TWENTY-FIVE

It was a little after nine that night. We were in Dwight Square, surrounded by bums—the Three, Danny Greer, and me. The Three had gotten here early and were somewhere in the black night, their objective for now to keep the bums and any other would-be distractors away from the scene of our action. Danny was off somewhere, checking out the perimeters.

I huddled against broken latticework with my tape recorder, in a dark hollow formed by the steps and foundation of the bandstand. I had dressed in Mrs. Binty's old gardening clothes—nondescript and a little worn. They were huge and baggy, and I'd teased her once that they were bag lady clothes. I have no idea what she thought when I'd asked to borrow them. Sometimes, though, it occurs to me that my life would be a lot less rich without Mrs. B.

It was a noisy summer night. Hot and humid, not a breath of air. The kind of night when tempers flare. Sirens wailed almost constantly; the emergency rooms would be filling up. Dogs wailed, too. Through it all you could hear the voices of the homeless, scattered throughout the park. Not all bums—a large percentage just people down on their luck. Some had been down all their lives, some only since the last recession, or Nam. A few were temporarily broke, as distinguished from those without hope—the forever poor.

I'd done a series on the homeless, and it had won me an award. I always felt a little like I'd ripped those people off.

Squeezed them dry for their stories, while not really participating in their lives.

I'd learned that anyone who had been sleeping in the park awhile had a special place. Some would seek privacy —or fragile safety—beneath a bush or next to a rock. It was poor shelter. Others chose to lie out beneath the stars, although they seldom slept. There was always the fear of being knifed for that final tuppence, the buck that would buy cheap wine.

I'd interviewed people during the day, when it was reasonably safe. I should have slept at least one night in the park. I'd been too lazy—and too much in a hurry. I'd used my imagination, instead, to come up with all the little "details" that had ultimately been the reason for that award.

Some reporter. It had struck me more than once that even in adulthood I was scamming my way through life— the way I had as a fourteen-year-old child.

I wasn't much in a mood to analyze that right now. I'd stepped in a pile of pigeon shit while walking from Danny's Blazer, and was digging it out of the sole of my Nikes with a stick when I realized I was sitting in it too.

Terrific experience, I thought, *for next month when I become a bag lady because I still haven't got a job*.

Well, I'd have plenty of time to prepare for winter. I could check around for a nice warm refrigerator carton. A watch cap. And a pair of those natty gloves with the fingers cut out.

I'll have to learn to mutter.

No, I won't. I do that now.

This bandstand—which, as Danny had said, was a fairly common meeting place for the drug crowd—had been erected in the 1920s in what was then the center of the park. Since that time, half the park had been sold off, so that now the bandstand was at the edge, along a street that had itself seen better days. An occasional car or taxi ambled by. Aside from that, not much moved. There was no moon yet—it was still too low on the horizon—and no stars that

I could see from here. The city lights reflected back from the sky to provide a fraction of light. Across the street, the windows of the old Kodak warehouse were black holes.

I glanced at my watch, a glow-in-the-dark, what-hour-is-it-in-Italy affair that Tark had given me a year ago as a sobering-up present. The meet was scheduled for ten, almost an hour from now. I was restless, with too much time to think.

Funny how Pop kept creeping into my life after all these years. Five, was it now? Or six? I hadn't really killed him —that much I'd learned in therapy at St. Avery's, years after the fact. But he'd died on a mission of mercy, saving me from just one more screwup I'd gotten myself into. True, he'd been driving drunk at the time, and I hadn't known it when I asked him to pick me up. Although, if I'd been thinking of anyone but myself, I would have known it, because Pop was always drunk at night.

The wheel of guilt goes round and round.

Mom had kept it turning awhile, by blaming me too. It was grief; everyone had told me that at the time. And things were a little easier now. She had loosened up in a lot of ways, since moving to California. Or was it just that she could be herself, now that Pop was out of her life? Living with a drunk makes you fearful; you learn to monitor every thought, every move. You learn not to trust.

I wondered about tonight. Had I led Danny and the Three into some awful scenario that I'd regret the rest of my life? Not having learned enough from the past, was I destined to repeat it forever?

On television, the hero does this stakeout sort of thing all the time. In real life, with real blood and living skin, you think about things like how a gun can go off and puncture that skin, let pour that blood. It's a sobering thought.

I moved irritably, feeling the pigeon crap soak through Mrs. Binty's thin cotton gardening pants. I wondered where Danny was.

On the way here, I'd told him some things we hadn't

gotten to during that rainstorm earlier. How I'd been grabbed in Atlantic City, and how the guy on the tape with the accent was the one who'd questioned me there.

"Who do you think he meant, when he said *he's too soft*? That *he* should have gotten rid of me? I don't want to believe it's Marcus."

"Don't worry your head about that, Jess." There was a raw, clipped edge to Danny's voice, the kind cops get when they're gearing up for work. We turned into a side street near the park, and all conversation ended while Danny looked for the right place to park—one we could get out of easily, if things went wrong.

Now, as I squinted into the dark, a shadow moved, drawing away from a patch of shrubbery. Crawling. They had the guerrilla tactics down to a T. No one watching would've known they were there. Hell, *I* didn't know they were there.

Rack was only a couple feet away before I realized it was him. Behind him came Percy, belly along the ground, skin and flat-top Afro black as night without camouflage.

I had tightened up into my corner, hoping not to be seen by whoever it was. Fat chance. When kids grow up on the streets, they know and see everything. I was a mere amateur, a two-bit thief at fourteen, while they were dancing circles around every cop in town.

Percy took my hand, turned it palm up, and laid a heavy object on me. I saw a faint gleam of metal. It was cold. I nearly dropped it.

"I don't want this," I whispered.

"Take it. You might need it," Percy whispered back.

"No, I don't want it."

Rack hissed, "What's the matter, Jess?"

"I hate guns. Do you have any idea how many people I might kill with one of these things? I'd probably take out the whole damned park if I heard a twig snap."

"You don't give yourself credit."

"Just don't give me a gun." I dropped it on the ground.

"Cripes, be careful," Rack whispered.

"It's cool, the safety's on. I think," Percy observed.

"Give me a break," I groaned.

They settled in beside me.

"Where's Abe?"

Rack answered. "Keeping watch. Most of the residents are settled down for the night. Where's your friend the cop?"

"Off looking around. He thinks they won't actually make the exchange of drugs and money here. Fournsey and Jack Hoffman will show they've got the dough, then the guy from Atlantic City will take them to wherever the drugs are—probably the trunk of a nearby car. Danny thinks it'll pull up along here at some signal from Atlantic City. He's checking out the side streets, to see if he can spot the car standing by."

"He know we're here?" Percy said.

"I told you I wouldn't say anything. Don't worry."

Rack snickered. "Don't worry, she says. Us on a stakeout with a cop, and she says don't worry."

"Just stay out of sight, back us up. If nothing goes wrong, he won't ever know you're here. If it does, and you have to help out—shit, you'll be *heroes*."

"Uh-huh. *Heroes*." Sixteen years of knowing how it really works was poured into that one word.

"You want to back out? It's okay."

"Shit, no, you kiddin', Jess? Never worked with a cop before. It's a challenge, as they say."

"A challenge," Percy agreed lazily. He yawned. "Gotta get back. You sure you don't want one of us here with you?"

"No. Too much clutter. I'll record what I can, and when they leave to make the exchange, Danny and I will follow. Just make sure no helpful citizens get in our way."

"You got it."

He stuck the gun in his waistband, and he and Rack made their return crawl to the bush.

I checked my watch again. Twenty minutes. Danny should be getting back soon.

I thought it was him, in fact, when I heard a footfall. My

hand nearly stretched out of the darkness to motion to him.
A second more, and it would have.

"You check up there," Jack Hoffman's voice said, so close
it scared the shit out of me. "I'll look around down here."

"Aren't you being a bit overcautious?" Fournsey replied.

"Never hurts. He could have planted somebody to take
us out the minute the money's flashed."

Fournsey muttered something in return, but by this time
I was only half listening—poised for fight or flight. Hoffman
wouldn't be fooled by this dark corner. It'd be the first place
he'd look.

Why did I never think these things through?

Footsteps went up the stairs. Another set began to circle
the bandstand.

The latticework behind me gave as I scrunched against
it. I turned in panic, stuck my fingers through it, and gave
an experimental tug. It came away from its frame, leaving
an approximate foot to crawl through. It also gave a squeak.
Rusted nails.

"What was that?"

I think it was Fournsey who said it, but I wasted no time
wondering as I skittered through that opening and underneath the bandstand. With shaky fingers, I pulled the latticework back into place behind me, holding it tight.

A large shadow approached—a thickening of the darkness, really, since there was so little light. I tried not to
breathe. I heard Hoffman say only a couple of feet away,
"Someone's been here." I could nearly feel his breath. He
was kicking at the dirt, then bending, searching through it
with his fingers.

Fournsey said, "Bums, that's all. They sit here and drink
all the time."

"I don't know . . ."

Hoffman straightened, hesitated, then kicked at the latticework. My fingertips took the blow. I held on tight. If I
were to let go, he'd see the panel was loose. He'd investigate. He'd find me squatting here.

He kicked a few more times. It occurred to me that my teeth were chattering—enough, possibly, to be heard. Fournsey said from above, "Leave it alone. I think he's coming."

Hoffman grunted, kicked again, then moved away. I heard him go up the stairs. I jerked my tape recorder from Mrs. Binty's pocket and punched the RECORD button, shoving the mike through a hole in the crisscrossed panel.

At first, the only sound to record was of tiny little things with tiny running little feet. Maybe not so little. I shivered and looked around. It was black as pitch in here, but in raising a hand I found the ceiling was almost tall enough to stand. The floor of the shell was a good five feet off the ground. I stretched sideways and felt tough, wiry cobwebs. Ughhhh. The smell was musty, of old earth that hadn't been turned in years. Like a grave. I tried not to think about it, and then I almost screamed as something closed over my shoulder.

"It's me," Danny hissed in my ear.

Shit! I guess I just mouthed it, instinct overriding fear. *What the hell—*

I felt him point to the other side of the shell. He must have crawled in from there, just as I had from here. He put a finger to my lips, not that it was necessary. My throat was so dry I couldn't have spoken a word. His hand ran down to mine, where I held the tape recorder. He nodded and moved slightly away.

"You're late," I heard Hoffman say quietly. Then more footsteps on the stairs. Atlantic City answering: "He was suspicious. I had to make certain he did not follow."

The sound of their voices, though low, carried easily through the rotting floor.

"And did you . . . make certain?"

"Of course. He is otherwise engaged this evening. You brought the money?"

"Right here."

"I must take a count."

"Go ahead."

The sound of a briefcase being opened. Rubber bands being snapped, bills being riffled. It took several minutes.

Hoffman said, "Hurry it up, will you?"

"I have people to answer to. These things cannot be rushed."

Finally, the briefcase was closed.

"How do you plan to move the drugs without SAVE's connections?" Atlantic City said.

"Gandolo is taking over. Personally."

"You will have nothing but trouble. Paulie Gandolo is a sick man."

"Better than SAVE," Fournsey said. "He's too soft. We've had nothing but argument over this latest recruitment phase."

"A man who puts children before his wallet?" Atlantic City's tone was dry. "Such a man has no future."

Fournsey murmured an agreement.

"Let's get on with it," Hoffman urged. "He thinks this meet is at midnight. He could show early."

They came down the stairs, and their footsteps faded in the direction of the street. I snapped the recorder off and made a move toward the latticework panel. Danny put a delaying hand on my arm.

"You stay here. I'll go after them."

"No way."

"It might get rough out there."

"I don't care, I want to be in on it."

"Jess—" His tone was impatient.

My hand was back on the panel. "Not a chance."

I didn't wait to see what he'd do. I pushed the panel open and began to slide through. He could have stopped me, but I'd have given him a fight, and he knew it. A tussle like that could blow everything.

We moved quietly through the shrubs between us and the street. Headlights drifted across the darkness, and the silhouettes of Fournsey, Hoffman, and Atlantic City were

clear at the curb. A dark, late model car pulled up. The
driver cut the engine and lights, and stepped out.

The nearest streetlights were at either corner, and we
were midway along the street. Still, there was enough il-
lumination to see that the driver was the big guy, the one
who'd come for me in the cellar in Atlantic City and chased
me through the house afterward. Manny, Ginny had told
me. He stood next to the car, keeping watch, while Atlantic
City opened the trunk. A small inside bulb came on.

There was some discussion as Fournsey and Hoffman
checked the contents out. Hoffman seemed in charge of
this. Fournsey just kind of stood by. Finally, Jack straightened and nodded.

"It's good," he said.

I turned to Danny. "Let's go," I whispered.

He had already drawn his gun. Gripping it with both
hands, he motioned for me to stay back. I followed anyway.
We stepped out from the trees and were eight feet from
the car.

"Good evening, gentlemen," Danny said.

Atlantic City and Fournsey whirled in our direction. The
big guy began to reach inside his shirt.

Danny, feet spread and gun firmly leveled, said coldly,
"Don't even think it."

The guy dropped his hand.

"Over here." Danny gestured with his head for Fournsey
and Atlantic City to move toward the front of the car. "You
too, Hoffman." Hoffman had begun moving backward into
the dark, but he stopped, shrugged, and joined the others.

We approached the trunk. "Well, now, looky what we
have here." Danny smacked his lips. There were drugs of
every shape and color. Loose bags, hard blocks. Pills. Pot.
Stuff I didn't even recognize.

"And you were going off without sharing?" Danny said
with a *tsk*ing sound. "That doesn't seem quite fair."

The briefcase of money rested on the pile of drugs. He
reached for it. "I'll just relieve you folks of this."

Atlantic City answered. "You won't get far. My people will track you down."

"C'mon, Jess. Let's go." Danny motioned with the gun in the direction of the parked Blazer.

I looked at the drugs and said, "I don't understand. Shouldn't we get some help—call somebody to pick all this up?"

A message passed from Atlantic City to Danny Greer. "Ah . . ." the man with the accent said. "She doesn't know."

Danny said again quietly, "Let's just go, Jess."

"Tell her, Save," Atlantic City said.

"Save?" I repeated it dumbly.

Danny's eyes closed briefly. It was like a light going out. His voice had that raw edge again. "I can't exactly call the cops, Jess."

"Why not?"

"Jess . . . little Jess." His tone was sad, a bit weary. He pushed me gently toward the other three. The gun was now pointed at all of us.

"Funny," he said, "I thought sure you'd catch on after you thought about that tape. I guess you don't remember." He flashed me a quick, nervous grin. *I know it's a bitch, but this is the way it is. What can I say?*

That's when it all came flooding back . . . the drama club in high school . . . Danny as the Music Man, playing the title role: the charming con who weaved his web of lies around everyone in town.

But not just a role. Danny himself was always the con, the scammer, the actor . . . Daniel X. Greer. Like on the trophies in his living room, Daniel Xavier Greer. "Xave" the guys had called him then. The guys on the team, not the girls. He was always Danny Boy to us.

How could I have forgotten?

SAVE said not to hurt her, just scare her.

Not SAVE—but Xave.

"Jess?"

Well, the truth was I hadn't exactly forgotten. It was one

of those things that you sweep under the carpet so it won't lie there looking ugly during the party.

"Over there, Jess."

I backed up until I was against the car. My feet tripped over themselves, and I stumbled. I braced myself against the open trunk lid.

"That's better," Danny said. "Now, I'll just take this money—which was supposed to be mine anyway, seeing as how I'd planned to double-cross you boys just the way you did me tonight—and then I'll be on my way—"

I reached with both hands and slammed the trunk lid on his arm. Danny yelped and jumped back, but his other hand, with the gun, came smoothly up to my level. For one horrible moment I saw his finger tighten on the trigger. Suddenly, it was as if daylight had broken. Floodlights lit the entire area where we stood.

"Drop it." The order came from the shadows of the Kodak warehouse.

Danny pivoted slowly to face the figure that stepped out of the dark behind him.

"I'm sure you'd prefer we handle this quietly," Grady North said. "Just drop the gun." Several police cruisers slid into position at either side of us. There were no sirens, no red and blue lights.

As Grady stepped closer, I saw he was carrying an automatic weapon, one of the big ones. Danny's Police Special was no match. He hesitated a moment, then dropped it.

Other figures moved in. Cops. All kinds of cops, carrying weapons. Jesus Christ, the whole fuckin' department, it seemed, was there.

I watched the procedure silently. There were searches, then, at some point, handcuffs. Everything was done in an orderly, matter-of-fact manner, it seemed—the well-oiled machinery of law doing its job. I remember at some point thinking that I was a reporter; I should take notes. But I didn't have any paper, and I wouldn't have used it anyway.

The commissioner, Danny, and Atlantic City were read

their rights. Hoffman, however, joined Grady North. "Perfect timing," he said, clapping Grady on the back. "Congratulations."

"Thanks," Grady answered. "I thought it went well."

"Feels good, after dealing with this scum all these months, to see the Department win one."

"You did an excellent job, Hoffman. We owe you."

I watched, feeling jaded and weary, as Jack hefted his belt over his paunch. He rubbed the back of one hand over his forehead. "Hell, I'm just glad it's over."

Grady turned to me then. "Jess." He smiled. Putting an arm around my shoulders, he gave me a squeeze. "We have Jess to thank, too," he said. "If she hadn't called me, and then seen this thing through . . ."

I removed his arm and stepped back. I felt sick, and tried not to meet Danny's incredulous eyes, but failed.

"Jess? You set me up?"

I couldn't answer. There was nothing to do now but walk away. I did not owe Danny Greer a thing. That's what I kept telling myself, anyway, and with every step that took me deeper into the park, I believed it more than with the one before.

"Jess?"

Oh, hell. I halted a moment, and finally I went back to face him—hands in my pockets so no one would see how they shook.

"How did you know?" Danny's voice and eyes were hollow. He'd been so sure of me—

I cleared my throat. "I didn't know, Danny. Not for sure. I just kept thinking, after our talk in the Blazer—when we were fantasizing about the prom—" It was awful, saying it in front of all these people, but it had to be done, the book had to be closed. I'd been reading in braille for too long—feeling, not seeing. *Poor Laura. What had I done to Laura?*

I plunged ahead, trying to get it over with. "I kept thinking how much we're alike. How you were always a con . . .

a pretender, like me. And I couldn't believe what you said about Jim North, Grady's father, being crooked all those years." I was having a hard time keeping my voice steady. "On the other hand, you'd been Jack Hoffman's partner. And I *did* believe he had gone bad."

There were things I'd missed, though. "I never did catch the SAVE/Xave thing. I guess I'm slow."

"But you actually told North about tonight?"

One of the young cops had begun to handcuff him, but stopped to listen curiously as his former fellow officer shook his head in disbelief.

I wiped moisture from my cheek. "It was too big . . . too big a deal," I stammered. "If I'd screwed it up—"

"I don't understand. You thought North was crooked! You told me . . ."

"I knew *somebody* was crooked, and I thought it was somebody in the department, somebody besides Hoffman. If it had turned out to be Grady . . . I . . . I had another backup." I glanced behind me and caught a glimpse of the Three. They faded into the park as all eyes shifted that way.

"I can't believe . . ."

I was incredibly tired. I passed a hand over my eyes, wanting, more than anything, a drink. "One thing about kids of alcoholics, Danny. They learn not to trust. Or they trust the wrong people—over and over. Sometimes I hate that side of myself."

I couldn't stand there any longer. I said to Grady, "I'll meet you at the station later, okay?"

"Don't be long. I'll need a full report."

I nodded and turned away. The only thing I could think about at that point was that I had something to do before I could even begin to put all this behind me. I had to go by and see Catherine and Laura Greer. I had to tell them about Danny—and how I'd destroyed their lives.

Otherwise, I'd always be waiting for them to come to me.

But the ordeal here wasn't over.

A late-arriving police car had been winding its way through the others. It came to an abrupt halt at the curb, and from it stepped a ghost. I stared.

Barbara Sloan.

She was dressed in jeans, a red shirt, and running shoes. Her blond hair was pulled back in a simple ponytail. She cast a look about the crowd, then lit out after Fournsey and Atlantic City, her eyes blazing. "You scum! How could you damage little *children* that way!"

Fournsey tried to back off. Danny, next to me, took it all in with an astonished look, and then an admiring grin.

"Goddamn," he breathed. "She's been working with the Department! What a sting!"

But Babs was still screaming about children. "Murderers! Don't you know what porn *does* to children?" Cops were grabbing at her, trying to hold her back as she tore into Fournsey, 120 pounds or so of rage behind her swinging fists.

And above the fray, suddenly, there were other shouts. "CHILDREN! WHERE ARE THE CHILDREN?"

We all whirled toward the apparition that stumbled from the park, into the headlights' glare.

"WHERE ARE THE CHILDREN?" it screamed.

It was Howard, the ex-schoolteacher, now bum. His lice-ridden hair was long and matted, his eyes wild. He screamed again: "WHERE DO THEY *GO*?"

Christ, the whole thing was coming apart. Howard was looking for long-lost children. Barbara Sloan was alive.

The cops were staring, distracted.

And Danny, the ultimate opportunist, took the moment and ran with it. In the next instant, he had me around the neck, pulling me back against him.

Grady swung around, his gun leveled. "Don't do it, Greer!"

"Too late." Danny laughed. "Jess and me, we're leavin'."

Grady's face was frightening. "You don't want to do this," he said. "Think, Greer. How far can you get?"

"With a hostage? As far as I have to. Now, drop it. And

give the order to them—" He nodded toward the surrounding contingent of cops.

"This is insane," Grady said harshly as he lowered his weapon. "Can't you see that?"

Danny's answer came swiftly. Before I could move, there were cold steel handcuffs around my wrists.

"We're taking a little ride, Munchkin. Say bye-bye."

CHAPTER TWENTY-SIX

Danny's hands made fists on the steering wheel. His eyes were fixed straight ahead. A few drops of blood stood out on the back of his right hand, where I'd hit him with the lid of A.C.'s trunk.

"Where are we going?" I asked. I thought I knew. We had been heading north on back roads for the past ten minutes. The moon was high now and full, but clouds skidded, pumped along by a fresh, stiff breeze off Irondequoit Bay.

Danny confirmed our destination. "Andrelli always keeps cash on hand."

"How do you know?" There was only one answer. He and Marcus were pals.

"We'll just drop by for a little visit," he said. "Pick up my pay. I'll bet he'll even give me a bonus."

"A bonus?

"For bringing you."

I sat sort of sideways, watching him as he drove. The position was a little awkward, since my hands were cuffed to something metal behind me, alongside the seat. My feet weren't tied, but there wasn't much I could do with them. Kicking Danny would only result in our going off the road.

I guessed the prom was over.

"You're bound to be caught," I said. "Where can a man with a wife and child run?"

"Nowhere. That's why I've got to leave them with some cash."

"You're leaving them."

"You got it."

"Just like that?"

"I can't stay here, Jess. I can't have Laura living every day of her life knowing her father's in jail. It'd cloud everything for her."

"There's not much you can do now that won't cloud everything for her."

Our windows were down, and cool night air sucked along my neck, whipping my hair as Danny's foot pressed the gas pedal.

"I can leave the country, go where there's no extradition. Sure, there'll be talk for a while, but people forget that kind of thing. Out of sight, out of mind. Not like having a father in jail. That's something the press never forgets, you should know that, Jess. They interview prisoners all the time. And when I came up for parole, it'd be a circus all over again. You know I'm right."

I didn't answer.

"I can't do that to Laura," he said.

"You'd give up seeing her, ever again, for the rest of your life? To make things easier for her?"

"I don't see what choice I've got now."

"What about Catherine? Does she know what you've been doing?"

He laughed gently. "Catherine. You wouldn't believe what she was like. Catherine was everything I ever wanted when I was growing up down on Dutton Street. I couldn't believe my luck when she went out with me in high school. I've always known I'd have to run to keep up with her."

"That's the reason you did all this? For Catherine?"

He looked surprised. "Oh, hell, no . . . I didn't mean to make it sound like that. And she doesn't know anything. Shit, Catherine's been great. She's had to put up with a lot—Laura's accident, and me being gone so much—and Catherine's even wanted to go to the support group they've got for cops' wives downtown . . . I had to tell her I didn't think she should, for now . . . the trouble being, there was no tellin' what she might say."

His voice had taken on a lilt, and was distant. Reasoning.

"What might she say, Danny? What could she possibly give away?"

"Well, you never know. Things they could use against me. It's harder to get proof against an undercover cop than almost anybody. If they see us with one of the mob, or a drug connection, we can always say we were working him—getting information out of him—like that. So they try everything."

I remembered Grady telling me once: There's no one more dangerous, or with less morals, than a cop who's gone bad.

But even the tough old pines along the road here were bent under the advancing winds off the bay. Anything . . . anyone . . . can warp, given enough distress. There was still time—

"Why don't you just turn yourself in? The D.A. would probably do a deal, give you a lesser sentence for turning state's witness. You could do your time, get out and get a job—"

Danny laughed. He licked at the blood on the back of his hand. "*Get a job?* You don't see it, do you, Jess? Funny, I thought you might. I remember that kid who used to boost cars in grammar school—well, I didn't know you then, not until you were older. But you were kind of a hero, or anti-hero, whatever you call it, with some of the kids who did. I didn't know you'd become all that straight."

"I was just a dumb kid, Danny. And I didn't make any bucks off that shit. We drove cars around, then dumped them. It was the thrill." Most of the time, anyway. We did heist a few.

"Still, the principle's the same. 'Up yours' to the establishment—"

"That was a long time ago."

But Danny had a point. I still had an 'up yours' attitude. If I thought I could get away with it, in fact, I'd probably steal right now instead of working for a living. One of the

joys that growing up takes from you is that it teaches you
not to steal.

"The principle doesn't change, Jess. No matter how hard
you work at a job, there's never quite enough. And there's
always somebody out there waiting to take it from you. The
insurance companies, the real estate sharks . . . People
have to think for themselves these days, make sure they
get their share, one way or another."

"That doesn't sound like you, Danny. What happened?"

"*Laura*," he said fiercely, jamming his foot on the gas
pedal. The Blazer leapt ahead. "Laura happened."

"The accident?"

Despite the cooling winds, sweat had popped out on his
forehead. "They don't *give* you the things you need, Jess.
Hell, no. The medical business? It's just that—a business.
There are kids dyin' every day because their parents can't
afford to buy organs or pay for operations." His expression,
in the dashboard's glow, became grim. We careened around
a curve.

I thought again about the stress cops go through. Had
Laura's accident been just too much, on top of nine or ten
years on the force?

"So you did it all for Laura."

His eyes crinkled momentarily. "That little girl . . . she's
been the brightest star in my life. Every ounce of real joy
I've had in the last ten years has come from Laura. And
every needle of pain. Jess, there are so many things I want
to do for that little girl. And all of them cost money. Too
many of them already have. Special training, private nurses
in the beginning. Special learning equipment. Books. Sure,
we've got free rent at the house—but Catherine's parents
can't help with cash. The reason they moved to Florida was
to save money. They didn't want to sell the house, and all
they've got is his pension now, that and Social Security."

He swerved as a cat ran across the road. The headlights
picked up trees, a road sign. We were nearing the cutoff
to the cabin. Danny slowed down.

"Take flowers," he went on reasonably. "Laura likes flowers. I make sure she has them, even in the winter. Good music. All the sensory things. And I want her to go to the best schools in the country for the blind, then on to a great university. I want her to have every chance in the world."

"Don't you think she'd rather have a father who's not disgraced and in jail?"

"That wasn't supposed to happen," he snapped. "Now that it has, I'll just have to change my plans a mite."

We rode in silence for a while. Finally, I said, "You and Marcus . . . you've been together in this thing all along? The drugs and porn?"

He chuckled. "Lover boy. I really got you going on that one, huh?"

I looked away. "Never mind."

"Ah, Jess. I didn't mean it. Okay, okay—look, I'll give it to you straight. I just wanted you to *think* he was doin' it, at least for a while. Keep you from knowin' what was really goin' on. Andrelli's just been paying me for information. I was already doing the same for Paulie, so I figured, why not? Then I began crossing the information, all three ways. I'd tell Paulie what was going on with Marcus, plus tell him who the cops were getting ready to move on in his organization, that kind of thing. And I'd tell Marcus what Paulie was doin', plus the cops—get it? And the cops—I was supposed to be undercover, gettin' information for them about Paulie *and* Marcus—but I'd just give them whatever I wanted. Sometimes what I gave them was true, sometimes it wasn't. I had it worked out real well—until your pal Tark showed up."

"*Tark?*"

"Yeah . . . now that is one big guy . . . in more ways than one. You gotta respect him, no matter what else. See, first off, he's at Paulie Gandolo's house one night, seein' Bernadette, Paulie's sister, and I'm there—and he overhears me talking to Paulie. Here I'm supposed to be gettin' information for Andrelli, his boss, and Tark finds out I'm double-dealing—givin' stuff about Marcus to Paulie.

"Shit, my ass was all but fried. I've got this drug deal tonight set up, and it's the last one, 'cause I can't go along with the things they're plannin' to do to kids, not anymore—and if Tark tells either Paulie or Andrelli I'm double-dealing them, I'm dead meat.

"So . . . I take Bernadette on a little trip that night. I hide her away. And I tell Tark if he says anything to any-body, Bernadette is dead." He laughed. "You ever see two hundred fifty pounds of tough guy turned into Jell-O in three seconds flat? That old boy didn't know where to turn."

I could imagine the rage that must have consumed Tark at his helplessness.

"Then Paulie, who thinks Bernadette is away at the shore—'cause that's the note I made her write—wants me to take the Sloan lady out. He's found out Sloan has the list of his drug contacts, and he doesn't know what she's gonna do with it, but he's willing to pay me a lot of dough to take her out. And even with this big drug deal, I need all I can get, 'cause I know I can't go much longer this way.

"But I can't get mixed up in killing the Sloan woman, either, and maybe get caught by one of Marcus Andrelli's goons and shot myself—or even worse, get hauled off to jail. Not with this deal tonight.

"So I says to Tark, 'There's one other thing, you wanta keep Bernadette alive. You gotta do this job for me, you gotta kill Barbara Sloan.

"And he does it, see? He offs her on the boat. Least-wise, I think he does, only from what we just saw back there, the cops have Sloan alive—either she's working with them, or she's turned state's witness. I still can't figure how they worked that one out.

"So anyway, Tark doesn't really do it, I guess. Then, right after he fakes the Sloan woman's death, Tark finds the warehouse where I'm keeping Bernadette, and he gets her out of there. And the two of them, they disappear."

The way he was gesturing as he drove, it was like Danny had slipped into a role. He probably had.

"Would you have killed Bernadette?"

"Hell, Jess, I'd like to say no—but I really don't know. I'll tell you this, she was better off away from Paulie's house. He was hurting her, bad. I just kept her cooling her heels a while."

We turned up the long drive leading to Marcus's cabin. Danny's turn was so sharp and so abrupt, my head banged back against the door frame. He didn't notice.

"So you see, Munchkin, how these last few weeks, they've been a little hot for me, and that's nothin' to do with the weather, believe you me. Only thing I can't figure out is why old Tark hasn't shown up or said anything to anybody yet." His eyes scrunched up in a frown.

"How do you know he hasn't?"

He gave a snort. "You think I'd be walkin' around like this, if he had? Hell, I'd be strung up somewhere by my thumbs. I never did kid myself I'm a match for that guy."

"I've seen him," I said.

"*Yeah?* Where?"

I shook my head. I wondered, too, why Tark was still hiding out with Bernadette. "I guess keeping Bernadette safe is the most important thing to him."

"Yeah. Who would have thought it—a big guy like him —turned all around by a girl?"

"The way you were turned around by Laura."

"Hmmm." He gave a bitter laugh. "Well, it doesn't matter now. I'm through."

"Are you going to kill me, Danny?"

"Not unless I have to." He looked at me sadly. "I always did have a little crush on you."

How many teenage years had I yearned to hear that?

"I just don't think it'll help you much now," he said.

CHAPTER TWENTY-SEVEN

A night man, not Lew or anyone I knew, was at the gatehouse to Marcus's cabin. Danny said hello, exchanged a few words of conversation with him like he'd done it often before, and we were passed on through. The Blazer's tires came to a jolting halt on the gravel drive. Danny reached into the glove compartment, took out a gun, then got out and came around to my side. He unlocked my handcuffs and pulled me out of the car. I stumbled ahead of him, my legs numb, along the pine-needled path to the cabin. The lights, it seemed, were on in every room.

Marcus answered the door himself. His eyes flicked to Danny, then me.

Danny pushed me through the door, almost into Marcus's arms.

"Yo, boss. I brought you a friend." He stepped inside cautiously, moved a few feet away, and quickly surveyed the room. It was empty, except for the three of us. An open book lay face down on one of the white sofas. A coffee cup rested beside it.

Backing up, the gun never wavering but pointed our way, Danny went quickly up the stairs that curved to a balcony bedroom. A lamp was on, its light striking the open beams and illuminating the platform bed, dresser, a comfortable chair that faced outward at a room-length window overlooking trees. Apparently satisfied that no one was there, he ran back down and crossed the living room to glance inside the L-shaped kitchen.

"Nobody here?" Danny said. "No bodyguards? Security? Doesn't look right. Where's everybody hiding, boss?"

"I didn't know I'd need anyone tonight," Marcus answered reasonably. He folded his arms. "What's going on, Danny?"

"Well, now, it seems we've got a little problem here. You've got something I need—money—and I've got something you want—our own little Jess."

Marcus continued to watch Danny, but he said quietly to me, "Has he hurt you, Jess?"

It didn't seem like much. His manner was calm, controlled. But the small white scar below his left eye throbbed.

"Not anywhere you'd notice," I replied.

He nodded. He leaned back against the arm of one of the sofas. "How much, Danny?"

"All the cash you've got."

Marcus appeared thoughtful. "The safe is in the barn," he said. "I'll take you there."

"Oh, now, don't shit me, boss. Why would you keep your money down there? You hoping for a chance to jump me on the way?"

"Tell him, Jess."

I hesitated, looked at Marcus, then nodded. "It's there. When we were working on the Whaler last year, I saw it. It's built into the ground beneath a pile of lumber that never gets used, never goes anywhere. It's on a hinged platform that swings up."

I was telling the truth, and my tone must have been convincing.

Danny said, "Okay. Let's take a walk." He closed the distance to me in three strides, took my arm, and twitched the gun toward the still open door.

Marcus didn't move. "Leave Jess here," he said.

Danny shoved the gun barrel into the back of my neck, making me stumble forward. "Jess comes along. Little Jess and me, we're close companions tonight." Marcus started for him, then heard the safety click and stopped. He backed off, his fists clenching.

"Now that we have that all settled," Danny said evenly, "move."

He shoved me ahead of Marcus, and signaled for him to follow. I glanced at Marcus as we passed through the door, and saw an eyebrow lift. A message of sorts. We followed the dark path, with the crickets and strange night animals hooting and chirping around us.

At the barn, Marcus stepped inside and snapped on the lights. Danny and I followed.

The Whaler's hull gleamed with its first white undercoat of paint. A smell of turpentine and oils lingered. Something scurried; one of the tiny forest animals that made its bed in here regularly at night. Danny started—then, at the sight of a flying brown tail, he gave an uneasy laugh. He herded us forward to an open space between the Whaler and workbench.

"Just stand over there. Nice and quiet like, while I check things out."

There were a lot of places where someone could hide. Inside the Whaler, for one. Or up under the eaves, where Marcus used to sleep when he first moved out here to build the cabin and work on the boat. Danny was visibly nervous with all the dark corners, with the creakings and groanings, the *wuzz* and *brrr* of insects and other creatures. He was out of his element here, a kid from the streets.

Marcus and I glanced at each other. The rest of the message passed. Grady had said once that Marcus and I worked in synchronization, like twins. Perhaps it was true.

Perhaps not. I couldn't be certain I'd gotten it right this time.

Danny seemed to realize, finally, that he couldn't search everywhere and still keep us within range. He came back, grabbing me by the arm and shoving me across the room with the gun. Marcus stood relaxed, hands on hips, and didn't move to stop him.

"Show me, Jess," Danny said.

We were at the wall where the lumber was stacked. Some of it—the pine and fir for the interior of the cabin—was still several feet high. The outer lumber was nearly gone. Marcus had been working like a madman out here since Tark disappeared. The Whaler was nearing its finish.

I turned and pointed to a neat stack of one-by-fours next to the workbench.

"Is there a switch? How do you move it?"

I pushed a button over the workbench, and the entire platform of lumber slid up, groaning, like an elevator on a metal vertical frame. It stopped about waist-high to me. A round metal safe was exposed in the sawdust and dirt below.

"Fuckin' fa-a-an-tastic," Danny said. "Open it."

"I don't know the combination."

"Christ." He grabbed hold of me, pulling me back. "Okay, boss, you get over here and open it up. And while you're doing that, I'll take care of our Jess here—just to make sure your priorities, like they say, are in order."

Marcus crossed to the safe, squatted before it in the sawdust, and turned the cylinder dial. I heard it ticking. The Whaler creaked on its platform. The insects *brrrred*. Other than that, it was so silent, you could almost hear the paint on the Whaler drying.

Marcus spun the dial left, then right, then left and left again. I had lied; I knew the combination by heart. He'd taught it to me—just in case. In case of what? I'd always wondered.

He pulled up on the handle, and the safe was open. Inside were tons of money. At least, it looked like that to me. I'd never seen more than a few hundred dollars cash at one time in my life.

"Now, start bringing it out, nice and easy," Danny said. His grip on my arm was firm, the gun barrel cold at my neck.

Marcus did as he was told.

Danny glanced around. "You got some kind of bag here? A trash bag or something?"

Marcus nodded. He glanced briefly at me. Then he reached into the box beneath the workbench. I slumped.

"God, I feel . . . faint."

Danny's grip loosened only a moment, but in that moment, Marcus straightened and swung our way with the propane torch. He punched it on. Flame automatically shot from its tube.

Danny gave a grunt of surprise, loosened his hold further, and I wrenched myself from his grasp. A second later I was on the ground.

Danny howled. I rolled back to see that Marcus had singed Danny's hand with the torch. The gun dropped to the barn floor. I scrambled to my feet. Danny backed up as Marcus advanced with the torch. He grabbed a hammer from the tools on the wall and swung. Marcus dodged. He shoved the flame at Danny's face. Danny yelled and dove for Marcus's legs, knocking him down. Marcus dropped the torch.

They rolled together, grunting, Marcus on top, then Danny. Marcus had the advantage, being taller and more muscular, but Danny had a wiry strength. Marcus grabbed Danny's head and began ramming it into the ground. Danny's fingers went straight out, punching at his throat. He connected. Marcus fell back, and Danny was on his feet. Marcus moved fast, lunging at him. He took him down. Danny groaned. His head hit the corner of the workbench. He slumped—unconscious—or so it seemed.

But Danny Greer, the actor, appeared insensible only until Marcus loosened his hold. Then he was on his feet, like a cat, shoving Marcus backward into the wall. An ax fell, slicing into Marcus's shoulder. Blood spurted. I screamed.

Danny moved in, going for Marcus's throat.

Marcus yelled, "Jess! The torch!"

It had fallen in dry sawdust, and flames were eating a path to the Whaler.

In the second or two that the fire claimed Marcus's attention, Danny grabbed him by the throat. Marcus, blood still pouring from his shoulder, weakened. His face turned dark. They struggled. I grabbed the propane torch and pointed it at Danny's back. He yelled and jerked away.

The fire attacked the Whaler's newly painted timber. As it ate, it gained strength. In the meantime, flames were spreading in the opposite direction to piles of old straw. I watched in horror as they flowered, then roared up a dry wall to the ceiling beams. The entire barn, within moments, was bathed in red. Sparks flew. The heat was intense. I panicked, my heart racing, throat beating. I couldn't breathe. A huge chunk of burning rafter fell at my feet. Flames lapped at the cuff of my jeans. I looked around frantically, my eyes tearing from the smoke. Danny was nowhere in sight, and Marcus—

God, where was he?

"Marcus!"

I saw him then, trying to lift a girder that had fallen across our path to the door. More timber fell, and he was enveloped, it seemed, by the blaze. I pushed forward, trying to help.

"Get back, Jess!"

His hair was scorched, his skin burning. Live ash flew everywhere, leaving welts. I felt heat then on my skin, and looked down. My shirttail was ablaze. Marcus saw. He plunged through the inferno and threw me to the ground, covering me, smothering the flames. Pain seared everywhere. Marcus shielded my head as more ash and timber rained.

There was a booming, exploding sound. A shattering of wood. I jerked my head up as a blazing section of the barn wall came apart and crashed to the ground. Illuminated by the fire stood Tark. He advanced into the barn, oblivious to the flames. They grabbed; he pushed them away. I don't know how he did it, but he made a path to us, shoving the burning timbers aside like so many Lincoln Logs. Marcus dragged me to my feet, and Tark, as he reached us, shouted orders, directions, which we followed without question. He cleared our way through the escape route he had fashioned coming in.

But as I stumbled out of the barn ahead of Marcus, I turned and saw that he *hadn't* followed. He had paused to look back, and was standing frozen, staring at the Whaler. Flames raced to engulf the mast that he and I had ridden down the bay from upshore the summer before. The Whaler's skeleton shuddered and began to fall. I sobbed and ran for Marcus, but Tark was ahead of me, pushing me back while he raced into the barn. He grabbed Marcus and yanked him out from under the burning skeleton just before it crashed in a massive heap of fiery rubble on the barn floor.

In moments, they were both beside me in the dark night. Flames towered into the sky, whipped by the winds off the bay, but we stood outside the fire's heat. The sweat on our faces shone red, like blood. I tasted smoke, and my lungs and stomach heaved. I could barely stand. Marcus and Tark were in worse shape, with burns and blood everywhere. We stood supporting each other, gulping in fresh air, and watched with stunned horror as the barn and the Whaler burned.

Gone within minutes. A seven-year labor of love.

I couldn't bear it. I began to cry silently. I rubbed the tears away but they came again and again. Finally, I reached up to Marcus, and rubbed them from his face too.

Marcus took my hand and held it in his. Then he gripped Tark's shoulder. "You could have been killed," he said. There was an entire lifetime of acknowledgment in the words.

Tark took a long time answering. Finally, he said simply, "I know."

CHAPTER TWENTY-EIGHT

Marcus sent me home with the guard from the hillside lockout who had shown up to help with the fire. And I didn't bother to keep my promise to Grady to stop in at Homicide. Instead, I dragged up my stairs, rummaged for iced tea, and crawled tiredly out on my porch roof to stare lethargically at the moon. Ice clinked in my glass as Janis Ian drifted through the open window from my stereo:

". . .sometimes it's all too much to say aloud. Sound's a shroud, meanings crowd . . ."

I would go by to see Laura and Catherine in the morning, I thought. Maybe they'd let me in. Maybe I could help them. Maybe that would help me.

". . . and all that's left are aftertones."

I wiped at the tears that had begun again on the way home—not quite sure what they were all about. I finally let them just pour on down. Who would ever know?

When they stopped at last it was 3:39 A.M. by the busy little watch Tark had given me last year. I was only half surprised when Grady's car pulled to the curb in front. I saw him climb out and look up, but didn't say anything. After a minute or so I shifted, to make room. His steps came up my gray wool-carpeted stairs and through my door, which I'd left open for the breeze. He crossed my living room. Stuck his head out.

"Permission to come aboard?"

"You've got the badge," I said crossly.

As he crawled through the window, he banged his head on the frame. He always did. I was glad.

He propped his back against the white siding of the house and stretched his long legs out. Light filtered from inside, and I saw that work boots finished off blue jeans that were, for a change, rumpled and stained. The sleeves of his smudged white shirt were rolled to the elbows. He smelled faintly of smoke.

"The state police caught up with Danny," he said, "on a dirt track leading from Andrelli's cabin to the state highway. He went without a fuss."

I didn't respond.

"I talked to Catherine," he added.

"Personally?"

"Of course."

Of course. Grady always did the right thing.

"I just came from there. She'll be all right, I think. She and Laura are stronger than Danny ever gave them credit for."

"So you know why he did . . . everything."

"Pretty much."

"You knew he'd been working for Marcus?"

He nodded. "That's why I figured he'd take you to the cabin. He'd need money to make his run. I called Andrelli and told him to expect you."

"And that's why there wasn't any security, other than at the gate."

"He was afraid it would drive Danny into doing something crazy, if there were all kinds of people around."

"You've been out at the cabin?" I noted again the stained boots and smell of smoke.

"As soon as Danny left with you, I headed out there with a couple of cars. We called in the fire. You'd already left."

When your scene is over, you get off stage. That's something Samved had taught me. It was Marcus who'd come along to add: *It's okay sometimes to let a man take care of things.* Good or bad, I was learning.

I sipped at my tea. "And Barbara Sloan?"

"She came to me a year ago, with a plan to get evidence against Marcus."

"Why?"

"She thought he was behind the drug and porn operation, and her son, Christopher, had had a bad experience."

"Christopher? With the porn people?"

"He was approached by a recruiter at his school. Before he knew he had a choice, they managed to talk him into letting them take a series of pictures, nude. The kid was so damn sheltered—and when Sloan found out, she nearly went crazy. She found the guy who did it, a sleazebag recruiter, but he threatened Christopher's life if she told anyone. From that moment on, she was dedicated to shutting down the child porn ring."

"So she got the job with Marcus, and set up her own apartment away from her son, so none of what she was doing would rub off on him."

"It damned near killed her," Grady said, "leaving him with her mother. It was a question of the end justifying the means. As long as that scum was around, she felt that Christopher would never be safe."

"And this is why Christopher has a bodyguard."

"Yes."

"Is Sloan the one who told you about Danny working with the mob?"

He reached to break a leaf off a branch of the tree that scraped the roof. He crushed and sniffed it, a country-boy quirk that didn't at all fit his normally sophisticated style of dress. "She confirmed what we suspected. There were odd things that Danny had told me, things Con Argento, the snitch, supposedly told him. They didn't fit together. I knew he was bringing in wrong information, that he knew more about the drug connections than he let on. Then, when Con was murdered, I suspected Danny had done it, to keep Con from telling anybody else what he really knew. It was time to haul Danny in."

"What about Jack Hoffman? Why did he go to Sloan's apartment and lie to the manager, saying he was Sloan's brother?"

"I sent him, to make sure nothing was left behind when

we moved Sloan out—nothing that would tell you she was alive. I figured you'd go there sooner or later."

"Why didn't he just say he was a cop?"

"Jack was working undercover for me. I didn't want him leaving a trail that Fournsey or Greer might find suspicious."

"I'd have sworn Hoffman was a bad cop."

I could feel his smile. "That's his strength undercover. He comes off as bland—even a little dumb. In reality, he's an accomplished liar."

"You haven't done so bad in that department yourself."

Grady shrugged at my sarcasm. He crumpled the leaf in a fist.

"You told me you were going to arrest Marcus," I accused, "then used my old friendship with Danny to bring your sting to a head. You hoped I'd be so hot to clear Marcus, I'd go to Danny with questions and stir things up. Make him nervous enough so he'd make mistakes."

"It seems to have worked rather well," Grady observed.

"Only because I decided to trust you. Christ, Grady, you *used* me."

"And you've never used me?"

"You had me running around— Dammit, you could have at least told me what the hell was going on."

"There might have been a better way, Jess, but this is the one that presented itself first. I knew I couldn't keep you out of it, with Andrelli being in it. I also couldn't take you into my confidence—not with Fournsey involved too."

"You knew about Fournsey all along?"

"I've suspected for years. A cop can be bad alone—but it helps to have cohorts in high places, someone to grease the wheels."

"Did you know Danny had ordered Tark to kill Barbara Sloan?"

His tone said he was pleased to reveal the next bit of news. "Tark told me that."

I blinked. *"Tark* came to *you?"*

"Paulie wanted Sloan taken out, and Danny agreed to do it for a fee. But then he was afraid he'd be caught and screw up tonight's drug delivery before it came down. So he coerced Tark into doing it instead, by kidnapping Bernadette.

"Tark was really in a bind. He knew that if he took out Sloan, Andrelli would be charged. But he couldn't refuse outright because of Bernadette. And he had his own reasons for not wanting to go to Andrelli. So he came to me instead."

I shook my head. "Tark . . . and you. I can't even conceive it."

"An odd partnership, I agree, but it worked. We figured out the sting together. I made sure Danny was scheduled to work undercover with Jack Hoffman that night, to get him out of the way. Tark, positioned on C dock, shot at Sloan and deliberately missed—"

"You *trusted* him with that?"

"We had to. Andrelli's security was stiff. Hell, Tark wouldn't have come to us with it if he'd planned to murder the woman. And he was the only one who could get within range."

"You were damned close enough, to get there as fast as you did. It's funny—I remembered something on the way home tonight. Marcus saying that he didn't even get a chance to check Sloan's pulse before your boys in blue arrived."

He ran fingers through his hair until it stuck up in irritated tufts. "The timing was right in a lot of ways. We couldn't leave Sloan in Paulie's camp much longer—he's been getting too damned crazy lately. Even Andrelli was getting ready to yank her. That prostitute, you know the one who was found headless a little while ago? She had worked for Paulie, and when she crossed him, he did the decapitation himself. We found this out through her sister, who went undercover with Paulie, pretending to be a chorus girl."

A chorus girl. "A *redhead? Ginny?*"

"That's the one."

"Did you know she—" I broke off and let him tell it.

"She's a P.I. from Seattle," Grady said. "She came to us with information after she'd infiltrated Paulie's camp."

But Ginny was working for Marcus. Was she also a P.I.? Or was that just the story she'd given Grady? I didn't think I'd be the one to raise that question. At least now I knew Ginny's reason for working on Paulie. She was avenging her sister's hideous death.

"So Paulie's going up now?"

"You'd better believe it. Sloan's given us enough to put him away for years. And we'll have Ginny's testimony about her sister."

"What about Marcus?"

"What about him?"

I set my glass down and dried my hands on Mrs. Binty's gardening pants—which, I was surprised to see, I still wore. They were stained with blood, and burnt. Mrs. Binty would be thrilled. Truly. It'd be all over the neighborhood. *I wonder what Jesse's been up to now!*

I finished my question. "Is Sloan—is she testifying against Marcus too?"

Grady sounded tired. "Funny thing," he said. "According to Sloan, Andrelli did nothing incriminatory while she worked for him. At least, nothing worthwhile bringing him up on." His voice turned cool. "I guess your pal goes free—again."

I almost felt sorry for Grady. He wanted Marcus so bad, and we women just kept getting in the way. Well, you could hardly blame Babs for keeping her kid's father out of jail.

I crossed my legs at the ankles and folded my arms. "Shit, Grady, I had a case built on so much circumstantial evidence, and most of it was wrong. I had Barbara Sloan dead by Paulie's hand . . . Jack Hoffman involved with the drugs and the child porn ring . . . and I almost believed that Marcus— Forget that. I even had Catherine Greer pegged as the problem in that marriage."

"The important thing is that you got it right in the end," Grady said magnanimously.

"Yeah, well, you could have saved me a hell of a lot of trouble if you'd just told me everything from the first."

"I'm up for promotion," he said bluntly. "And knowing your penchant for men on the wrong side of the law, I could hardly count on your help."

"You got it anyway," I reminded him angrily.

"That I did. And someday, maybe you'll even help me net Andrelli."

"When pigs sing opera," I replied.

"It doesn't matter." His jaw hardened. "I'll have him, and when the time comes, there won't be anything you can do about it. Where Andrelli's concerned, the same as with Greer, you're just one more element in the plot—one more ingredient in the soup."

Fish soup. Gray and oily. Suddenly, that was the way I felt.

The worst of it being that for too long now, I'd been like a salmon—swimming upstream. Over the rapids and through the dams, fighting my way against currents I didn't even know were there. It was the story of my life, and I was fed up with the whole damned thing.

Grady left. I sat there looking at the moon.

Well, hell, I thought, as Janis sang on about life and loss. At least I didn't spawn—so maybe I'd live to see another spring.

I found Marcus later that morning staring thoughtfully at the remains of the Whaler—a charred black frame, nothing more. The clearing around the barn had saved most of the woods from disaster. Piles of rubble were scattered throughout the clearing. Marcus must have worked all night, cleaning up. Across his back, arms, and chest were broad, blistered welts. The wound on his shoulder, from the ax, had been heavily bandaged. His jeans and athletic shoes were thick with black, muddy debris.

"Hi."

He turned, and I saw that his face was streaked with soot and sweat. It became worse as he rubbed a grimy hand over it. Everything smelled of smoke. Even the woods, on the way here, were thick with it, although a brief storm had come through around seven A.M. and left the ash and charred lumber a soggy mess.

"How are you?" Marcus said.

"Sick as hell, looking at this." I stood beside him.

"All the work we put into it is still here," he said philosophically. "It's just taken different form."

I made an attempt at a laugh. "Unfortunately, this form won't float."

"I'm not sure it was ever meant to, Jess."

I touched the charred bow. It was still warm, and brought back a too-vivid remembrance of the flames.

"Have you spoken with Tark?"

"He and Bernadette stayed overnight. We had breakfast earlier."

"Have you worked things out?"

"I guess you might say that. They're leaving later today for Italy. A vacation . . . and possibly a honeymoon, before they come back. They'll stay with relatives in Florence until the press gets tired of writing about Paulie. They'll have to come back to testify, of course."

"And when they come back? Will Tark work again for you?"

"I don't know. I don't think so, Jess."

I was silent.

"It was inevitable," Marcus said. "You can't keep people from growing—especially when you've picked them in the first place, whether as employees or friends, for their potential as human beings."

His saying that reminded me of the *Herald*, the way they treated employees, cutting off their growth before it even began. I said, "Charlie Nicks called earlier. They want me back at the paper. They want my firsthand view on this."

"And?"

"I don't know."

"A position is still open with me. I'll need a new bodyguard, and I'll pay for the training."

"You'd want me as a *bodyguard*?" I pulled back to stare. Janet notwithstanding, that vocation had never once occurred to me.

But Marcus misunderstood. "I wouldn't make the same mistakes with you that I did with Tark. Things would be much different."

"What kind of training?" I asked, curious.

"Self-defense . . . maritime security . . . you'd learn to shoot, to dive . . ."

"You want me to be a fuckin' underwater cop?"

He laughed, because he knew I was creating some distance between myself and the idea . . . it was too damned tempting.

"There are several schools in the country," he continued persuasively. "It's a tough job, Jess, but not without a certain amount of glamour. I'd pay you well, and you'd go with me everywhere, whether it's on a cruise or to foreign countries . . ."

"How much would it pay?" I was thinking of all the things I could do.

"Well, let's see . . . I could start you at somewhere around sixty thousand a year, plus living quarters, a car—"

"A car?" I think my nose wiggled at that one. I know my ears pricked.

"—a car, all expenses—"

"Stop!"

"What's wrong?"

"I think I just fell into the rabbit hole."

"You accept, then?" His tone was pleased.

"No . . . I don't know . . . I have to think."

"Not too long."

"No." Jesus. I had to change the subject.

"Barbara Sloan," I said. Talk about creating distance. "She has a son."

The shadows around his eyes became deeper. "Christopher."

"You know?"

"Yes."

I was afraid to ask, and just as afraid not to. "How much do you know?"

"You mean, that he's mine?" The weariness was back in his tone. "I've known since he was born."

"And you've never—"

"What? Claimed him? Accepted the responsibility? I've been sending Barbara checks from the first."

"Checks!"

He said angrily, "What would you have me do? Tell the boy I'm his father? Take him to Saturday afternoon movies, to ball games? What kind of life do you think Christopher would have if he knew—if *anyone* knew—he was my son? He'd be fair game for every reporter, every criminal, every nut—Christ, Jess, don't you think I *want* him to know? I just can't do that to him."

"And Sloan agrees with this?"

"It was her idea. It took me a while to realize she was right."

"Do you ever see Christopher? Spend time with him alone?"

"Never." His sense of loss was clear. "The risk, for him, would be too great."

I walked away from Marcus a little. Thinking. I kicked around some ash with the toe of my sneaker. "I don't suppose—I don't suppose you'd ever consider getting out of this . . . business . . . so you could make a life for your son."

He laughed harshly. "Get out of the family, you mean? Of course I've thought of it. Every day of my waking life. Do you think I'm blind to what people say about me? To what they say about you because you're connected to me?"

"And?"

"Jess, we've talked about this before. The way I live is a one-way street. I knew that when I chose it. And now that I have, I can't get to the point where respectability becomes a goal. I could no longer function that way."

"Not even for your son?"

"Don't you understand? It's too late for that. People don't forgive reformed mobsters. They send them to jail."

"So Christopher will grow up without knowing his father."

"When you have a better answer, Jessica, be sure to let me know."

The formal *Jessica* was my clue to let it drop.

The ensuing silence was broken when Marcus said, "You've seen Christopher?" There was so much longing in that one sentence, it nearly broke my heart.

"He's a wonderful kid," I said quickly. "Smart, and strong. He looks like you. . . ."

Marcus smiled boyishly and hooked his thumbs in the pockets of his jeans. "You think so?"

"He looks so *damned much* like you. When I was there, his grandmother became upset. She thought I'd come to hurt them, and she was angry. Christopher stood between us to protect her. His shoulders went back, the way yours do, and he has that sort of cocky tilt to his chin—"

I couldn't go on. The expression of half longing, half pride on Marcus's face was one I couldn't endure.

I reached into my tote. "I brought you something." I pulled out a slim white box. I'd picked it up a while back, and dropped it off to be engraved. I didn't know, then, how appropriate this gift might turn out to be.

"What is it?"

"Open it."

With a small smile, he untied the silver ribbon and opened the long thin box. Nested on a layer of cotton was a brass plate. The engraving read: WORK IS LOVE MADE VISIBLE. It was something Marcus had said once, when we were working on the Whaler. A quote from Kahlil Gibran. Marcus was the only man I knew who didn't scorn Gibran these days as being out of style.

The saying had stuck with me at the time because of the way I felt about my work at the *Herald*. The rest of the quote was: *And if you cannot work with love but only with distaste, it is better that you should leave your work and sit at the gate of the temple and take alms of those who work with joy.*

A question replaced the tiredness in Marcus's eyes.

"We'll rebuild the Whaler," I explained. "I'll help. That's for above the hatch, when we're through."

He drew me to him. His lips tasted like soot and ash.

"When you came into my life," he said a few moments later against my cheek, "I expected you to be a thorn."

"And?"

"You are. You irritate me into thinking and doing things I never would on my own."

"Thanks," I said. "I think." A *thorn*?

How did I always get the romantic ones?

EPILOGUE

The Flynns called to say their camping trip was over and they wanted to take Bastard the Dastardly Dog with them to visit Mrs. Flynn's sister in Iowa. I made all the appropriate "missing the mutt" noises, then hung up, did a jig, and celebrated. No Bastard for at least another week. And maybe he'd get lost in a cornfield.

Then I went out to Pittsford to see Samved.

He was in his spare, ascetic room, dressed in his flowing white robes. Meditation music played. The scent of lilies wafted. It would seem I had entered the New Age.

But old Samved didn't fool me. I marched straight over to the little nook opposite his prayer rug and whipped the curtain back.

"Ah-ha! I knew it!" A twenty-inch color TV. *Jeopardy* was on, the sound mute. "You old fraud," I accused. "And how dare you tell the *Herald* I haven't been around for counseling?"

"Unless you have been here on the astral plane," he said with dignity, "I believe that to be truth."

"And what do you know about truth? You sit here playing guru and collecting my hard-earned bucks, and the minute my back's turned you're watching TV."

"One man's reality is another man's dream," he said obscurely.

I'd have to think about that one.

I sat opposite him on the floor, my legs folded, and began. An hour later, we were still talking.

"So you wonder if you love this man," Samved said.

"I know I love parts of him. Some parts I just like. Others I'm not dealing with right now."

"Perception is everything."

"So I perceive him as good because to me he is. And loving. But what about the people he hurts with his illegal business schemes?"

"Each of us creates our own reality. They live in theirs, you in yours."

"And Marcus? Where does he live?"

"In the tower."

"The ivory tower."

"As you see it."

"And Tark?"

"Is creating a new reality for himself. As we speak."

"Marcus will be lost without him."

"The vacuum is always filled."

"But who can he trust as much as Tark?"

He merely smiled.

"*Me?*"

"Do you deny the thought even as it arises? You are creating a new reality too."

"That doesn't mean I should work for Marcus, though. The *Herald* wants me back. Maybe I should just stay there."

"It is for you to say."

"Why do you think I've been wanting to drink again?"

"It is the vision you have of yourself."

"As a drunk?"

"As someone not yet healed."

"I don't want to be that someone anymore."

"Then you will not."

"You make it sound easy."

"Perhaps—for reasons only you can know—you make it purposely hard."

"Look, don't give me that seventies shit, that 'relax and go with the flow.'"

"There's a new expression now, in keeping with the New Age."

"Yeah?"

"Gel out," he said.

"You are the goddamnedest fraud."

But that's what I did. I gelled right out and on over to *Newsweek*, who bought my stories about the nationwide growth of child porn, and took some other free-lance stuff I hadn't been able to move before. This helped me over my financial slump, and then some.

That night, I guess I was feeling a little empowered— and maybe a bit hyped—and I met the Genesee Three over at Clyde's. They helped me push my Ghia into the street, then several blocks away from Clyde's (who always disables the cars he's fixed when someone can't pay). Then, with that marvelous certificate from the radio station, which was for 200 miles of free towing, I had it towed to Syracuse— to a chop shop, to be remade. The new towing guy in town—who happened to be from Detroit—didn't know Clyde. He wouldn't be likely to say anything, though, even if he did hear the car he'd towed had been ripped. The Three took care of that, promising to set him up with the same kind of business he had in Detroit—which, wouldn't you know, was towing ripped cars.

The Three also took care of the chop shop mechanic. What they promised him, I don't know. I don't want to know. Ever. But what he did to that red and white Ghia is a miracle beyond compare. It already had the new engine I'd put in. It now has a new body on its classy chassis, new registration and plates, and looks like a collector's car. It can *almost* leap tall buildings in a single bound. And lest you think that my telling you this indicates that crime does pay, you should know that they did get one thing wrong.

I didn't want the Ghia back. Clyde would have grabbed it. What I wanted was an Olds, like Mrs. Binty's.

What they gave me in exchange for the Ghia was a *Dodge Dart*. I can't believe I've got to drive a fuckin' Dodge Dart around town.

Well, it's got a big trunk, that's one thing. Big enough to hold the exercise bike I picked up for me and Toni.

"Cool," she said, tossing her long dark ponytail. "Now you can exercise while you watch the soaps."

"I don't watch soaps!" I declared.

"You do too. Mrs. Binty told me she hears them on all the time since you haven't been working."

I muttered something mean.

The fact is, I *am* working. On a book. I told both Marcus and the *Herald* that I'd have to think about their offers. I wasn't ready to make a decision either way.

In the meantime, I've sent Mom a huge check, paid off most of Pop's old bar bills, installed a blender, and gone on a health food binge. And I've done all of this myself, thank you very much, without any help from anyone at all.

Maybe I am a genius instead of an apostle after all. Or at least becoming one.

Well, hot damn.

ELIZABETH GEORGE

"Exceptionally assured and impressive...Highly entertaining."
--Newsweek

Elizabeth George's internationally acclaimed novels A GREAT DELIVER-ANCE and PAYMENT IN BLOOD have placed her in the front ranks of writers of psychological suspense, earning her comparisons to P.D. James and Ruth Rendell. Her tightly woven tales of Scotland Yard Inspector Thomas Lynley and Detective Sergeant Barbara Havers blend rich textures and British locales with taut detective drama that places them in the company of some of the greatest fictional sleuths.

☐ 27802-9 **A GREAT DELIVERANCE** **$4.50**

☐ 28436-3 **PAYMENT IN BLOOD** **$4.95**

And now in hardcover:

☐ 07000-2 **WELL-SCHOOLED IN MURDER** **$17.95**

Buy them at your local bookstore or use this page for ordering:

BANTAM MYSTERY COLLECTION

NERO WOLFE STEPS OUT

Every Wolfe Watcher knows that the world's largest detective wouldn't dream of leaving the brownstone on 35th street, with Fritz's three star meals, his beloved orchids and the only chair that actually suits him. But when an ultra-conservative college professor winds up dead and Archie winds up in jail, Wolfe is forced to brave the wilds of upstate New York to find a murderer.